THE LIGHTBRINGERS

H. C. H. RITZ

grey gecko press

Published by Grey Gecko Press, Katy, Texas.

www. greygeckopress. com

Printed in the United States of America

Design by Grey Gecko Press

Library of Congress Cataloging-in-Publication Data

Ritz, H. C. H.
The lightbringers / H. C. H. Ritz
Library of Congress Control Number: 2012950917

ISBN 978-1-9388217-5-2

Second Edition

*To my dad, who showed me that
writers are the coolest people.*

Acknowledgments

Thank you first and foremost to my wonderful spouse, Benjamin, who wanted me to pursue my dreams and was willing to pay most of the bills while I did. All wanna-be writers should be so lucky.

Thank you to my friend and publisher, Jason Aydelotte, who gave me a compelling reason to finish this book (a publishing contract!). And thank you to Grey Gecko Press for having the only contract I've ever heard of that is fair to the writer.

Thank you to my awesome critique groups, without whom this book would never have been finished: Team Armageddon (Dominick D'Aunno, Shannon Winton, Erik Hailey, George W. Padgett, and Leo King) and Team Go-Go Gargoyles Galore (also Shannon Winton, plus Chris Lewis, Alyssa Woods, Wayne Basta, and Ian Everett). Thank you also to my beta readers Lindsay Nye, Eric Etheridge, and Michael Teegarden.

Thank you to Laura Stewart, Ryan "Iggy" Harrison, and Eric Etheridge, who gave me free IT consultations so that the technical bits of my book wouldn't make readers want to throw it against the wall.

Thank you to Eric Nelson, Anna Phillips, Chuck Coshow, and my mom, who reviewed and commented on my first draft's plot summary, and again to my mom, who provided feedback on the latest draft of the full book.

Thank you to my editor, M. K. Sidler, who took on the onerous task of editing a fellow editor and handled it beautifully, and who helped me become a better writer.

Thank you (a second time) to George Wright Padgett, author of *Spindown*, who graciously allowed me to co-opt his fabulously evil word "reduction" to describe what happens to the victims of New America.

Thank you to the Houston Sci-Fi/Fantasy Writers' Group, which inspired me every month to go home and write. Thank you to the organizer, Keri Bas, who keeps it going and keeps it useful.

And if I left you off by mistake, I'm sorry—I didn't mean to!

What Has Gone Before

2018　　The world economy collapses.

2019　　World War III begins

2022　　Martha St. Tala rises to fame; extols positive thinking as the way to create a perfect society.

2025　　WWIII death toll tops 200,000,000.

2028　　Martha St. Tala wins the presidency on an isolationist, positive thinking platform.

President Martha declares New America's "final independence" from the world.

2032　　President Martha accepts an indefinite term of office.

2035　　The borders are sealed; New American society reaches apparent perfection

2054　　President Martha I retires;
President Martha II comes to power at age 35.

2079　　Present day

Chapter One

President Martha St. Tala:

> *Exercising one's will over one's own mind is not automatic, and so you are all fortunate to have been born into a society which teaches you this skill from childhood. Remember, if there is anything you do not wish to have in your experience, practice your ability to overlook the reality of it now, and soon it will leave your reality. And you will hardly notice its departure or remember that it ever was there.*

Gaylen's wife didn't look at him as she passed through their small bedroom. Her tone exasperated, she said, "Sierra wants *you* to read to her," and she disappeared into the closet.

On the mandatory, government-installed wallscreen just a few feet away, the Brandenburg Concerto by Bach accompanied them, with a garden of bluebonnets, goldenrods, and daisies in tidy rows. It was a Beauty Moment approved by the Bureau of Entertainment.

Instead of going to Sierra's room, Gaylen got up and followed Serena to the closet. She had just pulled off her skirt and top, revealing her silky, white underthings. She tossed her clothing into the hamper beside her. Gaylen caught sight of the two of them in the mirror fastened to the wall. Both tall, slender, and dark-skinned, they made a striking couple. He had taken pleasure in the sight many times. Now, he noticed that his face looked worried, and he changed it back to a pleasant expression.

Meanwhile, Serena slipped into a nightgown, which slid invitingly along her smooth body. She flipped an errant shoulder strap into place, then glared at him. Her eyes flashed. "What do you want?"

He took a step back, his hands up. She glared at him, unmoving, until he had moved out of her sight.

A couple of months ago, she would have reached for him, given him a lingering, teasing kiss, then playfully slapped away his roaming hands. He would have left the bedroom pleasantly tantalized. Instead, he stepped into the tiny kitchen to eat a snack-size candy bar, then another, then a third, while he watched the too-loud wallscreen above the sink.

Gaylen didn't know why his wife had changed. She hadn't said, and it wasn't permissible to ask.

The Beauty Moment with its cultivated flowers faded into blackout. The evening's Good News report began, and the announcer cheerfully related that worker productivity had increased five percent over this same period last year.

Gaylen went into Sierra's room feeling somewhat fortified by the candy bars. As he went, he told himself, *I am happily married. I am surrounded by love. Everything in my life is perfect.*

Sierra half-reclined in bed with her handscreen in her lap. She stared absently at the wallscreen on the wall at the foot of her bed, which filled most of the room. The children's channel showed a cartoon with a little puppy—a yellow Labrador retriever with big, floppy ears—who turned around in circles in his flannel bed, then settled down to go to sleep.

Sierra lit up when she saw Gaylen. "Daddy!"

He smiled and snuggled into bed with her. "Let's get this book taken care of, shall we?" He kissed her on the forehead and picked up the handscreen to resume the book, which was reassuringly marked APPROVED FOR ALL AGES by the Bureau of Entertainment.

With his mind half on the story, he worried about his marriage. Yesterday, he'd added an evening session of positive affirmations to complement the half-hour morning sessions he'd been doing for a month, but there were no results yet. He reminded himself that he wasn't supposed to worry about results. They would come in time.

Sierra usually fell asleep as he read. Not tonight. Her little eyes closed a dozen times, but she kept shaking it off, and she was clinging to him. After he read the book once, she demanded another reading of it, then another. Finally, twenty minutes past her usual bedtime, she announced, "I'm always going to think about you smiling, Daddy."

He paused, trying to parse out the meaning and intent of her words. Finally, he settled for, "Thank you, sweetie."

She was quiet and still for a moment, and he thought maybe she had gone to sleep. Then she said, with an emphatic jerk of her shoulders, "I'm going to think about us always together, OK, Daddy?"

That comment, especially coupled with the previous one, struck fear into him. "What do you mean?"

She paused for a while. "Nothing," she said. But it came out in her "I'm in trouble and I'm telling a fib" tone of voice.

He decided that he needed to talk to Serena. He knew he was supposed to ignore anything that seemed negative, so as not to give it power and attract more of the same into his life, but it would be impossible to ignore this.

"You go ahead and think about the good things, Sierra. I will, too." He gave her a kiss on the forehead. "And everything will be OK," he added, hoping he sounded convincing.

Her little body relaxed, and she fell asleep immediately. He stay-ed with her for a few more minutes, watching the rise and fall of her chest and the little sleep twitches of her body. Apprehension built up inside him until it became unbearable. Carefully, he stood up and tucked Sierra into her bed. Then he went into his and Serena's bedroom.

Serena lay in bed and read something on her handscreen. She didn't look up when he entered. On the wallscreen, a comedian told innocuous jokes about family life. Gaylen slid into bed, his face blank but his mouth dry. He tried to ignore the wallscreen while he thought of and discarded a dozen inadequate openings.

Finally, he said, "Serena, are you . . . thinking positively . . . about our relationship?"

She scowled. "I'm thinking positively about my life."

"But about us? Are you thinking positively about us? Like you're supposed to?" He knew he sounded plaintive, but it was true. They were both supposed to think positively. How was he supposed to think positively for the both of them?

"I'm *not* supposed to. You know you're not supposed to get your heart set on any one person. People come and go, Gaylen. All that matters is being happy."

"So let's be happy. I am. I'm happy." He knew he sounded defensive.

She threw the magazine down onto her lap. "Fine. Me, too."

They glared at each other.

Serena shook her head once. "Look, I've decided I'm leaving. I'm not renewing our marriage contract this time. Sierra and I are moving out. I'm ready for something different." She picked her handscreen back up.

He found himself on his feet, facing her, breathless. His throat constricted. "No, no, no—don't take Sierra. Don't take her."

"She's my child."

"She's mine, too."

"Well, she can't live with us both, Gaylen!"

"Yes, she can—just stay here! Just don't go!"

"Stop it, Gaylen." She sat up fully and swung her legs out from under the blankets. "You aren't doing this right. Just think about the future and having someone else in your life. OK?"

"I don't want anyone else. I just want you. And Sierra. I *love* Sierra!"

"Stop it this minute. Let it go!" Her tone brooked no further argument.

Gaylen walked out of the room, her glare on his back. He went into the living room and sat on the edge of the sofa, his head in his hands. Serena didn't follow him. The sound of laughter did follow him, though, via the wallscreen in here. He stared at it uncomprehendingly. The comedian had finished a long joke and now waited out the laugh.

Breathe. She's not gone yet. You can still fix this. Think differently, Gaylen, think differently.

He went to the kitchen and got a glass of water with shaking hands and gulped it down. The cool water felt good, and he turned on the tap again to splash some on his face.

Your thinking is wrong. You're the one doing this to yourself. Just fix it.

I can do this. I can do it.

He settled onto the sofa and imagined Serena telling him that she had decided to stay. Over and over he saw it. By the time he went to bed, she had shut off the light.

All the next week, he brought home the most perfect bouquets of flowers for Serena every day, which she accepted with brief thanks and placed around the apartment. He complimented her at least three times a day, which she also accepted cordially. He spent forty-five minutes each morning and evening in meditation about his happy family. He prevented himself from entertaining any thoughts of Serena or Sierra being gone.

By mid-afternoon every day, he had a tension headache. He woke up several times every night, and each time he did, he recited affirmations with all his heart and soul while he watched Serena's peaceful, sleeping face.

And yet he came home on Thursday—a warm, sunny day—to find the apartment full of half-packed cardboard boxes. Serena sat on Sierra's bed and sorted through her clothing while she sang children's songs for her daughter.

Gaylen went straight to the bedroom and closed the door and sat on the bed. For three hours, he thought, as hard as he could, variations on *I have a happy marriage. My wife loves and appreciates me.*

My family is joyful. My home is full of love. His head ached and his body was rigid with tension by the time he fell asleep. But when he woke up in the morning, he found that Serena had slept in Sierra's room.

Before he went to work that day, Gaylen stopped at the wallscreen in the tiny kitchen and pulled up a digital copy of their marriage contract. It ran out on June 30th of each year—only one week away. To renew, they would just sign on the next year's line, and if they didn't sign, the marriage would expire.

He touched a button to pin it to the wallscreen so that it would remain visible. It read simply:

Gaylen Thomas Andrews

and

Serena Anne Tate

Are joined this day in love and joy.
For as long as love and joy shall
last, they shall forsake all others
and give one another their
unconditional happiness.

Love and joy are still here, he thought forcefully.

With determination in the set of his jaw, he signed the renewal line with his fingertip. Then he left the contract pinned so that Serena would see it. With all his hope, he left it there. He said nothing to Serena directly. Their earlier argument had reminded him of what President Martha taught—discussing problems only made them more concrete and attracted more of the same. All problems had to be ignored.

That night, after a long day of positive visualizations, he came home and looked into the kitchen with optimism, looking at the contract visible on the wallscreen.

The other signature line was empty.

The next day, it was the same.

And the next.

Serena continued to pack her possessions, and Sierra's.

Gaylen's optimism waxed and waned. He fought himself and he fought despair. And every day, he visualized more intently. On the final day, he put off what work he could so that he could sit at his desk in quiet visualization for most of the day. He knew he could not bring himself to go home until just past midnight, when Serena's decision would be final. After work, he went alone to a movie theatre and watched back-to-back romantic comedies, trying to summon the right wavelength of emotion and thought to align himself with what he wanted.

On the subway ride home, however, despair found its way into his heart. His wife and child were nearly finished packing. The flowers he had bought Serena had wilted and she had thrown them away. There had been no sign of a crack in Serena's inscrutable exterior. All his efforts were coming to nothing.

He admitted to himself that Serena was correct: he knew perfectly well that he had no right to insist on one specific person. Doing so violated the free will of others. He was supposed to ask for the kind of family and the kind of person he wanted and then let the universe find him suitable people—people who wanted the same things he did. And since Serena had already said she wanted to take Sierra, he had no right to argue with that, either.

But he couldn't seem to stop himself. He loved them too much. Especially Sierra—Serena had changed so much that he could hardly summon up his old adoration of her, but Sierra was his little girl.

Just after midnight, he arrived home with his head full of all the positive thoughts he could summon, but with trembling hands.

He walked into the kitchen and looked at the wallscreen only to find the contract ignored, silent and inert on the screen, a thing of disappointment and betrayal.

The next morning, the three of them stood at the door of Gaylen's apartment, Serena's and Sierra's suitcases around them in the hallway. Sierra clung to Gaylen, her face nestled into his chest.

Gaylen felt like his heart was physically breaking, coming apart into pieces, as he forced himself to pull Sierra away from him. He could not say goodbye. He would have broken down if he had tried. He struggled to stay composed, but Sierra saw his face, and she burst into tears. She threw herself against his chest and wailed.

Her mother knelt down with them. "Say, 'Only happy feelings,' Sierra," she commanded.

Gaylen took a breath and said, "Stop it now, Sierra."

The little girl tried valiantly to stop her tears. "I don't wanna go away from you, Daddy!"

Gaylen's eyes filled. "There's better things to come, honey," he said, trying with all his heart to mean it. "You'll be better off where you're going. 'Nothing bad ever really happens, unless you *think* it's bad.' Remember?"

"This *is* bad," Sierra cried, and she threw her arms around Gaylen's neck and clung to him as if for dear life.

He had always loved how she'd clung to him, from the first moments her tiny little limbs had been capable of it, when she was mere months old. It had always made him feel invulnerable somehow when she had held onto him like this. And this was the last time he would ever feel this way.

Serena had always been better at this than Gaylen. "Now stop it, Sierra. This minute!" She gently loosened her daughter's grasp and pulled her away from her father. "Do you want to make us have bad feelings, too? Do you want all of us to attract bad things into our lives because of you?"

"*No . . .*" Sierra wailed.

"Then stop it. Smile for your daddy and tell him how good everything is going to be for everyone. Tell him how happy we are all going to be."

Sierra struggled hard for a long moment and managed a smile through her tears. "Everything will be good, Daddy."

"Yes," Gaylen said authoritatively. "Yes, it will. Now go on and have fun with your mom!" He tried again to smile for her, and he succeeded this time.

Serena picked up their suitcases and the two of them walked down the corridor toward the skyrise's elevators. Sierra looked back twice, crying again. Gaylen forced himself to smile encouragingly each time. *My life is rich and good,* he repeated to himself as he watched them walk away. *My life is complete just as it is, lacking nothing.*

When they were gone, Gaylen turned and went into his apartment and closed the door behind him. He would never see or hear from them again. Sierra would have a new daddy in a few weeks or months, whenever Serena chose someone. And no one would permit Sierra to speak of her old daddy from this moment forward. He was in the past. He was over. And that was as it should be. Serena and Sierra didn't want the same things he did anymore. He couldn't do anything about that. He had been wrong—selfish—to even try.

As for himself, Gaylen would soon be assigned new roommates, unless he picked some of his own accord. Everyone knew that good company was important.

Gaylen hesitated in his living room. The digital frame on the wall over the faux fireplace held their family photos. He took it down and deleted every picture that included Sierra or Serena.

Tears blurring his vision, he went to the stereo and deleted all the children's songs they'd downloaded for Sierra, and then all the music Serena had contributed to their collection.

A plastic black-haired doll lay on the floor behind the sofa. Sierra had accidentally left it behind. He got an empty trash bag from the kitchen, shook it open, and threw the doll into it. He carried the trash bag with him as he moved through the house and looked for anything else that had to go.

I am so lucky, he told himself. *My life is rich and good. I have everything I want and need in this moment.*

In a bathroom cabinet, he found some of Sierra's hair ties. He added them to the trash bag. He also found some of Serena's old makeup she'd tossed into the bathroom trash. He emptied that trash bag into the one he carried.

He looked at himself in the mirror. He felt detached from the man he saw there, with his bloodshot eyes.

He went into their bedroom and came to a stop as he looked around. Serena had decorated the entire room. He would have to replace everything. She'd loved picking everything out. He'd walked hand-in-hand with her through the furniture store, not caring one bit what she chose but just loving the way her eyes glowed.

He dug an old blanket out of a chest and took it to the sofa in the living room. He would sleep there until he had a chance to buy new furniture. Numbly, he went into the bedroom closet. Serena had accidentally left some of her fabric-covered, perfume-scented clothes hangers. And all the little blocks of cedar wood tucked into the drawers—she'd done that. She'd organized his underwear and socks into little dividers, too. He stopped, defeated. Was there anything about the way he lived that she hadn't impacted somehow? How was he going to go back?

He went to Sierra's room with the faint hope that it would be easier. The room was empty, but there were stickers of cartoon characters all over the wall. He dropped to his knees and started scraping them off with his thumbnail while he tried not to think anything at all. Then he noticed the wall itself: the mural they'd painted while Serena was pregnant—a colorful, carefully cultivated garden of flowers reaching up to a blue sky and a big yellow sun. He would have to repaint.

The enormity of the task—of removing these people from his life as if they had never been there—crushed him. He slumped on the floor, his eyes unfocused, as he remembered family movie nights and walks in the park, shopping for clothes for Sierra, cooking together. Six years they had shared. Six years of family. He could not pretend they had never touched his life.

Slowly, his hands came up over his face, and he began to sob.

Late one night several weeks later, Gaylen pushed the "Request Ass-istance" button on the wallscreen opposite his bed.

The evening's good news report vanished and a live feed came through, of an older man of Chinese descent, with the standard short haircut of all New American men. "Gaylen Andrews?" he asked.

Gaylen nodded, surprised that they would know his name.

"Our records show"—the man glanced at something on his screen—"you haven't requested assistance since you were eight. You were . . . it says, 'Playing a prank on sister. Was informed as to the serious nature of the Assistance Response Team.' Correct?"

Gaylen nodded again, remembering with some embarrassment.

"How can we help you?" the other man asked, his tone disinterested.

"My wife left me. And she took my little daughter with her. A little over a month ago. I've done everything I'm supposed to. I'm trying to focus on the future and not think about it, but the thoughts just keep coming back. What do I try next? I—"

"Have you removed all signs?"

"Yes . . ." Gaylen said, but he remembered the one photo of Sierra he had kept on his handscreen.

"*All* signs?"

Gaylen hesitated. "It's really necessary?"

"It's the only way to move on," the responder said, his tone distracted, and he glanced at something off-screen.

Gaylen took a deep breath, resistant. What if he forgot what she looked like? Of course, he was supposed to forget.

Finally, he got his handscreen from the bedside table and pulled up the picture. He looked at her soft brown eyes, her braided pigtails, her beautiful brown skin. He struggled to keep his face composed. "I miss her," he said in vigorous protest.

The responder didn't comment.

Gaylen looked at the photo for long seconds while the responder waited. Finally, Gaylen took a deep breath and pressed the "Delete" icon and "Yes." In a flicker of the screen, the photo was gone. A jolt of pain lanced straight down into the pit of his stomach and demanded that he undo it, but it was too late.

He turned back to the wallscreen.

The responder said, "You're only making it worse by dwelling on it. It is your responsibility as a citizen of New America to let this go. Stop thinking about it."

"How?" Gaylen asked, his voice ragged. "I'm already trying. I've been trying. It's not working."

"That's the wrong thinking," the responder said in a monotone, as if it were a memorized script. "You can do whatever you *think* you can. Change your thinking and your life will follow. Here are your assignments." Gaylen saw the man's shoulders move and heard the clacking of his keyboard while his eyes focused elsewhere on his screen. A moment later, the wallscreen changed to white italic text on a background of drawings of blue daisies. It read:

> I *can* let this go. I am happy and at peace and grateful for everything I have. I distract myself every day with something fun and enjoyable. I am going on a date with someone new every night until I have a new partner who makes me just as happy as the old one did.

"Repeat these statements twenty times daily," the responder's voice prescribed.

"What about Sierra?" Gaylen asked.

"What about her?" the voice of the responder said.

"Am I supposed to just replace her, too?" Gaylen demanded, his voice rising.

The screen flipped back to the view of the responder, who recited, "This assignment addresses all aspects of the situation. Trust the assignment and complete it diligently. It is your duty as a citizen. All of your resistance only prolongs your pain. Stop resisting what is."

Gaylen felt as if he were adrift on an ocean, with no land to be seen anywhere. He had not known what help to expect from the ART, but this wasn't it. He already knew all of this.

"Isn't there anything . . . else?" he asked.

"This is everything you need as long as you complete it properly," the responder said. "If you don't change your mind, nothing else will change. Take responsibility for your experience."

The wallscreen went dark, and then it showed the assignment again. This time, a large "20" appeared beneath it. A warm programmed female voice said, "Let's complete your assignment! How great it is that you will be able to feel better so easily! Read this along with me, won't you?" Then she began to read the text aloud. "I *can* let this go. I am happy and at peace and grateful for everything I have . . ."

Gaylen stared disbelievingly at the text that was supposed to help him.

After a few seconds, the automated voice interrupted herself. "Come on, now, you have to play along!" she said, teasing. "This is your assignment and it is your duty as a citizen of New America to participate fully! Let's try this again!" She started over on the reading. "I *can* let this go. I am happy and at peace—"

Gaylen sank onto his bed and covered his eyes. "No . . . no, no, no."

"That's not a helpful attitude!" the voice said. She sounded as if she were scolding a small child. "Come on, chin up! We don't want to bring back the Assistance Response Team, now, do we?"

"No," Gaylen muttered under his breath. "No, we definitely do not." He took a deep breath and began reading along with the text, with a voice full of resentment.

Within a few seconds, the voice interrupted them again. "Now, that's not the right attitude, is it? Let's try it again, but this time, let's really try hard to mean it! You have to say it like it's already true. Try to feel it all the way down deep, in your bones. Let's go again!" And she started over.

Gaylen wanted to shatter the wallscreen.

Three or four tries later, he figured out how to fake a cheerful tone well enough to satisfy the program and was allowed to finish the twenty readings. By then, it was three o'clock in the morning. At least the effort exhausted him enough that he was able to go to sleep.

Thirty-eight days later—it was September now—the wallscreen still interrupted Gaylen every night at bedtime to read through the assignment. The words seemed to mock him even more than before. The voice replayed in his head throughout the day, though he begged it to go away. Sometimes he even hit his temple with his hand as if it would knock the words out of his mind—and then looked around nervously to see whether anyone had noticed.

As he forced himself to choke down a sandwich for dinner that particular night, dread of the readings brought tension that built in his chest until it hurt to breathe. After dinner, he ate five of the mini candy bars, as had become habit now that he didn't have Serena around to scold him. The dose of sugar only turned his tension into a more frenetic energy. It was so unreasonable to be forced to do this useless exercise every night.

He paced and watched the living room wallscreen and stared at the clock in the upper right-hand corner and waited for the readings. Gradually, he came to feel that he would commit some kind of violence upon himself or the world—although he could not imagine what—if he had to do this again. He went into his room after he brushed his teeth, and he changed into pajamas, all without processing anything he was doing. Tension rose and fell within him like ocean waves as he convinced himself just to get through the readings quickly, and then convinced himself that he could not bear to do them at all.

The moment he turned off the light, the wallscreen dimmed, and then the painfully familiar white italic text on the blue daisy background appeared. He screamed at the wallscreen before the voice could start. "No! I will not do this anymore!"

"That's not a helpful attitude!" the voice said, somehow both cheerful and scolding at the same time. "Come on, chin—"

"Shut up!" Gaylen yelled. "Shut the hell up!"

"We don't want to bring back the Assistance Response Team, now, do we?"

An unnamable and grim force driving him, Gaylen grabbed a water glass from the bedside table and threw it at the wallscreen, but missed. Next went the lamp; the cord ripped out of the socket halfway through, interrupting its arc toward the wall. Then he grabbed both pillows, one in each hand, poised to throw them.

The wallscreen clicked over to a younger white man. "Can I help you?" he asked.

Gaylen froze.

"I see you're on day thirty-eight," the responder said. "Surely you're feeling better by now?"

"No," Gaylen said. He still clutched the pillows. The grim force that had been driving him was gone as if it had never been. A lightness was in him now, hoping for some other solution. "Can you do something else? I can't do this anymore. I'm saying these stupid sentences over and over again and it isn't helping. I need something else."

The responder pursed his lips as if to speak, and then he shook his head. "Sorry. This is it."

Gaylen dropped the pillows, his arms going limp. "But you're supposed to have help for us—we just have to push the button. This is what we're supposed to do."

"Do your assignments. This is all I have for you right now." The man's voice was curt.

The wallscreen clicked back to the readings. The vacuous wallscreen voice started reciting again. "'I *can* let this go. I am happy and at peace and grateful for everything I have. I distract myself every day with something fun and enjoyable. I am going on a date—'"

Gaylen fell to his knees and dropped his head into his hands.

"Come on, chin up! We don't want to bring back the Assistance Response Team, now, do we?"

Gaylen broke down sobbing.

The screen clicked over again. It was the same responder. He glared at Gaylen and spoke in a hushed shout. "Stop it—you're making me look bad. You do not want to get their attention right now, I promise you!" And then the screen clicked over again.

Gaylen froze. Get whose attention?

Adrenaline rushed through his body and made him tremble. How could this be happening? The only source of help his society offered had threatened him. And they were watching him.

He got up and staggered to the bathroom. The readings showed up here, too, on the small wallscreen opposite the bathtub. He had never paid any particular attention to that wallscreen before. Now he couldn't believe it.

The voice was repeating, "We don't want to bring back the Assistance Response Team, now, do we?" It didn't seem to realize that the Assistance Response Team had dismissed him.

He wanted to cover up the wallscreen, but they'd notice that, too.

Gaylen staggered outside, onto the tiny balcony of his apartment. He inhaled the clean September air, just starting to cool off after the hot summer. He cast about for something to tell himself, some way to calm himself down, but he had nothing to turn to.

Then he noticed that, on the outside of the skyrise opposite his, a giant wallscreen covered several stories. He stared at it. Surely not.

Suddenly, he could hardly breathe.

Gaylen went back to his bedroom, eased under the covers, and used all of his remaining energy to go through the readings with perfect intonation. The voice was delighted with him. When they finished, it asked, "Are you ready for sleep?"

"Yes."

"Tomorrow is Tuesday, September 19. Tomorrow will be refreshingly cool in the morning and pleasantly warm in the afternoon. Would you like to wake up at eight o'clock in the morning again?"

"Yes."

"You will sleep well and wake up even happier."

Sure. Of course I will. He turned onto his side.

The wallscreen, and the rest of the room with it, went dark. He could still hear its electronic hum—it never truly turned off—and he was certain that they still watched him.

Keeping his movements small and casual, he pulled up the sheets and blankets and arranged them so that he could not be seen from the wallscreen. He allowed his neutral expression to dissolve, then, and his face contorted.

Why wouldn't they help him? Why were they watching him if they wouldn't help him?

He couldn't think of any answers that made sense. In the end, though, it all came down to him. He was the cause of all the trouble.

What is wrong with me? Why can't I just be happy like everyone else?

A few weeks later, on Thursday morning, October 5, Gaylen sat in a meeting at work. He and the rest of the data entry team for the marketing department of the Bureau of Entertainment listened to their boss talk about new software.

Without Gaylen even realizing it, his mind turned to the dark places he could no longer stay out of for any length of time.

Tommy Hiyashi's cheerful report on the software faded away until Gaylen heard nothing but his own inner voice screaming at him, "What is wrong with you? Why can't you be normal? Be normal! Be normal! *Be normal!*"

He returned to awareness and his eyes refocused, because the outside world had grown so quiet. The five coworkers seated around the table all stared at him. He realized then that he had crushed his paper cup and spilled the lukewarm coffee all over his hand and his arm and the table. Heat flooded his cheeks.

Tommy met his eyes; Gaylen saw a flash of concern. Then Tommy laughed and said, as cheerful and gregarious as ever, "Gaylen, you've had way too much coffee, haven't you? Go on, wash up—we'll clean up in here. Our meeting's almost over, anyway."

Gaylen could only nod and excuse himself. He hurried to the nearest restroom, his eyes downcast as if that would shield him from the eyes of others along the way. All the wallscreens in the hallways and in the restroom played an effervescent animated song-and-dance routine, and the catchy tune followed him as he walked. He locked the restroom door with trembling hands. He washed the coffee off his sleeve and hand while cartoon figures cavorted on the wallscreen at the corner of his vision.

He turned to grab paper towels and caught a glimpse of himself in the mirror. He looked drawn, haggard, creases starting to show on his forehead—far from the ideal of a happy, healthy New American. For a moment, he couldn't turn away from his own empty eyes. He ran the tap again and dashed cold water on his face.

As he gripped the sides of the sink, water dripping down his cheeks, he stared himself down. "You've got to stop this, Gaylen," he whispered to himself, his tone fervent. "You've *got* to."

Then something inside him broke. His face contorted and sobs burst from him. Tears ran down his face. He found himself on the floor, and he clutched at the wall as if it could keep him together. Moments passed while he watched himself having hysterics, as if he floated outside of his own body, unable to control it.

Then the wallscreen clicked. A black woman with her graying hair in a bun looked at him disapprovingly.

He was shocked out of his tears and back into himself. He stared at her, eyes wide, as tears dried on his face. He had forgotten that they were watching him all the time. It only made sense that they would be watching him here, too.

"Gaylen Andrews," the woman said in a commanding voice. "You have been working with the ART for almost two months, yes?"

"Yes," he said. He still clutched the wall.

"You are not completing your assignments satisfactorily. Stand up."

Gaylen stared at her.

"Stand up," the woman commanded.

He stood up slowly.

"Straighten up. Now smile. Repeat after me, 'Everything in my life is just as it should be.'"

Gaylen obeyed. His grief subsided into his core, like an animal that ran away, abandoned. It left emptiness behind.

"'I am happy and at peace' . . . 'I am grateful for my life' . . . 'I think only positive thoughts.'"

Gaylen repeated the statements in the pleasant, optimistic tone of voice he knew the ART required, but he felt dead inside.

The responder glanced at something on her screen. "Our records show you have not yet taken advantage of Love Today." That was the government-supplied matchmaking software, available on heart-studded kiosks all around town. "You must go on three dates per week. You will appreciate and enjoy the wonderful romantic options available to you. Understood?"

"Understood," Gaylen said with some approximation of a smile on his face.

The screen switched back over to the cartoon.

He kept up his blandly pleasant expression while he smoothed out his suit and washed his face and hands again and went back out into the office. He glanced around. The smiling faces around him seemed oblivious to all he was suffering.

As he returned to his desk, he noticed the wallscreens on every single wall and every ten feet along the hallways. He sat down at his desk and looked at the wallscreen to the right of him, which watched him in profile. It occurred to him then that he was never alone, that he didn't have a moment of privacy.

I'm trapped. I'm trapped and alone in a nightmare that no one can wake me from.

Chapter Two

President Martha St. Tala:

> *It is important that you know that we are here to help you. If you should ever experience distress, simply request assistance via the nearest wallscreen. We will do what it takes to help put your mind at ease. We are all friends. Together, we have the power to bring your mind to rest and your life to beauty.*

An hour later, Gaylen was struggling to focus on the wording of "Teal Sapphire Magic Sparta Tile" as he entered it into the marketing database when Tommy Hiyashi popped into Gaylen's cubicle. Gaylen's boss wore his usual broad grin.

"Gaylen!" Tommy said. "How's that new data going in? Loving that new line of tile, I bet?"

"Yes, of course," Gaylen said, and he quickly put away the half-eaten candy bar on his desk. "Great color selection." He glanced at Tommy nervously as he remembered how he had embarrassed himself at the meeting earlier.

"Got a sec before lunch?" Tommy asked. He gestured down the hall. "I've got more information for you on that Sparta Tile set."

"Sure," Gaylen said.

Tommy kept up a stream of chatter as they moved through the colorful hallways of the marketing department, but Gaylen soon noticed that Tommy was repeating himself. His boss also glanced frequently at the wallscreens and at the other people in the hallways. Gaylen faltered and fell back a couple of steps.

Tommy grabbed his elbow and continued to propel him forward. "Don't you want to hear all about it? This line is really outstanding because of the granite content of the tile," he declared for the third time, with even greater intensity. "That is by far the *best* value-add of Magic Sparta."

"Sure," Gaylen said. His chest was tight now. He had started to sweat. But he maintained a calm expression. If he had learned anything from recent events, it was to maintain a calm expression.

Tommy continued to babble as he watched a handful of boisterous people head toward the elevator, no doubt about to go out to lunch. As their paths crossed, he pulled Gaylen up close behind the group. They kept pace with the others for a few yards, then broke away to step through a doorway into a stairwell. Tommy shut the door.

The employees never used the stairwells. They worked on the forty-eighth floor, and they never had any emergencies that would call for taking the stairs. There were no wallscreens in the stairwell, either, and the silence was disconcerting.

Tommy's behavior was beyond disconcerting, and Gaylen's heart hammered.

Tommy leaned in close to Gaylen's face. He said, his voice low, "You need to take care of yourself. You're slipping. And I like you, Gaylen. I don't want you to . . . go to waste. You need to do something now, before it becomes too obvious." His eyes glittered unsteadily.

Gaylen stammered, "I—I—"

As if it were an incantation, Tommy said, *"Behind the door behind the smaller bar in the Lipstick Lounge. Spider sent you.* Repeat that."

Gaylen took a deep breath and did so.

Tommy made him say it twice more, then said, "Then do this." He placed his index finger against one side of his neck and drew it all the way across his throat. Gaylen had no idea what the gesture meant. "Do it," Tommy said.

Gaylen obeyed. His hands shook.

Tommy said, "It means 'death.' Don't forget that. And never tell anyone else about any of this, not *ever*."

"OK," Gaylen said.

A secret area in a bar . . . a passcode to get in . . . a warning not to tell: this could only be the underground that Gaylen had heard of before only in rumors and whispers. Gaylen had not even considered it as an option—he had half-believed it to be myth.

Before Gaylen had a chance to absorb this or ask questions, Tommy grasped him by the elbow again and pulled him toward the door. The older man cracked it open, watched for what felt like an eternity, then pulled the door open and dragged Gaylen back into the hallway and into step with another group of people. A pretty redhead looked at Gaylen but only smiled and winked.

Out of habit, Gaylen smiled and winked back.

Tommy already had his usual bounce in his step again, and he picked right back up with his fourth rendition of the merits of Magic Sparta Tile. It took Gaylen a few seconds, but he forced himself to join in. Adrenaline gave their conversation more intensity than made sense, but no one seemed to notice.

Back at his desk a few minutes later, Gaylen forced himself to resume his work. His hands still trembled, and he forced himself not to glance over at the wallscreen next to him, fearful that the ART would notice that something was amiss. But nothing happened.

That night, Gaylen lay sleepless for hours and tried to figure out what to do.

The ART had him under observation all the time, everywhere he went. He had lost control badly enough to slip up in public. Even his boss had noticed. The ART had nothing to offer him but vague threats. He was alone. Tommy had offered him what he thought was probably entrance to the secret underground, and his boss seemed to think that something there would help him—but going there was certainly a violation of good citizenship and he had no idea what would happen to him if he did.

And underneath it all, he missed his wife and child as badly as anything had ever hurt him in his life.

Maybe Tommy's instructions would give him the way out that he sought. Maybe something there in the underground, behind that special door in the Lipstick Lounge, could fix him. Maybe then he could be like everyone else—happy. Even without Serena and Sierra.

He still hoped every day against all reason that he would come home and they would be there again—Serena fixing something for dinner and Sierra playing with her dolls—as if they had never left.

He took a deep breath and forced himself to abandon the thought. Serena hadn't wanted him anymore. He'd had to let them go so that they could be happy without him. He had to find a way to make his own peace with that, because he could not go on like this anymore. No matter what it took, and no matter what the consequences were, anything would be better than this.

John Oldman sat at his desk in front of his workscreen, his head in his hands, and waited for his supervisor to come on the line. It was mid-afternoon on Friday, October 6.

John was an agent of the Domestic Awareness Agency, but his job didn't exist, and neither did the DAA, since there could be no need of either in a perfect society.

He stared into space while he waited. He tried not to look at the agency-only wallscreen in front of him. Every five minutes, the DAA's vision statement went by: "Protect the People While They Perfect Their Minds." Next would be the agency's mission statement: "Conceal All Crime, Reform All Criminals." After that, the statistics by which the DAA measured its success, or lack of it. Six numbers went by every few minutes: TC 7, IR 36, ASR 28, WC 29, BC 12, PC 135. The numbers represented the count of known crimes so far for October in D.C. and Virginia in each of the agency's six divisions: Terrorist Control, Interpersonal Relations, Appropriateness & Safety Reviews, Wellness Confirmations, Border Control, and Personal Control.

Monitoring the numbers was mandatory, and watching them tick upwards as the days wore on, month after month, was morale-destroying.

John caught a glimpse of himself reflected in his workscreen, and he grimaced. He didn't wear his fifty-four years well. His slumped shoulders, baggy eyes, and pensive face spoke of the constant weariness that multiple cups of coffee could not defeat. Sometimes, he was surprised that no one had reported him for his appearance.

John wished he had a stash of alcohol hidden somewhere in his office. He had been dry—or close enough, by his own estimation—for several years, but it was tough to make it through an entire workday without a nip of something. But private possession of alcohol was illegal and not worth the risk—even for DAA agents.

John's workscreen flickered to life and a doughy-looking man in his fifties appeared. He had thin lips and round cheeks. John pulled himself upright and put on an engaged expression; it was his boss, Russell Wallace, the manager of terrorist control for D.C. and Virginia. Wallace took a sip of his coffee then put it down and smacked his lips. When he spoke, his voice was cheery and patronizing.

"Gau is less than thrilled with the second-quarter reports, John. He points out once again that, since you *feelers* here in the DAA are the only ones in all of our society who are aware of and disturbed by the crime rate, you must be the ones who are still perpetuating it."

John made no reply. He was among the minority of agents whom the DAA employed despite the fact that they cared. Most of the DAA positions were filled by sociopaths—*socios*—like Wallace: those unusual people who lacked any sense of guilt, shame, empathy, or conscience.

It made a certain kind of sense. The government knew that people's emotional reactions and thinking reinforced reality. That meant they couldn't put people with compassion in a position where they would be forced into awareness of criminal activity. People would be damaged by such knowledge, dwell on it, and reinforce its reality.

But there weren't enough socios to staff the entire DAA. So they still had feelers, as the socios called them.

"Accordingly, Gau has increased your mandatory positive visualization time by another twenty minutes per day," Wallace went on. "Your total is now one hour and forty minutes per day." He took another sip of coffee and smacked his lips again.

John still said nothing.

Positive visualization was supposed to be the antidote for the DAA agents who did care. Every day, they were required to listen to affirmations and view images of law-abiding, happy people to erase the effects of the misery they witnessed in real life.

John found the repetitive and dull material sheer torture. He usually let his mind wander during the visualization exercises. Even worse, he too often spent the time thinking about how awful things really were in New America. He knew his lax attitude contributed to the ongoing failure of the system—dripping, one drop at a time, thick black sludge into the buoyant culture of New America.

"I trust you have some good news for me on your assignment?" Wallace asked.

As a terrorist control investigator, it was John's job to infiltrate and destroy domestic terrorist groups. His latest assignment called itself the Lightbringers.

John straightened up. "I've got an in." He was glad to be able to announce this after only two months on this case, given the nightmarish end to his previous assignment. He went on, "One of my leads is ready to deal. Nick Aglaeca. I've backed him into a corner he's not willing to try to duck out of. He likes his little empire and he wants to keep it."

"Is he in the terrorist organization?"

"No, he's just a run-of-the-mill boss, but he's dealt with the Lightbringers before, and he thinks he can bring me the leader of the local cell—Drew."

"And what's this man's history with them?"

"He wouldn't tell me the details, but it has to do with Drew. He . . . doesn't care for her." John tried not to recall the specific words Nick had used. That man had a talent for old-world profanity and vivid imagery that John didn't care for. And he obviously hated Drew.

"And what's your plan?"

"Nick is going to start working his contacts. He'll put the word out that, whatever Drew needs, he's the one to supply it. Cast the net. He'll let me know when he catches her in it. I'll keep the pressure on, but it may take some time."

"It sounds like you're moving more aggressively this time." Wallace's tone was approving and cutting at the same time.

John ground his teeth. He had moved too slowly before, and a lot of people had paid for it. He didn't need the reminder.

"I am. I know someone else will just take her place, but I should get enough intelligence from her to make it worth the risk. She should have information about how she contacts other cells, or whatever central leadership they have."

There were other people in his department who carried out stings in which they took away or dusted everyone they found—a short-term solution to specific problems—but John was an investigator. He used subtler methods over longer periods of time to try to understand and uproot entire criminal organizations, to bring a permanent end to them. He just hadn't been effective at it for a long time.

"Good, good. Carry on."

Wallace cut the connection and John slumped back in his chair and sighed. He pressed his palms to his eyes and chanted the DAA feeler mantra under his breath: "There is only good and right in the world. There is only good and right in the world. There is only good and right in the world."

It didn't take away his haunted feeling.

Again, he wished for something to drink, but he took a deep breath and straightened himself up. He had resolved that this assignment would be different. He had to stay on task, stay sharp.

He picked up the one file on his desk, labeled "Lightbringers," and started to thumb through it.

His eyes soon glazed over, and he decided that he was not going to be able to do this without more coffee. He headed to the break room.

The hallways of the DAA were narrow but colorful, with paintings of tidy rows of flowers and cultivated landscapes interspersed among the wallscreens, which currently showed a sitcom about family life. In the show, the youngest of the family had just locked himself in a closet by accident and now yelled for help. As John shuffled by, the family dog perked up his ears at the child's yells, and the laugh track kicked in.

John stopped in the claustrophobically small break room, the laugh track seeming to follow him via the wallscreens. He poured the coffee into a styrofoam cup and put in two creamers and five packets of sugar absently as his mind turned over the strange problem of the Lightbringers.

The group usually made strikes against government facilities. Rumors of attacks placed them in at least New York and Chicago as well as D.C. Numerous government workers had been injured or killed and several buildings damaged. Yet, somehow, the Lightbringers had a reputation as being too goody-goody for other denizens to tolerate. While John had not heard any specific anecdotes, he gathered that they drew arbitrary moral lines and then got self-righteous about them.

As a result, no one wanted to have anything to do with them. One denizen had told him in a whisper, as if frightened that they were listening, "They do something to your *mind*. And then you don't want to do anything *fun* anymore. And once you've joined, you never leave."

The terrorist control division had so far captured two Lightbringers. According to the notes in the case file, they withstood interrogation well, even with the application of mind-altering drugs. Under duress, they only babbled nonsense about light and darkness.

Unfortunately, both had been dusted before John had been put on the case.

He hoped to get a chance to talk to their leader, Drew. So far, he had heard only hushed whispers about her—she sounded almost superhuman.

Plus, anyone Nick hated had to be worthwhile in some way.

The wallscreen flickered and the volume and brightness increased. Brightly colored text, a raucous voice, and background cheers announced, "It's time for a Happiness Break! Come on, everybody!"

John nearly rolled his eyes, but he managed to catch himself and keep his expression neutral. He did let out a little sigh as he put down his coffee cup and turned to the wallscreen. He knew that, all around the nation, every other person would interrupt whatever they were doing—from making love to sealing a business deal to buying groceries—to do the same thing.

He followed along with a vigorously cheerful clown as they practiced big smiles, shouted along with happy affirmations, and did some light calisthenics to "stay focused and keep up your great energy," but he felt a sort of grim determination throughout.

He was one of the few people in the nation who knew the truth about the underground and the constant crime that belied the messages of positive thinking that President Martha taught. He found it difficult to get fully engaged.

It wasn't that the positive thinking stuff was a lie, he reminded himself for the thousandth time as he plodded through the calisthenics and fell further behind with every jumping jack. It just wasn't complete yet. *Eventually, it will work, once everyone is truly on board. It's just . . . taking a long time.*

It had taken his entire lifetime so far, and still it seemed to him that it wasn't any better. Metrics such as the ones that went by his wallscreen every few minutes weren't kept year to year, but he thought that he remembered them being about the same, or maybe even better, twenty or thirty years ago.

He had to abandon his line of thinking to keep up with the new sequence of aerobic moves the clown was demonstrating. This was the thing he hated most about Happiness Breaks, the daily visualizations, the evening Happy News hour, the Beauty Moments and all the rest of the positive thinking package: they were repetitive enough to be annoying but not repetitive enough to be completed on auto-pilot.

He finished the last few bouncy steps and then straightened his suit. At least the break got his blood flowing again. He headed back to his office with a frown and sat down heavily. He needed to get somewhere with this case.

He picked up the Lightbringers file again and paged through the file for the hundredth time.

In his meticulous handwriting, he'd written out dozens of reports of meetings with various *denizens*—the low-life people who made the underground their permanent home. Usually, denizens could no longer pass for normal, due to tattoos or piercings, or sometimes age, illness, or weight. *Tourists*, on the other hand, stopped by the underground from time to time for drugs or banned entertainment, but otherwise lived out normal lives in New American society.

He reviewed his notes several times again, his forehead wrinkled in concentration. He traced one finger down the pages as he read until his finger settled beneath one name: Chloe. The entry read, "The criminal who calls himself Demon Dog says that he knew someone named Chloe who went straight as a Lightbringer. Last time he saw her, she had purple dreadlocks & an eyebrow piercing. Says that she had returned to her old favorite, the Karma Café under the First National Bank on 19th NW."

It was a good place to start. He stood, patted all his pockets until he found his office keys and wallet, locked his door, and trudged out of the building.

CHAPTER THREE

> *Everything—every detail—is a microcosm of the whole.*
> *If you want happiness, beauty, wealth, and success, every*
> *detail must reflect happiness, beauty, wealth, and success.*
> *Every single expression a smile; every bloom in the bouquet*
> *placed just so. Make every action, every detail, perfect now.*

With every city block he walked, Gaylen's heart beat harder and his breath grew tighter in his chest. Two days had passed since his stairwell meeting with Tommy, and now he made his way through the bustling streets of D.C. toward the Lipstick Lounge. He checked his watch for the third time; it was just after nine o'clock on Saturday. Tommy had not given him a specific time to go, and he hoped that the hour was neither too early nor too late. He wrapped his coat around himself and lifted his collar against an unusually chilly October breeze.

Despite how distracted he was with his mission, the happy people of New America drew his attention as they went in and out of stores, shared coffee in open cafes beneath standing heaters, ate their dinners and drank wine. Everyone was always laughing, everyone was always beautiful. For some reason, it all just made Gaylen grind his teeth.

Plastered in varying sizes on every building, all the wallscreens blared an advertisement for hair gel, then went back to a comedy routine. All of them had a small "Request Assistance" button, the very sight of which turned his stomach now.

With every step he took toward the Lipstick Lounge, Gaylen fought the urge to turn around and go back home. Voices warred in his head: *I have to do this. I have to do something. But what's going to happen to me? What if I get caught?*

I can't do this. I should go back.

No, no, I can't go back. I can't keep living like this.

Twice, he did turn around and head back toward home. Each time, he caught himself and retraced his steps again.

He wondered if he should be trying to hide, but hiding was impossible—wallscreens and people were everywhere.

He took a left turn onto N. Lynn Street and saw the neon glow of the sign halfway down the block, on the left. The Lipstick Lounge was on the bottom level of a multi-story mixed-use building. Against his hopes, this street was just as busy as the rest.

Across the street from the bar, he leaned against a wall between two stores and tried to summon the courage to go in. He cast a suspicious look at the wallscreens here. Would the ART have kept track of him as he moved through the city? When a stranger slowed to give him a second look, he realized he was drawing attention to himself. The realization gave him a jolt of adrenaline, and he took advantage of it to make himself go to the bar.

He pushed open the door. It seemed to be a typical place—oversized wallscreens and beautiful people drinking, talking, and laughing. Most sat around tables. The waitresses and waiters all wore black unitards with giant cardboard cutouts of red lips strapped across their rear ends. He grinned a little.

Every wallscreen showed the same thing, since the Bureau of Entertainment provided only one channel for adults, plus the one children's channel. Right now, they broadcast the evening news. At that instant, an image appeared of a peanut superimposed over the state of Florida, and Gaylen guessed at the announcement of a bumper crop.

He scanned the room and spotted a wide doorway leading off to a darker, quieter area of the bar. He headed that way. The bar was overly warm, and he took off his coat as he walked.

He made it halfway across the room before he heard his name. He jumped and turned and searched the crowd. A hand waved in the air, and he traced it down to its owner—a brunette with bright red, glistening lipstick that highlighted her broad smile. It was Rachel, a near neighbor in his skyrise. Two more of his neighbors sat with her. He held back a groan. He would not be able to avoid them. After all, as far as they knew, he had come here to drink and relax with friends, just like everyone else.

He headed toward their table. Rachel shifted her chair to give him room.

"Hey, gorgeous!" Rachel said with a wink.

"Hey, gorgeous yourself," he said. He pulled up another chair next to her. "What's new?"

"Big bumper crop of peanuts in Florida," answered Stan, one of Rachel's roommates.

"I saw that," Gaylen said. "That's great."

One of the waitresses approached. "What do you feel like, sugar?" she asked. She flashed her scanner at him. Gaylen knew that it would register his height, weight, metabolic speed, and current state of inebriation and that the waitress would know in a few seconds that he hadn't had any alcohol yet today. He would be allowed a few drinks—just enough to get buzzed. Then he remembered that it would also record his photo, name, and Social Security number. His stomach turned over. Just what he needed—proof that he was there tonight.

He had hesitated too long, and the waitress raised her eyebrow at him. He put a smile on. "Chocolate martini," he said. "Extra chocolate syrup."

She nodded and turned away while she punched in the order on her scanner.

"Did you hear the humor broadcast today?" Stan asked.

"No, I missed it," Gaylen said. He tried to sound disappointed.

"Oh, no! It was sooo funny," Rachel declared. "There was that one—what was it, Stan—the dog one—"

Stan laughed, remembering, but it was another woman at the table who jumped in with the joke. Gaylen had met her before, but he didn't remember her name. She was another brunette. Her hair was longer than Rachel's and her lipstick was more subdued and her eyes were hazel, but otherwise they could almost be the same person. "Oh, yeah—so, what's the difference between a new dog and a new husband?" she asked.

Rachel grinned at Gaylen and waggled her eyebrows.

Gaylen said, "OK, I give. What?"

"A dog only takes a couple of months to train." The brunette and Rachel doubled over laughing. Trying to be a good sport, Gaylen chuckled a little.

Rachel jumped in. "The other one I liked was, 'The only reason my husband likes to go fishing is because it's the only time anyone ever tells him"—she paused for dramatic effect—"'Wow, that's a big one!'" Everyone laughed again. "If only I had a husband," she added, and she looked at Gaylen pointedly.

Gaylen had always liked Rachel just fine—she had even come up as a good match for him the one time he'd been able to bring himself to browse his options on a Love Today kiosk. And she had asked him out on a date the moment she learned that Serena and Sierra had moved out. But the thought of dating anyone turned him off entirely right now.

He knew he was going to have to crack and bed Rachel soon, simply to avoid rumors that something was wrong with him. It was rude to turn down anyone's advances—why hurt people's feelings by not having sex with them? But even if he could stand the idea, if he encouraged her tonight, she would disrupt his plans.

"I'm sure it'll happen soon enough," he said. Rachel's lips tightened and she turned to Stan. She leaned in against his chest, and he put an arm around her shoulder, looking pleased. Safe in her refuge,

Rachel looked at Gaylen with volumes in her gaze, but he ignored it. Memories of Serena and Sierra ran through his mind and renewed his grief.

"Anything else fun in the good news report?" he asked, wanting a distraction.

The other brunette said, "They had a neat story about a little girl who almost got hit by a car."

"Oh, no," Gaylen said. The waitress brought his drink, and he downed half of it.

"Yeah," Rachel chimed in. She seemed to have forgotten her petulance for the moment. "The little girl—she couldn't have been more than six years old—she was thinking bad thoughts about her older brother and she ran out into the street."

"But the driver was a wedding officiant who had just come from a wedding and was feeling like a hero already—so he saw her and stopped just in time," the brunette said.

"That little girl was so cute," Stan said. "She said she would never think any more bad thoughts about her brother. What a sweet story!"

Everyone chuckled. Gaylen fought back a bitter response, which instead came out as louder laughter than was appropriate, but no one seemed to notice.

The conversation went on, but Gaylen lost track of it. Something about the brunette's hazel eyes seemed familiar to him. It came to him quickly. She reminded him of Chandi, an old girlfriend from long ago. Someone he'd hurt.

He stifled a sigh. As always, the haunted feelings returned whenever he thought of her. He cursed his mind for not leaving him alone about it. It had been fifteen years, for goodness' sake.

Chandi was probably part of why he was too passive now, why he had let Serena go without much of a fight. Partly it was because no one was ever supposed to fight, but partly it was because he had learned that he could hurt other people if he pushed too hard.

He remembered where he was and shook off the thoughts before actual memories flooded back. Everyone still chatted about nothing. He finished his chocolate drink and looked for the waitress and signaled her to bring another martini. Then he refocused on the conversation, despite the sick feeling in the pit of his stomach.

Two hours later, the others decided to call it a night. By then, Gaylen had had his allotment of drinks, which had eased his nerves a little. The wallscreens had all shifted to a Beauty Moment, with a presentation about the flora and fauna of the ocean, with swaying sea plants and chiming music. Gaylen pretended to be entranced so he could wave off the others.

He sat and watched for another fifteen minutes, just in case Rachel came back. He wondered if he should even go through with it, especially since he'd been scanned and friends had seen him there. He vacillated a hundred times in those few minutes, but through it all, a sense of inertia carried him along his original plan, whether he even consciously meant to do it anymore or not. And as he thought about what he was doing, adrenaline rushed through his system again. It sobered him up and made him tremble.

A few minutes later, he stood up and strolled into the back room, despite the pounding of his heart.

It was darker and quieter back there. Thick carpet absorbed sound, as did the deep, plush sofas tucked into semi-enclosed nooks. A smaller bar stood against one wall. Just behind and to the far side of the bar was the unmarked opening to a hallway. That had to be Gaylen's destination.

He crossed the room, sure that he looked out of place. He scanned the room for anyone who might be watching him. He saw the tops of a few heads over the backs of the sofas and heard voices and laughter just breaking through the ambient music. No one took any note of him. Not even the bartender looked up from wiping down the bar.

Still, Gaylen kept his eyes down and hunched his shoulders to make himself look smaller. He kept expecting to hear a voice call out accusingly. He made it to the corridor without incident, but worried that there had been eyes on his back. He hoped he was just being ir-rational. The hallway was empty, without even a wallscreen, and he leaned against the near wall and tried to breathe normally.

"OK, Gaylen," he whispered. "Get yourself together."

He took another breath and looked around. There were two doors, both of which said "Employees Only." The first one led to behind the bar, and the other should have led to the kitchen or a storeroom—at least, that was what he would have expected, before.

He hesitated. This was it. He could still walk away and claim that he had just gotten lost looking for the men's room.

He swallowed hard and pushed on the second door.

It opened with a click that echoed on the other side.

He peeked through the crack.

A dozen yards down a dull, dimly-lit hallway, two rough-look-ing white men leaned against opposite walls, talking. They turned their heads and saw that the door was open.

Gaylen jerked back and let the door close. Then he realized that it was too late for that.

"Dammit!" he muttered—it was the only old-world curse he knew—and opened it again, now with shaking hands.

The two men were already at the door, their size imposing. "Employees only!" the taller one said with a glare.

"Spider sent me," Gaylen said. Just in time, he remembered the movement Tommy had taught him, and he drew one finger across his throat, even though he felt like an idiot. Surely nothing would come of any of this.

But the taller man barked, "What does it mean?"

Gaylen gaped. "What?"

Both men stepped forward.

Suddenly, Gaylen remembered. "Death!" he said, too loudly. He quieted his voice. "It means death." Sweat broke out on his forehead.

The two men stepped back and opened the door wide to let Gay-len in.

Gaylen stood there, hesitating, and then, despite his doubts, he forced himself over the threshold and walked into the underground.

The door clicked shut behind him. It sounded final.

The taller man said to the shorter one, "You take him."

The shorter man made an odd gesture—putting one hand up to his forehead and then snapping it down—and said, "Aye, aye, boss." He sounded like he was being sarcastic. He took off down the hallway without a word to Gaylen.

Gaylen hesitated, and then followed.

At the end of the hallway stood a door with a number pad on it. His guide punched in a string of numbers, and the door made an audible click. As the other man opened the door, Gaylen realized that the door had been *locked*. How bizarre. No one in New America locked their doors—they had no reason to.

They went down a flight of stairs to basement level. The low fluorescent lighting flickered. The stairwell smelled like old urine.

Then Gaylen's escort opened the door at the bottom of the stairwell, and they entered into chaos.

Screaming and shouting and electronic screeching blasted Gaylen's ears. Bright flashing lights made everything in the room seem to stutter as it moved. Dozens of men and women thronged in the room, pushing and shoving recklessly, surrounding something in the center. They screamed and cheered with raw voices. The mood of the crowd seemed dangerous, ugly.

Gaylen's guide walked around the people, and Gaylen hurried after him, adrenaline pumping, eyes wide. Heavy drumbeats thudded beneath the rest of the sounds. A smell of something rotten and acrid came to his nostrils. Trash littered the floor in his path. It was like a pep rally from his high school days twisted by the darkest nightmare he had ever had.

Gaylen caught sight of several people circling around each other in the center of the seething crowd. The tallest man had blood smeared all over the side of his face, and one of his eyes was purple and swollen closed. The man let loose with a furious blow to a woman's face. The crowd roared and Gaylen gasped and stopped as the woman dropped out of view in one flash of the light, dark blood spraying. Gaylen's stomach clenched. Then his guide disappeared around the corner, and Gaylen dashed after him.

The fight continued and the crowd surged with it, back and forth, like stormy ocean waves caught in too small a space. Gaylen ran past, his breath coming hard. People stood around in the room's corners, wearing outfits that were garish or ugly or indecent or bizarre, smoking cigarettes and, weirdly, blowing smoke into the air from their mouths as they leaned close to one another to shout over the noise. A few people were well-dressed and well-groomed—normal, like Gaylen—but they were acting no different from the rest.

A surge of the crowd caught Gaylen in its path. The press of people took him off his feet—he staggered and fell across the lap of an emaciated blond woman sitting on the floor. She was just lifting a needle out of a vein in her stick-thin arm. The corners of her lips lifted in the caricature of a smile. She moved her arm and the syringe out of his way.

"I'm sorry, I'm sorry," Gaylen shouted over the noise. In danger of being trampled by the crowd surrounding them, he tried to scramble up. He had to put his hands all over the girl, and they found skin and bones so delicate he was afraid they would come apart under his weight. She just smiled at him, oblivious, cavernous dark circles under her eyes.

He got to his feet and pushed himself backward through the crowd, backing away from her skeletal grin and vacant eyes, which followed him in the flashes of light. He dodged out from among the roaring people as they surged again, and he ran after his guide, his heart hammering. He had never before seen a person who was anything other than healthy and vibrant.

As they moved down the corridor, they left the music behind them. The flashing light gave way to buzzing, dim fluorescent lighting that hung from the ceiling. Wide tunnels opened up before them, roughly cut out of the rock and then painted with thick yellow latex paint. Gaylen stuck close to his guide. No way was he going back into that room alone.

Questions came to his mind and fell away, incomplete. He had no words for what he had just witnessed. He realized he was nearly hyperventilating, and he tried to calm down. The other man never even looked at him.

A few turns through the hallways—some short sections of them unlighted—and then his guide stopped and knocked on a door.

Gaylen waited, trying to steady his shaking hands.

"Come in," called a voice from inside.

The man opened the door and motioned for Gaylen to go in first.

Inside, Gaylen saw an office with dark, busy wallpaper, wreathed in that weird cigarette smoke, and a short white man behind a desk.

Gaylen took a step forward and saw the man inside more clearly. He had a pot belly and graying hair and a somewhat scraggly goatee, none of which Gaylen had ever seen before. The other man also wore all black and had both ears pierced, which was simply unusual. His gaze was sharp.

The man stood up and mashed his cigarette out in a metal dish overflowing with ashes and stubs.

From the door, Gaylen's guide said, "New one for ya, boss. Spider sent him."

The man cast a cutting look at the other man. "He had the name, gesture, and passcode, I'm assuming."

"Yeah," the other guy said. He left quickly.

"Good," the man in black said to the closing door. He smirked at Gaylen. "All right, son, let's see what I can do for you." He walked around the desk with his hands spread. "Welcome to my humble domain." He sounded like he was mocking himself with the words. "My name is Nick, and I am pleased to be your lord and savior."

At a loss, Gaylen said nothing.

Nick grinned. "My best jokes are always lost on you sleepers. Oh, well." He sat on the edge of his desk. "Have a seat, son." He gestured toward one of the chairs in front of the desk.

Gaylen sat down cautiously.

"Spider sent you. So I know what that means. It means you're having a tough time with life up there." Nick pointed upward. His tone was sympathetic if grandiose. "And that is sad, sad news, my friend. But the good news is that you have me now. Your supplier of all things that will fix you right up and make your life more than bearable."

Gaylen both did and didn't want to know more about what Nick was offering, but then he remembered all that he had seen so far. He blurted out, "Do you know what's going on out there? The fight?"

Nick laughed, sounding genuinely amused. "Yeah, son, I know about the fighting. Are you worried about them? Well, aren't you cute. Don't worry, they'll be all right. More or less."

Heat rose in Gaylen's cheeks and he wanted to leave the room.

Nick went back around the desk and lit up another cigarette. He took a drag before going on, "So, you're a total sleeper, right? You have no idea even what you want? Drugs, girls, violence?"

Gaylen shook his head tentatively, the urge to run growing stronger.

"That's OK. But first, the rules. The basic rules for you tourists." Nick's face became grim and his voice harsh. "And you want to listen close and not fuck this up, you get me?"

Taken aback, Gaylen nodded.

"First rule. This is my fucking domain. Spider sent you to me, and that means you belong to me. Everyone who comes here has to belong to someone who's responsible for them when they fuck things up. So you're mine, for better or worse, till death do us part, you get me?" The man grimaced and pressed one hand to his gut in a way that looked habitual.

"Second rule." Nick took another drag and tapped off some ash. "Blood price. The rule that keeps the underground functioning, such as it does. You break something or spill blood in my domain, you pay me the blood price. You break something or spill blood in another part of the underground, you pay them the blood price. If you don't pay it, I have to pay it, and then I come and take it out of your hide, and I tend to mean that pretty literally. So don't fuck up. Or be ready to pay." He stared at Gaylen intently, his gaze piercing.

Gaylen nodded again. There was a sinking feeling in his stomach, and he wondered what he had gotten himself into and whether it was too late to get back out of it.

"Third rule. This one is my own personal rule. Around here, we feed the wolf. Because that is my gift to you. That is how I fix you. You're lucky Spider sent you to me. Because I teach you to feed the wolf inside, and that means you're going to end up stronger and better than you can even imagine right now."

Gaylen had no idea what the other man was talking about.

Nick sat down in his chair behind his desk again. "Let me tell you a little something about me, son. Hey, what's your name?"

He hesitated, but reluctantly said, "Gaylen."

"All right. Gaylen. So let me tell you about me."

Gaylen shifted uncomfortably in his seat. He didn't want to learn anything about Nick, but he didn't think he had a choice. He disliked this person—which was an extremely unusual feeling.

Nick went on, "There's an old, old saying from people who lived on this continent before your people or mine ever got here. They said that a man can feed either the dog or the wolf inside him. Do you understand what that means?"

Gaylen shook his head.

"If you feed the dog inside you, that means you learn obedience and loyalty. You learn to be a good dog. And you do what you're told. And they reward you with scraps from the table.

"But you feed the wolf inside you, then you have strength. Power. Freedom. Wolves are vicious creatures, though, son. You know about wolves?"

Gaylen hesitated and then shook his head. "A little. I mean, they're wild animals. They don't live in the cities."

"Right. But the wolf inside us is always there, waiting to come out. You want more than what loyalty and obedience get you, you've got to feed the wolf. I have. And it's a hungry, demanding beast, but it set me free."

Nick took another drag from his cigarette.

"Once upon a time, a long, long time ago, I had no power. I was the victim. And then I set my wolf loose one day, although I didn't think of it that way back then, and I nearly killed my father."

Gaylen flinched.

"And then he learned better. He was afraid of me after that, instead of the other way around."

Gaylen just waited, hoping this conversation would be over soon.

"Now, that's not what they meant." Nick gestured with his cigarette. "They wanted people to become dogs. But I don't want you or me or anybody to be a dog, Gaylen. And that's what you are right now. A good dog."

Gaylen said nothing. He only had the vaguest idea of what Nick was trying to tell him.

"You do what you're told, don't you, son? You think positively with all your little heart? You drink your allotted amount of booze?" Nick's tone had become mocking.

Gaylen stayed quiet.

"And what has it gotten you? Panic attacks? Depression? Erectile dysfunction?" Nick smirked.

Gaylen had never heard of any of those things before.

"It doesn't matter. We'll fix you up." Nick took another drag and then set the cigarette down on the metal tray as he stood up again. "I have the perfect cure." He stood up and gestured elaborately at the walls.

Gaylen glanced around, and only then came to register what he had thought was a busy, dark wallpaper. They were photographs.

He looked closer. Each photo depicted a human being who was naked and bound, with visible wounds—cuts, burns, and bruises.

Gaylen stared, making out one horrifying detail after another. He couldn't pull his eyes away, even though he wanted to, and even though the sight made him feel sick. He had never seen anything like this before. Accidents and injuries were incredibly rare and trivial—a cut finger, perhaps. These wounds . . . some of them were surely life-threatening.

"What happened to them?" Gaylen asked.

Nick laughed again. "Mostly, I did."

Gaylen stared at him, unable to take his meaning. Then he remembered the fight in the other room. He did a double take. "Why?"

"Feeding the wolf, Gaylen. I told you, it is a beast. It is hungry for blood. But it is strong. And it is free. You can't even imagine, right now, what it will be like for you when you let yours out." Nick smiled in what looked like anticipation.

Gaylen shuddered. He found himself on his feet. "No. I don't know what this is all about, but I don't want to be—you can't do this. Things like this. It's bad. And I don't want to—almost kill people, or these pictures—" He realized he was practically incoherent as he backed up toward the door.

Nick closed in on Gaylen, his face serious and his eyes piercing. "Stop right there. You're not going anywhere."

"You can't do this!" Gaylen said, gesturing at the walls. His heart pounded and his throat had gone dry.

"I can, and I do. And so will you."

The two men stared at each other. "No," Gaylen breathed. "No. I won't. This is crazy."

Nick stepped even closer to him. The other man's eyes glittered unsteadily. "You don't have a choice, son. You came here, to my domain. You belong to me now. I have people all through this city who are going to watch you wherever you go and whatever you do. They'll know whether you're following my orders or not. And if you don't, then I will have them bring you to me, and then you are going to be the subject of a whole series of photographs for my wall. Is that clear?"

Nick's words struck Gaylen like blows, each sentence hitting harder, taking away his breath.

"But we can't! We can't do these things!"

"Why not?"

Nick smirked. He stepped away and went back behind his desk to put out the cigarette that had been burning down. It was as if Nick knew he had already won the fight.

"Because—because it will make things worse. For everyone."

"Why? How?"

"Because whatever you see, whatever you do, that is what you're going to attract into your life," he said, repeating the government's teachings. "'Hear only good, see only good, speak only good.' Or it will show up everywhere. It will hurt everyone." He realized that he was trapped in a room, underground, lost, with someone who hurt others on purpose. His hands were shaking and he clasped them together to make them stop.

Nick lit another cigarette. "I know that's what they say," he said. "I know that's what you've heard every day of your miserable little life. I know, I used to live up there, too. But is it true?"

Gaylen blinked at him.

"Is it true?" Nick demanded.

"Of course it is."

"No, it isn't," Nick said. "It's a lie. The wolf is in all of us. And it doesn't go away if you ignore it. It will never go away. And you can't pretend it isn't there." He gestured at the photos on the walls. "None of this could happen if the 'Hear only good, see only good, speak only good' thing actually worked, would it?"

"Maybe it's only here because you didn't try hard enough to disbelieve it."

Nick shook his head. "It's always been here. Remember the whispers you've heard about the bad old days? It was alive and well then. And it's still here, because it can never go away. It can't. " He took another drag and blew the smoke out quickly. "That's what Old Man Watts taught us all." He gestured to a photo on his desk—an old man with bushy eyebrows and piercing eyes. "Wayne Webster Watts. My hero. Taught me everything I know. Look, if the lies that President Martha spews actually worked, then wouldn't you be happy?"

Gaylen looked away.

"I know, you think you're defective, don't you?" Nick said, not unsympathetic. "But you're not. That's what none of you stupid sleepers ever realizes before you come down here and become a tourist or a denizen. Everyone is just like you, Gaylen. Everyone is on the verge of breaking down all the time. And it's not because you're all defective. It's because the system Martha's little cult cooked up doesn't work."

He spat on the floor, a motion so revolting it startled Gaylen.

"It's not you," Nick repeated. "The wolf is inside all of us, and it will never go away, and you can't ignore it, and there's no point in trying."

Gaylen looked away, fighting back insane laughter that threatened to burst out. Here he had spent years trying so hard to do something that was . . . impossible?

He found himself sitting back down. "You mean . . .," he said, "if everyone is like me . . . then other people aren't happy, either?"

Nick laughed. "Yep. You're all pretending. It's the stupidest game in mankind's history." He let a few minutes pass while he finished up his cigarette and then rubbed it out in the filthy ashtray. Gaylen meanwhile tried to adjust to this new worldview.

Apparently speaking for the entire underground, Nick spread his hands and said, "So, that's why we're here. Providing a public service. Because the only way to deal with the wolf is to embrace it. Befriend it. Feed it and nurture it. Let it help you get through your day. It takes a little time, a little trial and effort, but you'll never go back."

Gaylen shivered. Nick's certainty was compelling. He spoke like someone who had years of experience and hundreds of case studies—and Gaylen believed he probably did.

"It's not good," Gaylen protested, but he knew he was defeated.

Nick grinned. "Yeah," he said. "That's kinda the point."

He leaned forward in his chair. "Here's your assignment. You spend some time in my playground, in my anarchy. You find something that's more horrible than anything you could possibly imagine, and then you do it. You have one week. And I'll have my people watching you, so don't think you're going to get away without doing it." His voice grew harsher and he met Gaylen's eyes dead on. "You do something despicable inside one week or I'll just have to go with you and help you do it. And I think you'll like my way a whole lot less than whatever you come up with."

Chapter Four

President Martha St. Tala:

'Hear only good, see only good, speak only good' is one of the most important teachings of our society. I know how tempting it can be to worry and gossip about anything that you perceive to be a bad thing. But if you simply let nature take its course while you focus only on the desired outcome, the imagined problem simply melts away. Trust the universe to handle all these so-called problems for you and for our society, and you can save yourself all that time, trouble, and worry.

After staying too long in bed and then taking a shot of bootleg whiskey, John Oldman managed to get himself dressed. His destination this afternoon was the Karma Café, where he hoped to find Chloe of the Lightbringers.

The café was an underground spot he had never heard of before. He put on his bulletproof, stun-proof vest and hoped that the denizens he ran across wouldn't have newer tech imported from the outside world. Technology had been stagnant in New America ever since the borders had closed forty-five years ago. With the economic classes evened out, most wages set, manufacturing taken over by the government, and the country theoretically perfect anyway, innovation had taken a nosedive.

He buckled on his gun holster and slid in his gun, then put on his jacket and overcoat. The vest and gun were a dead giveaway that he was DAA, but if anyone saw them, something would have already gone wrong.

He was feeling too lethargic to walk all the way to the entrance to the underground closest to the Karma Café, so he picked up a community electric car a few blocks from his house. He only needed to swipe his ID card for the car to unlock and charge the time to his bank balance—or, in his case, to the DAA. Soon after, he pulled up at the Francis Scott Key House at George Washington University.

He got out of the car and pulled his jacket tighter against the wind. The basement of the north wing held an entrance to the underground. He'd already acquired the new name, passcode, and gesture from another contact.

He hoped everything would go smoothly. Every so often, some denizen did something stupid and he had no choice but to dust him.

Then he remembered that he wasn't supposed to think that way. With a grimace, he ran through the mandatory antidote—a positive visualization of people stopping carefully at stop signs, walking on the crosswalks, paying for their purchases, and smiling all the while.

Just shoot me, he thought. Then he shook his head. He visualized the thought, struck it out in his mind, and turned it into *What a lovely day I'm going to have*. It didn't particularly help, but it never particularly helped.

He entered the building and took the stairs down to the basement. He walked through the laundry facilities, catching a few glances from students doing laundry along the way, and went around a corner to the boiler room door. He shoved open the door, and an ungainly teenager confronted him. "Hey, man, you lost?" the kid demanded, looking him over.

Pressing his palms together and bowing slightly, John said, "Reverence. Sent by Ian."

The kid nodded. "All right, sorry. Just doing my job."

"No worries," John said.

He left the kid behind and went on into the narrow, rough-hewn tunnel behind the boilers. It expanded after a few hundred feet into a hallway with flickering fluorescent lighting and an occasional ventilation shaft. He tracked his progress using the digital compass on his handscreen. The hallway took a contrary turn to the north before straightening back out toward the east and the supposed location of the Karma Café.

The hallways that had been dug out under D.C. over the past for-ty-five years formed a meandering, inefficient maze. Some trips that took five minutes by foot topside took thirty minutes underground. Lighting was unpredictable, the footing sometimes treacherous. Still, the existence of the tunnels was remarkable, especially given that they were dug out by people who were too lazy, depressed, or high to do anything constructive topside. It had taken thousands of people and dozens of laser dozers several decades to pull off this feat.

A literal underground like D.C.'s could exist only in some parts of the country—places where the ground and water tables were right, and where existing basements, sewers, and subway tunnels provided good jumping-off points. Other cities had to hide their "undergrounds" in the backs of various buildings, and denizens could rarely live there full-time. Denizens in cities like D.C. had it easy by comparison.

Once John was sure he was alone in the hallway, he touched his jaw. A hidden subdermal switch activated his facial tattoo. Gold na-nites that were embedded in his flesh reversed polarity and rushed to the surface of his skin in a pre-programmed pattern, stinging and burning along the way. His eyes teared. He checked his reflection in his darkened handscreen to confirm that the gold mask was in place. The sleek oval covered the center of his face, from forehead to chin, and from cheek to cheek.

The tattoo was the same he'd used for his cover with FPU. He'd called himself Goldfinger, in tribute to the James Bond villain, but it usually got abbreviated to "Finger"—too appropriate, if they had known his real job. It was easy for him to keep using the same cov-er on his new assignment. He could simply claim to be one of the survivors—one of the lucky few who had been elsewhere in the underground when the DAA had shut down the FPU cell. In some sense, it was even true.

Against his will, John remembered again the moment when Russell Wallace had told him that his assignment had been terminated. Wallace had looked self-satisfied as he'd related that the DAA was, at that moment, releasing swarms of nanotech nukes throughout the area the FPU called home. It was the DAA's first official trial of microscopic nuclear weapons.

Weapons of mass destruction were the only area where technology was still progressing, but the DAA still struggled to find a method of extermination that would meet President Martha's mandate to "cause no additional fear or pain."

In this case, Wallace had bragged about how the scientists had said that there would be no fallout with such a tiny amount of fissionable material. The terrorists were being efficiently massacred, with DAA workers standing by to clear the area of corpses, and then it would be safe for reoccupation. The deaths would be relatively painless. Wallace was optimistic that President Martha would have liked this weapon.

John was speechless, frozen in his seat, his heart thumping dully in his chest. He sat quietly while people he had known for years died because he had failed.

"Why?" he asked. "What good will this do? Killing all of them?"

"Not much," Wallace said. He leaned back in his chair and twirled a pencil in his fingers. "These terrorist groups—like a plague. Cure one patient, it's already spread to another. But we bought a year or so before they fill their ranks out again. Maybe then we'll have someone on the job who's competent to handle the situation."

This time, John would not get so close to his targets. This time, he would not delay.

John started encountering denizens as he approached the café. It was common to see all types of people down here, so no one gave him a second look, other than in appreciation for his gold mask.

The café itself turned out to be innocuous. It was just a corner of a large room, with glass walls, a handful of small tables, and counter service. Speakers played Bob Dylan's song "A Hard Rain's A-Gonna Fall"; the wallscreens were off network, playing the old movie *Bonnie and Clyde*. Both had long been banned. A banner across the windows said, "For freedom." The menu above the counter advertised a mean falafel sandwich plus gyros and burgers.

John kind of liked the place.

For a moment, he debated whether it was good or bad to like the place. Liking things was positive, but this was illegal stuff he wasn't supposed to like.

He glanced around. The café was empty of customers.

He went up to the counter and ordered a falafel sandwich with fries, then pulled out his off-network card to swipe for payment. In the underground, anyone could get himself a rechargeable card— and entrance to the underground economy—by bringing down something valuable to sell to one of the fences. In John's case, he got his card recharged back at the DAA.

He asked the guy behind the counter, "You know a girl with purple dreadlocks? Chloe?"

The guy looked him up and down. "Who's asking?"

"Looking for the Lightbringers," John said. "Demon Dog told me she was the way to go."

The guy shrugged. "I don't give out info. Sorry, pal."

"No problem," John said. "Ring me up for another $500." With his lunch costing just over $30, $500 was a decent bribe.

The guy stared at him for a moment, then keyed something into his register and nodded toward the card reader. John swiped his card.

"Stay till seven," the guy said. "She'll be here. And yeah, she's your hookup."

John nodded. "Thanks." He took his order and sat down with it. He ate, then he sat back and watched *Bonnie and Clyde*. It was so much better than Bureau of Entertainment tripe, even with the language and violence.

John kicked himself mentally for thinking that and found himself reciting the feeler mantra while he watched.

A few minutes after seven o'clock, a girl with purple dreadlocks and an eyebrow piercing came in along with two young men. John observed that she had a sweet, round face, a small chest and curvy hips. She popped her chewing gum. Her shirt said, "Meh."

John watched the guy behind the counter to make sure he didn't warn the trio in some way.

The kids, meanwhile, were just acting silly. The older one, who had tattoos peeking out of his shirt sleeves, kept pulling at Chloe's dreadlocks from behind her back, then acting innocent, driving her to exasperated laughter. She pummeled him while he pretended to cower, then she stopped when it was her turn to order. The younger boy paid for all three of them, and they sat at one of the tables.

The café was pretty quiet, so it was easy to overhear their conversation. They exchanged gossip about mutual friends and then made fun of the movie that had just come on—*Missing in Action* with Chuck Norris.

John had trouble imagining any of them as dangerous criminals, even though their appearances confirmed that they were permanent residents of the underground. His mind flashed back to old friends from the FPU—friends who were dead now because of him. He reminded himself that he couldn't do anything about it now. The DAA would have executed them all eventually anyway.

John sighed heavily. He'd gone off into negative thinking again. This time, he lacked the energy to counter the thoughts. He just let his mind go blank. It was easier.

He got up and headed down the tunnel a short distance. There he leaned against a wall and waited. The whiskey had long ago worn off and he fought the desire for more alcohol, but it kept coming back. The Karma Cafe didn't serve alcohol, he didn't think, but he wanted to go back to check.

Twenty minutes later, the trio left the café. They headed his way together, unfortunately. He'd hoped they would separate.

They slowed down when they saw him and recognized him from the café.

He stepped forward, his hands out in a gesture of peace. "Hey. Can I talk to you a minute?"

The three stopped and exchanged glances, their faces sober. "What do you want?" the older boy asked, stepping forward, his hand going under his coat.

John talked faster. "Demon Dog told me I could find you, Chloe. Said you could introduce me to the Lightbringers."

Chloe looked dubious, and cast a look at her friends for moral support. They shrugged at her. "I . . . don't know," she said.

"OK, I understand," John said. "You don't know me from Adam. I don't blame you for being nervous. Look, can I just walk with you guys for a minute and talk to you?"

Chloe shifted her weight from one foot to the other.

The older boy stepped up again. "I don't think she wants to talk to you."

John looked down and tried to collect his thoughts. Chloe looked like a sweet girl, so he changed tactics. "OK. I just thought you might be recruiting. I was with the FPU. You heard what happened to them? All my friends are dead." He shrugged, and he didn't have to fake the way his face twisted with grief.

An expression of sympathy swept Chloe's face, but the boy shook his head and spoke first. "They don't need anybody right now." He took Chloe's arm and they walked away.

John watched them go.

Hardly a success. But he'd gotten Chloe's attention. He just needed to get her alone next time.

He waited for a few more seconds, then followed them.

Chapter Five

President Martha St. Tala:

> *You have an obligation to everyone you know—every friend,
> lover, coworker, and family member—to be happy. When
> you're happy, you cheer others up, and that turns into a
> ripple effect that affects so many other people. Now, the
> opposite would be true as well, wouldn't it? And you don't
> want to be responsible for that. So remember, the people
> around you deserve to see you smiling.*

The next morning, Gaylen woke up with his heart pounding and
his breath tight in his chest. From his bed, he listened to President
Martha's extended Sunday morning Good News message intently,
all the while applying his new perceptions of his society.

Today's lesson was about the perfection of the body, how it
could—and did—heal itself from all injuries or illness so long as
the person entertained thoughts only of health.

As usual, President Martha emphasized the importance of the
quarterly Wellness Confirmations. "Our questions are deliberately
chosen," she said, her tone soothing and persuasive, "and answering honestly is very important. If your thinking has been slipping
and you've been experiencing dis-ease in your body, you should tell
your Wellness Consultant. They will give you the tools you need to
recover immediately."

Gaylen had heard this information many times before, and he
had always taken it for granted as true. No one he knew had ever had

anything worse than a cold or a headache or a splinter. Such minor ailments were considered warning signs that one's thinking was going off track, and after a few days of focusing on health, they always went away.

But now he considered the injuries he had seen in the underground, in Nick's photographs. Would those gashes close up from positive thinking? Would the burns and bruises disappear? The thought seemed ludicrous.

He also thought about how the Assistance Response Team had treated him. If the Wellness Confirmation team was similarly trained and offered the same skills as the ART, would their prescribed treatment even work?

"So what if it's not just me?" he murmured to himself. Then he remembered that they were surely watching him from his wallscreen. Careful to keep his thoughts contained to his own mind, he asked himself again, *What if it's really not just me? What if it doesn't work for anyone?*

He wondered how many people went to the underground on a regular basis. It could be thousands of people. Even hundreds of thousands. Incredible. And if the cure was to "feed the wolf," then what awful secrets did the smiling faces all around him conceal?

Surely all of them weren't like Nick. The ugly man confused Gaylen immensely. He seemed to care about Gaylen and people like him enough to try to help them, yet he did awful, violent things to other people. It didn't make sense.

Surely there were other options in the underground. How could committing acts of violence resolve his unhappiness about his wife and daughter leaving him, anyway? He hated the thought of hurting anyone.

He kept his eyes on the wallscreen while he reviewed the few facts he had. Judging by the photos in Nick's office, Nick was more than capable of punishing him if he failed to comply with his "assignment." Gaylen couldn't report Nick to the ART—he had lost that option when he had gone to the underground, becoming a criminal in the process. He didn't know the extent of Nick's power. He didn't know who Nick's men were, or how to avoid them.

Since Gaylen's boss, Tommy, was a member of Nick's underground, then surely Nick could go through Tommy to get all of Gaylen's personal information and hunt him down. Although Gaylen wanted to believe that Tommy would protect him against Nick, he had no reason to hope that he would.

And if Gaylen went to the underground and took Nick's medicine . . . Nick had suggested that Gaylen could do these things with no consequences from the universe, and that they would fix him. "Powerful and free," Nick had said. Gaylen wanted those things badly.

He thought that over for a few minutes. No consequences. No punishment from the universe. No punishment at all. But as Gaylen contemplated that, he realized that his revulsion at Nick's path had nothing to do with the fear of punishment or consequences. His revulsion was just there, attached to the very idea of hurting others. Just looking at Nick's photos had made him feel sick.

But what other choice did he have? He had entered Nick's territory.

He rubbed his hands over his face.

Maybe he could find a way to placate Nick without doing anything too bad, and then he would be free to search out other cures down there in the underground. After all, if Nick had told him the truth, then lots of people found cures down there.

Maybe everyone seemed so happy not because of positive thinking, but because they were getting fixed in the underground. Heck, maybe he was one of only a few who weren't, yet.

Gaylen told himself that his mind was made up, even though his stomach still felt uneasy. He threw aside the covers and got dressed. He went to the Golden Dragon Chinese café and coffee shop on the ground floor of his skyrise, where he passed the day by watching the wallscreens and reading a novel on his handscreen.

The novel bored Gaylen—it was standard Bureau of Entertainment fare, this time about a young man who steals due to his thoughts of lack but who is redeemed and discovers he has everything he really needs after all—but he tapped through the pages anyway. Mostly, he watched the other patrons of the café, looking for signs that might reveal which of them were faking their smiles, which ones were going to engage in some depraved activity underground that night.

The task fascinated him, but he was unsuccessful. He wished he could tell the difference, because that meant he would be able to tell the good people from the bad people. On the other hand, he was glad that he couldn't, because that meant he should be just as undetectable to everyone else.

Finally, the sun went down. His heart hammering, Gaylen buttoned up his coat against the October chill and set out for the Lipstick Lounge.

Gaylen had to stop and psych himself up before entering the big room at the foot of the stairs coming down from the Lipstick Lounge, but to his relief, only a few people stood around, smoking those old-style cigarettes and talking. The music was the same as before, but the light held steady instead of flashing.

The people looked too much like Nick for Gaylen's taste. He hurried through the room, feeling eyes on him, and then, as he walked down the next hallway, he realized he was going to get lost in short order. He pulled out his handscreen so he could take notes on which turns he made through the hallways.

He took a left turn, made a note of the crude drawing on the wall as a landmark, and moved purposefully down the hallway. He wanted to look like he was on his way somewhere, as if that would be safer. He put his hands in his pockets so no one could notice that they were shaking.

He soon passed a small group of thugs who all had heavy, permanent-looking markings on their faces. He kept his eyes averted. These people must be committed to the underground lifestyle, since they could never appear above-ground with those facial markings. They glanced at him but kept walking.

A few yards later, a door on the right hung open, and moans and grunts emanated from inside. Against his better judgment, he glanced inside as he passed. A woman lay naked across a mattress, her head thrown back and three half-naked men at work on different parts of her. Gaylen walked faster. Sex was hardly taboo in New America—it was a form of casual recreation, with not much more significance than a game of tennis—but it was done privately.

However, he'd much rather be part of a public orgy than do the things Nick had suggested. He half-grinned, his anxiety easing for a moment, and wondered whether that would satisfy Nick. Probably not.

He hesitated at the next intersection, then dictated to his handscreen, "Took next right at the words 'GIVE UP.'" As he saved the note, screaming and shouting come from the passage on the right.

He peeked around the corner. A group of rough-looking men and women charged in his direction. Two men carried ropes and led a chant of "Take 'em, hang 'em, make 'em pay!" Others dragged along a man and a woman by their elbows, their hands bound behind their backs. Both screamed and kicked out in all directions.

Gaylen ducked backward, out of their path. He didn't know the exact meaning of "hang 'em," but he could tell that the man and woman were captured and resisting. The mood of the crowd was ugly.

To his dismay, the mob turned directly toward him.

For the second time in as many days, he rushed to get out of the way before he was trampled.

The woman's long hair was bright green mixed with black. The man had drawings on his face and neck. He sobbed, tears falling on the ground below him.

Gaylen took a deep breath and reminded himself that he was, however reluctantly, looking for something terrible enough to satisfy Nick. Feeling sick at heart, he fell in behind the mob. Already, adrenaline rushed through his system again.

As they hastened along, people in the back cried out, "No, don't do this! They didn't do anything!" Others yelled, "They have to pay! It's the law!" An overweight blond girl screamed, "Laura!" over and over; it seemed to be the name of the captive with the green-and-black hair.

Her cries went straight to Gaylen's heart. He had never heard anyone sound so distraught. Terrible things were surely going to happen. Surely he should try to do something to stop whatever it was going to be, but he was helpless against such a mob. And on the other hand, the raw energy of the crowd surged through him, making him feel stronger and more alive, just as Nick had said, but mixed with nausea and trembling.

The mob passed through several turns and sections of hallway. Other people came out of rooms and hallways and joined the throng. Dozens of people now surrounded Gaylen.

The blond girl screaming "Laura" managed to force herself through the crowd and throw herself on top of one of the men who held her friend captive. A brief scuffle broke out, not all of which Gaylen could see, and then everyone surged ahead again, leaving the blond girl laying on the floor. She cowered and cried while people stepped over her or even on her. Gaylen stepped around her, looking down at the blood on her hands and face even though he wanted to look away. He hated to leave her there, and he feared the wrath of the crowd if he helped her, and in the end, he kept walking.

After what seemed like a long time and a great distance, the crowd stopped in a room with a high ceiling and several entrances and exits. A wooden frame had been built against the back wall. The men with the rope tugged two large hooks down from the structure. They made loops with the ropes.

The mood of the crowd became even more volatile. Loud voices got even louder. It seemed that everyone was screaming at someone. Another scuffle broke out.

In the distraction, the male captive made a break for it. Two other people jumped on top of him and dragged him to the ground. Laura wailed. The two men put the loops over the hooks.

Gaylen hugged the wall, trying to stay out of harm's way. His heart was beating so hard he thought he might black out. He was definitely part of some awful thing that was going to happen—something he was helpless to stop.

Three men worked together to lift up Laura. Despite her struggles, they held her firmly enough that a fourth man could secure the rope around her neck.

Finally, Gaylen understood the purpose of the structure and the ropes and the full meaning of "hang'em." His heart lurched in his chest. He stepped forward. "No!" he screamed as loudly as he could. "No, don't!"

The sound of his voice was lost in the crowd's shouting. The men let go of Laura at the same moment the fourth man pulled a lever on the wood structure. The woman stopped screaming as the rope yanked her three feet into the air by her neck. Her legs churned in the air, her body jerking stiffly back and forth. Screams and cheers echoed through the hallway. Five men worked to subdue the male captive, who had gone wild with fear.

Tears sprang to Gaylen's eyes. He was part of this. He had let it happen. She was dying right in front of him, and it was his fault.

Then, suddenly, new shouts and screams erupted.

"DAA!"

"Sting!"

"Fuck, *fuck*, get out!"

"Run!!"

It took a few seconds for the voices to be heard. Then everyone fled in every direction. They pushed and shoved and trampled one another as they went. The male captive ran alongside his previous captors.

Laura was left kicking in mid-air.

Gaylen had never heard the words "DAA" or "sting," and he didn't know what the threat was, but Laura's plight was more important than anything else. Maybe it wasn't too late to save her. He shoved through the panicking roil of people.

At the wooden structure, he climbed up to the lever the fourth man had pulled, and released it.

Laura dropped the three feet to the ground and collapsed with one leg twisted underneath her.

"Dammit!" Gaylen said. He jumped down to rush to her side.

At that moment, he heard a strange sound—like a distant whine with a sudden stop—and Laura and the three people to her right dissolved from their insides out to their heads and hands and feet. Their clothing fell to the ground with a fine mist of dust following them.

Gaylen sucked in a panicked breath and looked up.

Uniformed figures held small devices that they pointed around the room. Everywhere they pointed one of the objects, people disintegrated from their insides out. One of them looked directly at Gaylen and raised his device.

Gaylen took off and dashed down to the hallway to his left faster than he had ever run before in his life, and faster than he had known he *could* run.

A whine came from behind Gaylen, and a man with a bald, tattooed head disintegrated a few feet in front of him, and he knew that the men were right behind him.

He cried out and his speed began to flag with the futility of knowing that he was about to be turned into dust.

And then an odd blur coursed through the air from his right, and a small but strong body crashed into him. He was already off-balance, in mid-stride. He bounced off a door jamb hard, stumbled into a room, and collided with a desk. He fell, and his attacker landed on top of him.

She was so petite that he could have shoved her back off of him. But she leaned close to his face and commanded "Be still!" with such intensity that he froze. She slapped one palm against his mouth and held it there. A cold metal ring bit into his bottom lip. Squinting down, he could just see that the top of the ring bore a flashing yellow LED.

She stared at him with a threat in her eyes that told him that he must not move.

He tried to suck in enough air through his nose to stay conscious. Had his mouth been free, he would have been gasping for breath.

Men tumbled into the room behind them, shouting for them to stop, while weapons whined outside. Gaylen would have struggled to get away, but the girl leaned even closer and her gaze grew even more threatening.

Inexplicably, though the men stood only a foot or two away, they did not seem to see the two of them on the floor. Through the roar building up in his ears from oxygen deprivation, Gaylen heard one of them curse and say, "Where the hell did they go?" The other one kicked at something, perhaps a chair. A few seconds passed, suspense hanging thick in the air, and then their pursuers left the room.

The girl's hair was honey brown and straight and cut to the level of her chin. Her eyes were green, her face triangular, her lips full. She was small enough to be described as a waif. But in her eyes was a strength and power Gaylen had never seen in any person before. He lay unmoving, his lip throbbing where she pressed the ring, feeling her slight weight on top of his body, transfixed.

Outside the room, the shouts and footsteps continued for a few moments. Then the sounds faded into the distance.

Finally, the girl climbed off of him. She took his hand and pulled him up with compact strength and led him out of the room.

She checked both directions and pulled him down the hallway back in the direction they had come, then down another hallway, then through another room and into another hallway. Gaylen realized that he had stopped taking note of the turns way back when he was part of the mob.

"Where are we going?" Gaylen asked quietly.

She glanced back at him. "Doesn't matter," she said, and she looked around a corner before proceeding.

He went another hallway length before saying, "What are we doing?"

She looked at him with one raised eyebrow. "Saving you."

Gaylen let that process for a moment before asking, "Why?"

"I always save someone."

And then she led him up a dark stairwell. They would be back at surface level now. He could see artificial light edging the doorway.

She pushed him against the wall next to the door and grabbed his shirt collar. He found himself bending down to make it easier for her.

"Up there, they won't use the dust guns," she said with intensity, her green eyes all but glowing. "They'll have to get in close. If you see anyone coming up to you, stay away from them. Don't run. Don't look frightened. Just look distracted and keep following me. Do you understand?"

"Yes," Gaylen said, although he didn't really understand, and then she pulled open the door and walked out ahead of him into a surprisingly busy shopping area. Gaylen sucked in a breath and followed.

The wallscreens on the buildings were lit up with circus spectacle. A block party filled the streets with hundreds, if not thousands, of people. There were vendors of snacks and drinks all around them, in addition to the stores all being open and advertising special block-party prices. The air was a cacophony of music, laughter, and cheering, plus fireworks here and there.

All around them were the beautiful, happy people of New America.

They walked about a block before a pretty redhead carrying flyers singled Gaylen out and approached him from across the street. He averted his eyes and hurried toward his escort.

Then a blond girl called out to him from one of the shops. "Gaylen! Try some of this cologne!" She came out into the street with a bottle in her hand, trying to close in on him. He mumbled an apology and dodged around a family standing clustered together and all but ran a few paces to leave her behind. His heart beat wildly. How did she know his name?

Twenty more paces, and then a man at a hot-dog stand called out, "You want a hot dog, don't you, son?" He and his partner both beamed at Gaylen, who looked away and kept moving. Both men broke away from the crowd waiting to buy hot dogs and followed him several steps as they called after him. Gaylen pretended to find something very interesting on the other side of the street, but he knew his expression was frantic, his face sweaty. People stared as he passed by.

Only a few minutes had elapsed since they'd left the underground. How was it possible that they already knew who he was?

Within a few more moments, the girl was leading him into another stairwell and through an unmarked door, and then they were racing down corridors without wallscreens. She slowed enough to catch his hand and then dragged him along.

"Who were those people?" Gaylen asked between breaths.

"The DAA," she yelled back.

He still didn't know what that meant.

They spilled out onto a subway platform and raced across the tracks just before a train shot by, blaring its horn, and then through another door, through another hallway, down another stairwell . . . And finally she threw open a final door and flung herself inside, onto a bare mattress on the floor in an empty, dirty room. Only a blinking white light on the wall provided light.

Gaylen collapsed on the floor near her.

Moments passed as they caught their breath.

"We're safe here?" Gaylen asked.

She nodded and straightened up into a cross-legged position.

"Safe as houses. Which is to say, not in the least, but it's as good as you're ever going to get."

He could see her only on every other word, as the light blinked on and off.

She looked him over and grimaced.

"What?" he asked.

"You dwell in shadow."

"What does that mean?" he asked, defensive.

"You live in darkness! It's all over you." She surprised him by leaning over and punching him on the shoulder and then laughing.

"I don't know what you're talking about."

"Of course not. But you'll learn." And she looked at him for a long time, her face expressionless again. She seemed to be waiting.

"What now?" he asked.

She only kept watching him.

It dawned on Gaylen that he was shaking.

Suddenly, everything that had happened came down on him all at once. Laura hanging, kicking in mid-air, and then disintegrating, the long moments as the DAA walked right past them on the floor, the beautiful but threatening people accosting him as he worked his way through the crowds outside. He had trouble breathing, and he suspected that the girl had been waiting for this reaction to hit him.

The look in her eyes was softer now.

He tried to catch his breath. He looked around for something to distract her, to make her stop watching him. He was too close to breaking down in front of her. He wanted to scream, cry, and punch things, all at the same time.

She leaned toward him, still giving him all of her attention. "Just breathe deeply. It will pass."

He met her eyes and tried to anchor himself to the kindness he saw there during the flashes of the light. He took deeper breaths for a minute, as she had said, and it helped.

"I . . . I nearly died."

"Yes," she said, not without compassion. "And now you can never go back."

"Never go back?" He stared at her. "To the underground?"

"To your life. It isn't safe for you anymore. They saw your face."

Gaylen tried to register this. "No. This . . . can't be."

She looked at him—no, *into* him—with such sad certainty that he could not doubt her.

"What do I do?"

"You belong with us now. You will become part of the Light-bringers."

"What's that?"

"We work against the government. We undermine it. At least, we do what we can. And you're going to help us."

He balked. He shook his head. "Against the government?" he echoed. "Why? Would I do that?"

"Because we saved your life," she said sharply. And then her fierceness dissolved into compassion, and her voice softened. "And because you have no other life now, not without us."

Again the piercing gaze, and again her conviction calmed him.

She reached across and took his hands in hers, this time not shrinking away from whatever darkness it was that contaminated him. She said ritualistically, as if she had said it many times before, "You are a man without a life or a home. And we will give you life, and we will give you a home. And you will find strength with us."

Chapter Six

Wayne Webster Watts, from his underground book, **9 Lives:**

> *Sleepers are afraid. That's what it comes down to. They're afraid to see what they're really made of, what humans are really capable of. Being a true denizen, well, that means you don't look away. But you don't just look. You dive in until you really understand what it's all about. Because it's all part of being alive. You want to be alive, there's nothing you reject.*

John Oldman's mother lay unmoving in the bathtub. Rich, dark-red blood surrounded her. Her long blond hair and iridescent blue dress were sodden with it. Eleven-year-old John noticed that she had put in the plug; blood pooled around her feet and covered her ankles and elbows and hands.

Her pale face was fixed in the remnants of a sob. Her glassy eyes were turned toward the two of them standing together at the door, as if her last thought had been how they would find her there. On the floor by the tub were two empty bottles of vodka.

John's father still held the doorknob. He just looked, silent, his face impassive.

It was only a year after the closing of the borders of New America. The wallscreens had not yet become mandatory. John's father could still telephone the police, and that is what he did.

In the real world, young John stayed in the bathroom and observed every detail of his mother's corpse with dread fascination while his father made the call.

But in the dream, John sobbed while he watched his father pull out his phone. He screamed at his father, and then began punching him. "How could you let her do this? How could you? *I hate you!*"

His father ignored him, and John hit him harder and sobbed louder.

Just as the sobbing became both deafening and heart-wrenching, John came back to the waking world. He looked around to discover that he had fallen asleep sitting up against the wall in a little nook outside a clothes store in the underground. He touched his face, but it was dry. The sobbing in the dream was always so vivid, he always thought that he had started crying in real life, too.

He tried to shake off the memories. He was supposed to be watching the store for Chloe to come out.

If President Martha's system had been fully in place when his mother had died, the ART would have taken the two of them away for rehabilitation. The negative thoughts spawned by such an event were uncontrollable by the average will. Thus the DAA's mission statement: "Protect the people while they perfect their minds."

It was true enough. John and his father had been unable to control their responses. His father had spiraled into depression. For about three years, he'd done little except watch the new wallscreen programming and sleep. Then, for the next two years, he'd added binge eating to the list. Then, when John was sixteen years old and just starting to pick up his drinking habit, his father had decided to move to Florida.

At least, that's what the postcard had said.

Some years later, John learned that the DAA sent out forged postcards when they imprisoned people.

Whenever those two facts came too close to colliding in his mind, John thought about something else.

Now, John tried to refocus on his mission. It was early afternoon on Sunday. John had been following Chloe for a full twenty-four hours. So far, she had not gone anywhere that looked like a terrorist cell's safe house. She'd gone out dancing, gotten drunk, and stayed overnight with a girlfriend; the rest of the time, she'd been shopping, eating out, and listening to music.

John found it confounding. Had she been shopping for approved items, listening to approved music, and keeping her appearance up to approved standards, she could have had the exact same lifestyle topside, except for not getting quite as drunk. What was the allure of the underground life, anyway?

As he had watched the girl with the purple dreadlocks and the eyebrow piercing go about her day, he had found himself thinking about his own daughter. Suzy would be twenty-five years old now—not much different from Chloe, he suspected. Though they all still lived in D.C., he'd been out of touch with his ex-wife and their children since the kids were teenagers. They had grown aloof and resentful, he had run out of things to say, and his ex-wife had hinted that his presence in their lives had become superfluous.

He'd loved Rebecca. He really had. He still smiled at the thought of her round, cheerful face and auburn curls. Jack and Suzy, their kids, had meant everything to him. He just hadn't been able to stop drinking when he needed to, after the new head of the DAA, Gau Bidarte, had busted him down the ranks just for being a feeler and he'd started his long, useless work against FPU.

He should have remarried—everyone had told him so—but he had quailed at the thought, and no one had seemed interested in him, anyway.

It was ancient history. It was all long behind him now. Now he had nothing but his work and the constant, haunting presence of failure.

He tried to shake off the desire to find an underground bar and drown his misery.

Just then, he saw Chloe leave the store. Good, he hadn't missed her. He decided it was time to approach her again. It was partially an attempt to distract himself from the dream and from his thoughts—and especially the urge to drink.

He hastened to catch up to her. Right as she turned to see who was behind her, he said her name.

Her body stiffened, and she stopped walking, her face tense.

John had expected to alarm her, and he was quick to respond. He raised his hands in a placating gesture. "I wasn't following you, I swear. I was surprised when I saw you in front of me. But I'm glad. I—I wanted to talk to you again. Will you please just hear me out?"

Chloe half-turned away, but she stayed put.

So far, so good. He appealed to her sympathy. "You're the only person I've met who can get me into the Lightbringers. And I can't explain why, but I think it's . . . I think it might be . . . my only hope." His shoulders drooped even more than usual. He was playing it heavy-handed, but the intelligence he had gathered so far suggested that the Lightbringers would be receptive to emotional disclosure. It was in these moments that he regretted his mask. It tended to obscure his best acting.

She still said nothing, but she put one end of a purple dreadlock in her mouth and chewed on it.

John pressed, "I know your buddy said you're not recruiting . . . please tell me that isn't really true."

Chloe hesitated.

John waited, tense. This moment could make or break their connection. He let the silence draw out while he fought back the nervous urge to speak again.

Chloe said, "Not exactly. I mean, we might be recruiting. I don't really know." She shifted her posture toward him.

"How can I get an interview?"

Chloe shrugged. "It's not like that, exactly. I mean, I don't think we interview, exactly." She bit down on her dreadlock again. She glanced around, as if to see if anyone else was nearby.

He let a moment of silence go by, to keep the pressure off. He said, "Then what do I do?" He spread his hands and stared at her with the most pleading, puppy-dog look he could muster.

The girl dropped her head for an instant. It was a small gesture of sympathy. "I don't know if Drew is taking anyone right now. She has another new recruit right now, and we have a big mission coming up . . . I don't know if she has time."

John nodded and tried not to get ahead of himself. "She only trains one new recruit at a time? How long does that take, then?"

Chloe shrugged and looked around again. Her movements became agitated. "I dunno. Look, I really shouldn't be talking to you. I should go."

John cursed to himself. He'd lost her, for some reason, and it would be counterproductive to push her. "I understand. But—can I talk to you again later?"

Chloe looked reluctant, but apparently she was too nice to tell him no. "Sure," she said, and backed away from him.

"My number is 202-GFINGER," John said. He hated giving out this ridiculous number, but it was memorable, and that was the important thing. "For Goldfinger, like James Bond." He pointed at his mask.

She grinned and nodded and kept going.

John sighed as she moved out of sight. He waited a few seconds, then tailed her again. He still hoped that she would eventually lead him back to the cell's safe house.

She walked down two hallways and around two corners before she glanced back with a frown. John saw her slow down and her head start to turn, and he dodged behind the corner just in time.

He waited a long count of three before chancing another look. A flash of purple dreads disappeared around the next corner. He hurried to catch up, although he second-guessed himself the whole way.

He peeked around the next corner. She was just turning away from another backward glance, and walking faster now.

Then, while John watched from the corner, she stopped and brought her hands together in front of her where John couldn't see them. An instant later, a swath of shimmers enveloped her from head to toe, and then both the shimmers and Chloe were gone.

John blinked.

She was definitely gone. The hallway was well lit here; there were no shadows, and there were no doorways anywhere near her. She should be—*had* to be—standing right there halfway down the hallway. But she had vanished.

John stared intently and strained his ears, but he saw and heard nothing. He stepped out and walked to where she had stood. He waved his hands through the air, half-expecting to touch her, but nothing was there.

He stared into the emptiness for a long time.

Only a few hours after the DAA sting in the underground—it was in the early hours of Monday morning, now—Gaylen sat in another bare and ugly room with his rescuer, this time inside a house. This room had once had a wallscreen, but it was shattered. It was the only broken wallscreen Gaylen had ever seen.

They'd come in through underground tunnels, including one long, dark, damp tunnel that Drew said was taking them under the river, and ultimately up through a trap door into what turned out to be the laundry room in this empty house.

Two men had met them as they'd entered. They'd hugged the girl and given her a warm welcome, which is how he had learned that her name was Drew. They had given Gaylen a brief and distant, though cordial, welcome.

Gaylen wondered why they weren't more friendly. Perhaps they knew that he had nearly fallen into Nick's underground. Even worse, perhaps they thought he was a regular there already, engaging in the kinds of activities that Nick did.

Yet, oddly—or perhaps it wasn't odd at all—a part of him rebelled as he sat on the wood floor next to Drew and stared at the broken wallscreen. He had just yesterday come to accept that there was something wrong with the society he'd known all his life and begun the difficult process of embracing a new reality, and now they'd come and pulled the rug out from under him again. How many groups like this were there? People who thought they knew all the answers, who would try to tell him what he needed to do and who he needed to be? Earlier today, he'd had a job and a home and a place in society, whether it made him happy or not. Now what did he have?

After they'd met the two men, Drew had gone into the back of the house and come back out with a backpack that she had tossed to him. "Your recruit's kit," she'd said as he'd opened it and looked through it. He'd found a set of nondescript men's clothes and a toiletries kit.

"And don't worry," she'd said reassuringly, "you'll always have enough to eat and a safe place to sleep."

Gaylen had just stared at her. It had never occurred to him—not once in his life—that he might ever go without these things. No one ever went without them. But at this moment, it seemed like she had lied to him, because he was hungry and had nothing to eat.

Now she sat next to him, cross-legged, her hands on her knees and her eyes closed. Her face was beautiful and serene. She had been that way for a long time. Gaylen was mystified by it. Had she learned to sleep that way?

He tapped her on the shoulder.

Without moving or opening her eyes, she said, "What?"

"What's going to happen to me now?"

A moment passed before she answered, again without moving. "You have to be trained. And you'll help us on assignments. Now be quiet. I'm meditating."

"You're what?"

"Meditating."

"What's that?"

A moment passed, and the corners of her lips twitched in a little smile. She responded lightly, "Where I sit still with my eyes closed and don't talk to anyone. I'll teach you how sometime."

Gaylen rolled his eyes and got up and went into the kitchen, hoping to find some food, or at least something else to see or do.

The kitchen was bare, though the pleasant aroma of coffee came from the coffeepot. The cupboards were mostly empty. The wallscreens in here were broken too.

He imagined that all of the screens in the house were broken. He hated it. He didn't have anything to *look* at.

A girl with her hair in purple dreadlocks and a ring in one of her eyebrows walked in with a coffee cup. She caught him glowering at the broken screens. With a smile and a shrug, she said, "You get used to it," and reached out her hand. "Hi, I'm Chloe."

"I'm Gaylen," he said and shook her hand.

"Oh, I know. Everyone's heard." She went to the coffeepot and poured herself a fresh cup.

"Heard what?"

"About you. Drew's new pet," she said. She smiled over her shoulder.

"I'm not anyone's pet."

"Well, of course you are. It's OK. I was Drew's pet once, too. It's not so bad." She opened the cupboard and pulled out creamer and sugar. "Do you want some coffee?"

"Yeah, I guess so." It might help fill his empty stomach.

She poured him a cup while he looked at the floor. At least this one was being friendly to him—even speaking to him.

He cast about for something to talk about to prolong the moment. "What is Drew's story? How'd she get to be . . . who she is?" Despite his general frustration, he couldn't find adequate words to describe how impressive he found her.

"That's a long story," Chloe said as she handed him his coffee. "She was in the underground from when she was a teenager. Then Don found her. Don was the head of this cell of the Lightbringers back then. But really, she should tell you the story, not me." She took a cautious sip of her coffee, suddenly looking shy. She pulled the tail of one of her dreadlocks to her mouth and chewed on it.

"She's so . . . tough," Gaylen said. "For someone so small. It's . . . weird."

Chloe tossed the dreadlock over her shoulder and lowered her voice conspiratorially, grinning. "Wait till you see her mad. She's like a rabid Chihuahua."

Gaylen laughed. Then he took a deep breath. "I'm glad you're being nice to me."

Chloe looked at him for a long moment. "I remember what it's like to be you right now. I even miss my old life sometimes." She took another sip of her coffee, her eyes downcast.

"Did Drew save you from the underground, too?" Gaylen asked. He leaned against one of the counters and tried to adopt some sort of nonchalance.

She looked away. "Sort of, I guess. I didn't think I needed saving, though. I liked the drugs I was on. I liked the parties I went to. Drew says I'm avoidant. I have to keep choosing to stay here, where reality is." She looked at him awkwardly, as if she was uncertain what his reaction might be, and chewed on her dreadlock again.

He wasn't sure what his reaction was, either. He wasn't accustomed to emotional disclosures.

Drugs were a routine part of New American lifestyle, so long as the Bureau of Entertainment carefully chose and administered them to provide a minimal, yet pleasant, effect. He was sure, though, that Chloe's drug use hadn't been monitored in the usual way. He happened to glance at her arms and saw small round scars and dark patches on the insides of them, near her elbows. He remembered the frighteningly thin girl he had seen in the underground his first time—the girl pulling a needle from her arm. He shuddered at the memory.

Chloe saw where his gaze was, and she folded her arms and turned away.

"Sorry," Gaylen said. "I've just never . . ."

"Yeah, I know. Sleeper." She said it gently enough, but she left the kitchen.

Gaylen sighed and drank some more of his coffee. Then he went back to the room where Drew meditated. He sat down in front of her and mirrored her cross-legged posture and looked at her closed eyes in a silent plea for some company.

He guessed that Drew could feel his gaze, because she soon opened her eyes and looked at him. Her eyes were kind. "Ready for training?"

He spread his hands to show confusion. "I don't know what training is, but sure, I guess so."

Drew relaxed her posture and rested her hands in her lap. "OK. What do you know so far?"

"About what?"

"About the underground and the true nature of our society."

Gaylen hesitated. "Only what Nick told me."

Drew frowned. "Nick Aglaeca?"

"I don't know his last name."

"Older man who wears black, smokes, overweight? . . . Sadist?"

Gaylen didn't know the last word, but the rest of the description was close enough. He cringed on the inside, but he said, "Yes."

"Ah." Drew pondered that for a moment. "How did you meet him?"

"Um—that's—isn't that where I was? Nick's area?"

"You were close to it, but not in it."

Gaylen had wandered for quite a while with the mob. And there weren't any signs saying which boss owned a given area. Maybe Nick's area was smaller than he'd imagined. He kicked himself mentally. He had only followed that mob to prove something to Nick, and maybe it wouldn't even have counted.

"So what did Nick tell you?" Drew asked.

Gaylen took a deep breath. He hated thinking about Nick at all. "Only that no one else is happy, either. Is that really true?"

Drew tilted her head. "For the most part, yes, that's true." She closed her eyes thoughtfully for a moment. Then she launched into what seemed to be a well-practiced lecture. "What you must understand first is that New Americans are like children, despite our physical ages, and most of us stay that way all our lives. We're rarely tested, and when we are, we inevitably fail, because we haven't been taught how to be strong and healthy adults. Our society tells us that we must be happy, but it doesn't teach us how to be happy. That's its chief failing."

Gaylen remembered what had happened when he had called the ART about his grief. For the first time, he considered the possibility that the ART had let him down, rather than the other way around. It was a bizarre thought. But he remembered something else, too. "Nick said that the failing of our society is in trying to ignore . . . Well, he called it 'the wolf inside.' I'm not completely sure what that meant. Something that wants bad things, I guess."

"Here, we call it 'darkness.' Others throughout history have called it 'evil.' And it's true that trying to ignore it doesn't work. That's the single greatest problem with Martha's perfect society. But what Nick doesn't know, or what he refuses to recognize, is that the darkness strengthens when it's indulged. Darkness must never be indulged. It must be faced, it must be accepted, and it must be renounced over and over again."

Gaylen looked away. He regretted anew how he had participated in the mob that had tried to hang Laura.

Drew scrutinized him. "It's time for you to renounce some of your darkness, Gaylen, but you have to start by facing it, which I'm now going to teach you how to do."

Gaylen's heart beat faster. "What do I have to do?"

"Close your eyes. Find the worst feeling that you're having right now. I know you don't know the words for negative emotions yet, but just try to catch it and feel what it feels like."

Gaylen dropped his head a little. He knew that a part of him wanted to scream and throw things right now. He tried to grasp the feeling. Trying to do so went directly against everything he had ever been taught about positive thinking.

Drew said, "The part of you that feels this feeling, and that wants you to keep feeling it, is a real and valid part of you. It's your shadow. It wants to feed on it, to grow stronger from it. And that's natural."

She paused for a moment, then said, "Dwell on the feeling. Let it get stronger. Encourage it. Don't worry, it can't harm you."

Gaylen opened his eyes. "I thought . . . you said we couldn't indulge it."

Drew shook her head. "This isn't indulging it. Indulging darkness is when you let it act out in your words and deeds. You're doing this meditation in order to bring it to the light. When it's fully exposed, it will disappear, and it will no longer reveal itself in either word or deed. Darkness is always destroyed by light."

Gaylen was mystified by all this, but he trusted her certainty. He closed his eyes again and tried to obey her instructions. He had never delved into his own mind in this way before. He didn't know how to make his mind do things the way she was suggesting. It was like trying to build a structure out of soap bubbles that kept evaporating.

Besides, echoes of President Martha's teachings rang in his ears—"Never entertain a thought that is not a happy one; it will only cause it to strengthen and multiply."

But he kept reaching into this intangible space and directing his feelings, and somehow they began to move as he directed. The violent feeling drew nearer. His face and shoulders tensed.

"Do you feel it?" Drew asked, her voice low.

He nodded, his eyes still closed. The feeling set off an adrenaline rush. His skin began to prickle as the small hairs on his arms lifted. The tingling moved up his spine.

"Draw it closer. Let it become bigger than you until it envelops you. I know it feels threatening, but it can't harm you."

He did so, even though the better it worked, the more his heart pounded. His brow furrowed as he tried harder.

"Relax," she said. "Take a deep breath. Don't try so hard. Just let it come."

He took a deep breath, still obedient.

He teased the darkness out again, remembering how it wanted to do violence. It latched onto the memory of Laura's hanging, and it liked it. It hungered for more of the same. He let it grow stronger and stronger. The image came to mind of him lashing out now, smashing Drew in the face—a wrong and perverse image.

And yet, the more he coaxed the feeling out, the more it seemed to dissolve, as if a part of him that was entirely new to him calmly recognized its foolishness. Unlike how he usually pushed away and fought against his "bad" feelings with President Martha's advice, he simply saw the emotion for what it was.

Yes, he was rightfully upset about everything that had happened, and some part of him wanted to lash out. But the rest of him knew that he didn't want to lash out. He knew better. And with that realization, the upset feelings simply dissipated, evaporating into nothing, but leaving peace instead of emptiness.

He opened his eyes, eager to share what he had just experienced.

Drew waited, her face kind. Her luminescent green eyes played across his face.

"That's amazing," he said. Could it have been that easy all along, if only he had known how to do this?

"Good. Very good. Now, resolve that whenever you're feeling this way, you'll bring it to the light. Say this now, in your mind."

He closed his eyes and repeated her words to himself. A lightness opened within him, expansive, clear. A deep breath freed itself and released the remaining tension in his chest.

He opened his eyes again. He met Drew's gaze for a moment, and then he felt awkward, and he had to look away. It was as if she had been looking into his mind the whole time and now she knew him too well.

She squeezed his shoulder again. "And now you're uncomfortable. That's to be expected, because now you're in a place of vulnerability that you're not accustomed to, and that can be difficult. This will be easier, because it's only an after-effect. So bring it to the light, and let it be dissolved."

Gaylen teased out the feelings of discomfort. He let them grow larger and stronger, while his face grew hot and he wished he could disappear from Drew's sight. Quickly this time, the bubble burst. The truth was that Drew was a safe person to do this with—possibly the only safe person he had ever known. He looked at her again. Those green eyes held no judgment.

Drew smiled at him, her face radiant. "Good," she said. "Remember that technique. It will serve you well as time passes. Now, I have orders to go collect."

She surprised him by leaning forward and embracing him. Then she got up and left him alone in the empty room.

She really was beautiful.

Monday morning, Gaylen awoke late, or so he judged from the amount of light peeking in around the bed sheets that were taped up on the windows. He was alone in the bunk room. Other Lightbringers had been there, already asleep, when he had turned in, and now they were gone.

He'd slept fitfully. He had returned again and again to the meditation Drew had taught him, and at four in the morning, he had awoken from a fitful doze with sudden clarity about something that had been haunting him: fear for Serena and Sierra.

Instinctively, he felt that Serena was innocent of the truth—that the law of attraction failed so many people. Surely Serena had never visited the underground. But she might someday go there. Worse yet, his daughter might someday go there.

Somehow, someday—before it was too late—he needed to warn Serena. He needed to tell his family the truth.

This was the first and only substantial goal he'd ever had in his life. Everything else had simply fallen into place without much thought. Standardized tests had identified his basic personality traits, skills, and interests, and funneled him into a suitable career. The Love Today kiosks had supplied him with well-matched dating partners until he found one he wanted to settle down with. Everyone always had everything they needed, and the Bureau of Entertainment provided safe, enjoyable recreation for all. Life was simple.

Now he had to figure out how to make something important happen, something that he had never encountered or even thought of before, and he had to do it with real actions and not just optimistic thoughts. But how?

He stared with increasing agitation at the empty walls. With no wallscreens to distract him, he could only take in the slight odor of mildew, the cracks in the plaster, the cobweb in the corner of the ceiling, the blankets on the floor, and the backpacks and bundles of personal possessions piled around the room. His eyes went around to everything again and again while his thoughts went in similarly useless circles.

Finally, he could bear the unchanging quiet no longer and got up. He went out through the hallway into the kitchen, which was empty. Despite knowing it was sure to be useless, he checked the cupboards again, and again found nothing to eat, and no chocolate. At least someone had made fresh coffee. He poured himself a cup.

He still didn't see anyone around, so he peeked out of the back door to see what he could find.

Chloe sat on a bench in the back yard. She was staring at nothing in particular, as far as he could tell.

He stepped out cautiously. When she looked toward him, he said, "Am I allowed to be out here? I mean, I guess I am, if you are ..."

She smiled. "Yeah. You can be out here. Don't go out the front, though." She scooted over and touched the space on the bench next to her.

Gaylen sat down, pleased by her welcome, though once he'd sat down, she just stared down at the ground and chewed on the tip of a purple dreadlock.

He took a cautious sip of his coffee, and, finding it cool enough, drank half of it. The sugar and caffeine would do him good.

The backyard was badly overgrown. Once, there had been a swingset, now a twisted wreck of rust. There had been a sandpit, now mostly full of grass. Through the partially collapsed fence, he saw other yards that were equally unkempt. Trees reached up to the sky. There were no taller buildings, so there were no wallscreens to break the quiet. The only sound was birdsong. The air was clear and sweet and the sun was warm.

Chloe remained silent and stared at the ground while she fidgeted.

Gaylen turned toward her. "How can I warn my family? I mean, my . . . ex-wife . . . and my daughter? About the underground?"

She looked thoughtful. "Um . . . well . . . I mean, you can just tell them. Do you know where they live?"

He shook his head. "I tried to let them go. Like I was supposed to."

"So you would have to find them first, I guess."

"Is that something that you all can help me with?"

"I can't speak for Drew. She's in charge of our cell. So, you would need to ask her if we can do that."

Gaylen looked down. "But . . . is it possible? If she agrees?"

"I think so. I don't see why not." But her tone of voice was uncertain. "You should probably just ask her about it."

Gaylen nodded and tried to relax his shoulders. The overgrown backyard and rusted swingset caught his attention again. "How can this even be here? Why is it here? These houses are empty. I've never seen empty houses."

Chloe's face brightened. She seemed happy to have an answer this time. "This area used to be military housing. We're close to Fort Myer."

"Oh." That made sense. The bases had been abandoned long ago, when New America's borders had been closed and the military permanently retired. Naturally, no one would want to live here.

Thinking about the nation's history set off a chain reaction of questions. If positive thinking was a lie and the nation had an entire secret underground he hadn't even known about, then what else was a lie?

Thoughtfully, he asked, "If positive thinking isn't true, then how did New America get to be perfect?" He looked at Chloe, who laughed, and heat came to his cheeks. Things weren't perfect at all. "You know what I mean."

"Yes, I do," she said, sounding apologetic for laughing. "The original President Martha just made everything look perfect, that's all. Nothing actually changed."

"Well, where did she put the imperfect things? How did she make them go away?"

"That's why most people live in city centers. Anyway, that's what Drew told me. Martha took all of the people who used to work in the military or medicine or law enforcement or whatever and had them start cleaning things up. But keeping everything all shiny and new all the time takes a lot of work. So people were encouraged to move into the cities, where they can keep everything nice." After this speech—the longest Gaylen had heard from her—she lowered her gaze self-consciously.

Gaylen drank some more of his coffee while he absorbed this. The Martha whom Chloe was talking about was the first Martha. She had turned over her office to her younger replacement when Gaylen was a teenager. No one actually knew whether Martha I had ever died, but logically, she had to have—otherwise, she would be over a hundred twenty years old now. But the transition had been seamless. The two Marthas had been nearly identical, and everything continued just the same as it had, as if Martha had simply been rejuvenated and made decades younger.

"How did she get rid of sickness and old age?" he asked.

"She didn't. She just took away the people who were sick or old. I mean, she tried to get them to learn how to think positively enough to get healthy or stay young, but when it didn't work . . ."

She let her voice trail off, but Gaylen didn't know how to complete the sentence. "When it didn't work . . . then what?"

"Well . . . maybe I shouldn't be the one to explain this." Chloe chewed on a dreadlock.

A new voice said, "Explain what?" The back door of the house had just opened, and a stocky Hispanic man stepped out and approached. Tattoos covered both arms. He had a goatee and a mustache, and his head was partially shaved—just a short, round shock of black hair came from the top.

Chloe answered, "You know, the usual stuff. He's a sleeper."

The guy pulled a pack of cigarettes out of his pocket, along with a lighter, and lit up. He looked at Chloe and gestured at Gaylen, asking, "Who is he?"

"Sorry. This is Gaylen," she said. "And that's Kevin."

Kevin extended a hand. Gaylen stood up to shake it and then sat back down.

Kevin said, "So what needs explaining?"

"I was just trying to tell him about what happens to NCPs." Chloe glanced at Gaylen and clarified, "Non-Compliant Persons. The ones who get old or sick or depressed."

"Oh, they kill them," Kevin said, sounding cheery and helpful in a dry sort of way. "Dead as doornails."

Chloe's shoulders dropped, and she cast a mild glare at Kevin. "I was trying to break it to him easy," she said.

"Sorry," Kevin answered with a grin. He didn't sound sorry, but he didn't sound unpleasant about it, either.

Now Gaylen was trying to accept the idea that President Martha killed people. He couldn't believe it.

Every person in the nation knew President Martha's face and voice by heart. The perfectly calm, perfectly coiffed brunette now in her fifties addressed the country via wallscreen multiple times every day. She relayed good news, made announcements of fun events, taught lessons about positive thinking, and continually reassured and reminded all of her citizens that they lived in the wealthiest, happiest, and safest country in the world. And she did it all without ever having a hair out of place.

After a moment, still not able to believe it, he asked again, "President Martha kills people?"

"No, not her," Kevin said. "The DAA. President Martha doesn't even know about it. It's the DAA you have to worry about."

Gaylen remembered that term from when Drew had rescued him the previous night. "What does 'DAA' stand for?"

Again, Kevin answered. "The Domestic Awareness Agency. Also known as Douchebags and Assholes Anonymous."

Chloe grinned and shook her head a little, but Gaylen didn't get the joke. He was noticing that Kevin always had a dry but humorous tone of voice.

Kevin went on, "They're the secret police. Like the Gestapo back in Germany or the Oprichniki in Russia."

Chloe recognized Gaylen's blank look and said, "Never mind. The point is, they're the part of the government that does all the dirty work."

Gaylen said, "But how could President Martha not know about them? That doesn't make any sense. She's the president."

Chloe looked at Kevin, but he gestured toward her, inviting her to answer, while he took a drag off his cigarette.

She pulled her knees up to her chest and folded her arms around them. She spoke hesitantly and kept her eyes down most of the time. "So, supposedly, the way it happened—I mean, this is what Don told us—is that President Martha—the original one—was teaching everyone to think positively, but of course there was still crime and sickness and accidents and all of that. And at first, Martha taught everyone to just look away from anything that was 'bad.' Like homeless people, fat people, sick people, accidents, or whatever. And also to think something positive to undo what they'd seen. So, if you saw a disabled person, you were supposed to immediately think about people who are 'normal.' But that's actually pretty hard to do. And also, incredibly offensive. But, anyway."

She paused and ducked her head and wrapped her arms around her legs even more tightly, as if to make herself seem smaller. "The point is, it's harder to think positively when you're seeing things that are negative, and Martha wanted to help people with that. So she wanted to make everything look really perfect. Plus, the people who had these problems—well, obviously, they weren't thinking right or they wouldn't be that way, so she wanted to help them. That's really all it was, I think. The people she took away, she really was trying to fix them.

"Don is older than us—he's the leader of all of the Lightbringers—he lives in Atlanta—and a long time ago he talked to some of the old-timers who were the first ones who went in and out of treatment because they were sick or overweight or whatever. He said that they were really trying. And it was really . . . upsetting for them, actually, when they couldn't fix it by thinking right. Which is why New America's suicide rate is really, really high."

Gaylen asked, "What's suicide?"

Kevin cheerfully supplied the answer. "Self-killing. Like when somebody throws himself in front of a subway train. Or cuts his wrists open to bleed out. Or deliberately takes a drug overdose. Or hangs herself from—"

"Kevin, shut up." It was Chloe, her face stormy.

Kevin winced. "Sorry. I forgot." This time, he sounded like he meant it. He looked away and focused on his cigarette.

The two men waited in uncomfortable silence while Chloe drew a deep breath in and let it back out. Then she went on. "So, like I was saying, when it still wasn't working . . . I mean, she had to do something, right? Because everyone who keeps on thinking wrong is attracting the bad stuff. So, sedating the NCPs was the first step, so that it was impossible for them to think anything bad anymore. Putting them in stasis. The plan was that when she figured out how to fix everyone, then she would wake them up and . . . well, fix them."

Kevin interjected again, but more soberly. "The problem is the numbers. Hundreds of thousands of people still getting sick or old or depressed or having accidents." He tapped ash off his cigarette. "The nerve of them."

"It's kind of creepy, if you think about it," Chloe said. "All those people in stasis in stacked-up caskets—skyrises full of them."

Kevin went on, "Martha knew they had to do something. But you can't kill off a bunch of people and think positively at the same time. So that's when Gau got involved."

Gaylen looked to Chloe for the explanation. She said, "Gau Bidarte is the head of the DAA. He's the one who suggested creating the DAA and making only socios work there."

Gaylen shook his head. This was all coming too quickly. "Socios?"

Kevin answered, "Sociopaths. People who are born wrong. They don't feel bad about doing things that are wrong. The rest of us feel at least a little bad." With a glance at Chloe, the comment became an apology for whatever he'd said wrong a moment ago.

Chloe grinned at Kevin and went on, "So, Martha told Gau to just . . . take care of it. Hire socios and take care of it. She didn't want to know. Because it would affect her thinking, and since she's the president, her thoughts are more important than anyone else's. Or so she thinks, anyway."

"So President Martha . . . OK, so President Martha really does believe in positive thinking?" Gaylen felt more confused than ever.

"Yes," Kevin and Chloe said in emphatic unison. Chloe continued, "Now, keep in mind, all of that was the old Martha. The new Martha didn't have anything to do with the DAA or Gau Bidarte. She doesn't even know any of it—not in any detail, anyway. I mean, that's all we've ever heard.

"The old Martha really thought that when we all started thinking right, everything really would be perfect. She thought it was just a matter of time. If the new Martha does know anything about the underground and the crime rate, she probably believes the same thing."

Gaylen rubbed his hands over his face and left one hand covering his eyes. His head felt like it was stuffed full of cotton. "Well, could it be true? That it's just a matter of time?" he asked hesitantly. When he got no answer, he dropped his hands and looked up.

Chloe was just looking at him sympathetically. Kevin was taking another drag from his cigarette. After he blew out the smoke, he said, "No."

Chloe said, "That's kind of the problem with all of this. Because if . . . if things aren't perfect yet, then you just aren't doing it right, right? So, until things are perfect, you can never know whether it's not true or whether you're still just . . . not doing it right."

"That's why it's fucking evil," Kevin said flatly. "If anything is wrong, it's always your fault."

Chloe shrugged a little. "Anyway, no one outside of New America believes in the law of attraction, and the fact that we have this underground is pretty much proof to them that it doesn't work."

"It *doesn't* work," Kevin said. "It's total stupidity."

"Wait a minute," Gaylen said. "'No one outside of New America'? How would you know?"

Chloe touched his shoulder gently for a second. "The borders aren't really sealed. We get books and news and tech from the outside world. I mean, not directly, but through some of the other groups."

Gaylen didn't say anything. This was all too much.

"Maybe we shouldn't tell you everything all at once?" she offered weakly.

Kevin laughed again. "Oh, just give him the red pill," he said.

As usual, Gaylen had no idea what he was talking about.

Chloe waved at the tattooed man in a shushing motion. "You're not helping," she said. "This is always hard for them."

Kevin grinned and went on, "It's not that bad outside the walls, Gaylen. It's actually pretty decent. I mean, it was rocky for everybody else when the United States just closed its doors. But they figured out how to function without us. They were able to put their economies back together. Mostly because of the New Republic."

"The New Republic?"

"Yeah. We used to have states called Texas and California, plus a couple of others I forget the names of, and there used to be a country called Mexico to the south. It's all the New Republic now. They have almost all of the oil and technology that the United States used to have. We should have fought to keep them, but President Martha just let them walk.

"These days, the whole rest of the world pretty much hates us and doesn't give a crap what we do with ourselves. They're just watching and waiting for us to self-destruct. The Lightbringers, though, are descended from a group of people who chose to stay inside to try to save America from itself.

"A lot of other people fled this country in the beginning—not just Texas and California. People are still leaving. You can even leave, if you want. We smuggle people out sometimes."

Gaylen couldn't even process it. The firmly secured borders of New America and the barbarism and chaos of the outside world were just facts to him. Facts he had known all his life. He rubbed his face with his hands again.

"OK," he said weakly, "so, the DAA kills the NCPs, who are anybody who still gets sick or old or whatever, which is—a lot of people. And President Martha doesn't know because . . . what was his name? The head of the . . . socios?"

"Gau Bidarte," Kevin supplied.

"Because Gau Bidarte runs the DAA in secret with socios who don't think killing people is a bad thing." He looked at the two Lightbringers, his eyebrows raised in question.

Chloe nodded, the end of a purple dreadlock in her mouth again. "That's pretty much it."

"So then how can there be this huge underground? Why haven't they all been killed by now?"

Chloe shrugged.

Kevin said, "I don't think they have the manpower to keep up with us. They've done mass exterminations down here before, with chemical weapons and nanotech. But there are a whole lot of people who just disappear when they do that, and it's a bitch to cover that up. So they don't do it very often. Just when there get to be too many of us. Like sewer rats."

They sat quietly for a while again. Gaylen's mind was mostly blank. Eventually, he found himself saying, "I can still see how it could be true, though. I mean, that President Martha could be right.

If all these people in the underground are thinking wrong, that's got to—" He caught Chloe's gaze and stopped. She was looking at him with sympathy again. He sighed.

CHAPTER SEVEN

Wayne Webster Watts, from his underground book, 9 Lives:

If you really want to know life, you have to face death. I recommend being on the killing end. And then, there's nothing like a conversation with a corpse to make you really get it. Then nobody can preach to you—nobody can claim that they have some insight you don't. You get the biggest picture there is to get. You know the end.

That afternoon passed in a blur of awkwardness for Gaylen. Kevin announced that there was no time like the present to give the new guy some training, and he disappeared into the house. A few minutes later, he emerged with a gleam in his eye and an armload of weapons.

First, Gaylen nearly hyperventilated, because these weapons were like the ones the DAA carried that turned people into dust. Once Kevin explained that the guns also had a stun setting which merely put people to sleep for a short time, Gaylen was able to calm down. He made careful note of the dial on the side. He had to keep it below the red line to keep from disintegrating his targets.

He also asked, out of morbid curiosity, how the guns worked—turning people into dust while leaving their clothing intact. In his usual dry, cheery way, Kevin talked about "molecular breakdown" and "chemical disassembly." What it seemed to come down to was that the stream of nanobots identified the victim's DNA based on a skin sample and then disassembled all matching living material down to its component parts, even including the water molecules.

After a moment in which Gaylen simply nodded, Kevin added, "It's actually pretty damn humane. This is how all the people in the hydrorises are killed off, too. It's quick. Martha insisted on it. Just identify the unique DNA and zap—it's gone. Same for abortions."

"For whats?" Gaylen asked.

"Never mind," Kevin said. "We'll explain that one some other time."

Kevin also taught him how to use two other types of weapons. "Just in case you lose your weapon during a fight and pick up someone else's."

One was called a revolver, and it fired a small but hard projectile Kevin called a bullet. He described the weapon as hopelessly inefficient and archaic because it required precise shots to the body, neck, or head and carried a high risk of accidental mortality. Then he showed Gaylen another modern-looking weapon and explained that it was the precursor to the dust gun. It had a stun setting, but when turned to the highest setting on its dial, it delivered a jolt of electricity strong enough to kill the person. "It leaves a corpse, which can be problematic. And it's not as easy a death for the victim. But it'll get the job done.

"No matter what weapon you're using, just watch carefully for who's nearby and behind the person you're targeting," Kevin impressed upon him. "If there are allies or civilians near them, don't shoot. It's better to do nothing than to take out an ally or accidentally kill a civilian."

Privately, Gaylen thought that perhaps doing nothing was his best bet. He was very out of place here, especially compared to Kevin, who seemed to relish the use of the guns. The tattooed man fired with quick precision and made every shot when he was demonstrating the weapons.

The rest of the afternoon was spent in the back yard doing target practice on a couple of metal trash cans. While Gaylen had no experience aiming anything at anything—he had never even gone in for basketball—they determined that he had some natural aptitude for it. By the time dinner was served, he could reliably hit a man-sized target at short range—which, Kevin assured him, was all he had to do.

In the early evening, Drew walked through the house and called everyone to assemble in the living room.

There were around two dozen Lightbringers in the living room. Some leaned against the walls while others sat on the floor. Chloe stood to Gaylen's right side. She was chewing gum, and she played with it, stretching it out of her mouth and then pushing it back in.

Drew stood at the front of the room with a warm smile. "Orders are in from HQ," she announced. "We have a serious mission. It's on a tight timeline, and it has a lot of moving parts. And it's important enough that we're breaking out the cloaking devices for the first time on a real mission."

Gaylen assumed that by 'cloaking devices' she meant the ring she had used to make them both invisible to the DAA.

He glanced around the room. Everyone looked serious but calm. Chloe snapped her gum.

Drew went on, "I've never heard Don sound so excited about a mission. This could be the strike the Lightbringers have been hoping to make for decades. And we get to make it, because of our location here in D.C. The other cells will be waiting and watching to see what we do."

At that, a few whispers rustled through the room, and smiles appeared on a few faces.

"The next step is going to be recruitment, because we need more manpower than we have here. We're going to see what we can find at the Bureau of Provision. The rest of the orders will be revealed to us all as we go.

"Nine of us are going on this recruitment trip. Once we pick up the recruits, we won't be able to get more behind the cloaking devices we have. Gaylen, you're coming. Kevin, you're my second. Pick your third. The rest of you, self-select five more. We leave in ten, so say your goodbyes." She looked over all of them with the warmth of a mother surveying her much-loved children. "Let's bring the light."

"Let's bring the light," the revolutionaries echoed.

Gaylen was caught off guard, and he missed the moment. He felt very much out of his element.

The revolutionaries gathered into small groups or milled around as they broke into quiet conversation. The leaders of the group went off together and talked too quietly for Gaylen to hear. Again, Gaylen felt like an outsider, and he decided to pretend to do that *meditation* thing. He sat down and kept his gaze down.

After a couple of minutes, he overheard Chloe say that she was going to self-select to go on the mission. He glanced up at her, and she caught his eye and stuck her tongue out at him, revealing a silver tongue ring. He grinned and then returned to his meditation.

The group exchanged what sounded like goodbyes. It sounded suspiciously as if they were expecting not to see one another again. It worried Gaylen.

The rest of the team then recited some words together, with several others gathered around to join in. He heard only fragments: " . . . as I walk into darkness, may I never forget that it has no power over me that I have not given it . . . as I go out into the world of darkness, may I act out of the light that I carry within me . . ."

Someone entered his field of vision. It was Chloe. She knelt in front of him, leaned in slowly, raised his head, and gave him a soft kiss.

He looked at her, surprised, and she shrugged with a fragile grin. "Goodbye, Gaylen," she said, sounding hesitant. "I enjoyed talking to you earlier, and I enjoyed that kiss just now, and I hope that we can have more of those if we both come back from this mission. Because you're nice-looking, and I think that you . . . are a . . . nice person."

Gaylen was used to being hit on, but Chloe was struggling to be genuine in a way that he had never seen before. Usually, women just wanted to get in bed and then get on with their day. There was rarely anything so sweet or sincere about it.

He gathered his wits and tried to think of the right sort of thing to say in response. But then Drew called for their attention again, and Chloe stood and stepped away.

Kevin handed out weapons to each team member. Gaylen took his dust gun and a holster and inexpertly strapped it on. His heart beat faster—he was going to have to use one already.

Drew, Kevin, and two others gathered in the center of the room and called the others close. They put on the rings and pressed the LEDs. The lights began blinking, and then a stream of glittering particles spilled out from the rings faster than the eye could track and settled in a translucent field that surrounded the nine members of the group.

Some of the revolutionaries still in the room looked them over, one of them through a handheld camera. "You're gone," he said, and the others nodded confirmation.

Drew glanced at Gaylen. "Here are the rules, for those of you who don't know them.

"First, stay within three feet of a ring at all times or you'll lose the field.

"Second, once we get around other people, don't move too fast; the field follows your body but it doesn't adjust instantaneously. If you don't move, you're perfectly invisible, but if you try to move too fast, you'll cause a shimmer in the air that people can see.

"Third, if we're around other people, you must be quiet. The rings do nothing to mask sound.

"Finally, the different fields join up if we're all close together, but if your group gets separated, you won't be able to see the rest of us anymore. The team leads are wearing subvocal gear so we can communicate"—she tapped her ear—"but it'll make things harder if we can't see each other. So stay close."

Everyone nodded, then Drew pulled open the front door, and they all stepped out into an overgrown yard. The area around the house looked deserted, as if not part of the city at all. It was fairly dark, with only the occasional working streetlight, and no lights inside the houses. With the faint illumination, Gaylen could make out broken windows, overgrown yards, and ugly bright-colored markings that marred many of the buildings.

It was chilly, and Gaylen pulled his coat closer around him.

To his surprise, Drew called his name. He stepped up next to her and they walked side by side, with Kevin at Drew's other side.

"Gaylen, you've already seen some upsetting things," Drew said. "And now you may see more. And if you see one of us do something that bothers you, you'll need to be able to keep moving. So, there's something you should hear now."

He waited for her to go on.

"Think now about this fact: no action is inherently of the darkness. Right is what comes from the light. Wrong is what comes from the darkness. But light and darkness are not static things. They are living things, and they speak to each of us differently. You may not be able to tell from the outside where something is coming from. You will need to suspend your judgment and trust in the actions we take until we have time to debrief."

"'No action can be judged without judging the state of the mind that inspired it,'" said Kevin, his words taking the tone of a recitation. He sounded more serious than he had in their earlier conversation, his dry humor missing.

Drew nodded at Kevin, then said to Gaylen, "One of our aphorisms. You'll learn a few in time."

They were speaking another language, it seemed. He tried to understand what they were getting at, but he only understood that he was being told that he didn't know right from wrong anymore. He was willing to believe that. He hardly seemed to know anything anymore.

He stumbled and almost twisted his ankle because of a pothole in the street—something that would never happen in a civilized area of New America—and became sharply aware that he was in danger on many levels. He had spent his whole life making sure he was safe—every New American had 'stop work' authority for everything they ever witnessed, and crying foul was second nature to everyone—and now unknown risks threatened him at every turn. He didn't even know why he was here. Surely he was unprepared for a real mission. He'd had exactly four hours of training. Why had Drew made him come along?

As he walked, the situation took on an increasing sense of unreality. These people were insane. But he had witnessed so much insanity in the past few days, he had no idea what was normal anymore. And *he* wasn't exactly sane either. That was what had started this whole thing—his inability to keep himself together. For a moment, he hated himself.

He wondered whether a short life ended in the company of these people was better than one that ended in cracking up and being taken away by the ART.

"Drew?" he asked.

She looked over at him.

"So if I had given myself up to the DAA, I would have been put in stasis?"

"Actually, here in D.C. and in a number of other cities, they've stopped doing stasis these days. They just dust people if rehabilitation fails. Which it usually does, since they have no idea what they're doing."

"What's rehabilitation?"

"They try to train you to be happy. Except that they have no idea how to do that. They try to indoctrinate you, they give you drugs—some left over from the old days, and some experimental ones—basically, they do whatever they think might work, but without any understanding of what human happiness is really about. So it doesn't work. Almost never. Some people are able to fake it well enough to be let out again, though."

This information squared with what he had noticed about his encounters with the ART—especially the part about faking it well enough to be left alone. But now a new thought had come to him, and he found himself compelled to ask it. "Does the DAA . . . take away children? To do rehabilitation and . . . the rest of it?"

Drew's face and voice became somber. "Yes. Usually because they've witnessed something upsetting and the DAA knows they won't know how to apply positive thinking correctly. Children are imprisoned and dusted from the time they begin to understand the world and form long-term memories—usually about twenty-four months."

Gaylen's face went hot as he imagined the DAA taking Sierra.

He could not allow this—not ever.

This thought propelled him into saying what he needed to say—as frightening as it was to try any tactic in life besides ignoring bad things and thinking good things.

"Drew . . ." He took a deep breath. His heart thudded. "I don't even know why I'm here or how I'm supposed to help your group. But I will help, and I will do my best, because you did save my life, but listen to me. You have to help me find my family and tell them the truth about New America, to keep them safe. When this mission is over, when I've done my part, the Lightbringers will help me find my family. OK?"

The group had stopped walking, and everyone stared at him. Chloe smiled. Drew looked at him intently, but with her head cocked to the side as if listening to something else far off in the distance. Moments of silence passed while Gaylen bit his tongue. He wanted to apologize and take it back—he had never deliberately caused trouble for anyone before, not once in his life—but this was more important to him than anything else had ever been.

At last, Drew said, "Agreed. We will help you." She extended her hand, and Gaylen shook it. His tension drained away, and weakness followed it. He let out a long breath.

"There are several parts to this mission," Drew said, "but it should all be over within a few days. Then we will keep our end of the bargain. In fact, I look forward to it." She smiled warmly at him, then resumed walking, and the others followed.

The pleasantly warm flush of victory came up Gaylen's cheeks. He found himself walking taller.

Soon after, they came around the corner and found themselves in New America again—where everything was cheerful, clean, new, and safe.

They slowed to a crawl as soon as crowds appeared. Each group of two or three Lightbringers hugged its cloaking device. The crowds forced the three groups apart, and the team leaders resorted to their headsets to stay in communication. They inched across a street, entered a subway station, and crowded into one corner of a subway car where they were unlikely to get too close to anyone else.

Sweating and shaking, Gaylen struggled to stay silent and move slowly and smoothly. Too many times, someone had nearly bumped into one of them.

They switched trains once—a delicate procedure to manage without coming within three feet of anyone else. They traveled painstakingly down the crowded night streets and then into one of the Bureau of Provision buildings in the Southwest Waterfront.

What were they were doing here? Drew had spoken of recruiting, but these were just hydrorises, tall warehouses set up with hydroponics and artificial sunlight to grow crops for the vast population of New America.

They took an elevator and came out on one of the huge, humid hydroponics floors about a third of the way up the building. Gaylen, who had not been inside of one of these since a tour he'd taken as a child, gaped up at the rows and rows of green crops stacked warehouse-style to either side and the blinding lights that hovered above every layer.

They continued on, faster now that there were no people, toward the center of the building. The groups rejoined and the cloaking fields merged. Seeing one another again was good.

Long minutes later, they stopped before a door that had a keypad on it, like the one on the door to the underground that Gaylen had first encountered. Gaylen looked at the door blankly. Why on earth would a door above ground be locked?

"Passcodes," commanded Drew.

Kevin stepped up with an electronic device while the others kept watch, and soon they passed through this door, too.

Inside the center of the building, the environment changed. Now they walked through dark metal corridors with rubber floors that hushed their steps.

They passed a lobby with a booth where two uniformed men stood and chatted—they crossed this room one step at a time—then another hallway, and then they reached a quiet room full of individual wallscreens.

The screens showed dozens, or perhaps even hundreds, of tiny rooms full of women and men. They sat around chatting or slept or watched their wallscreens. Some fought. In his quick survey, Gaylen caught a glimpse of one man beating his head slowly against the metal wall of his cell.

He looked at Chloe. She leaned close to him and whispered, "Prisons. For rehabilitation."

Kevin was hard at work with another electronic device on a terminal near the wallscreens. Moments ticked by.

Gaylen watched the prisoners, remembering what Drew had said about how people were "treated" when they had to be taken away. He wondered how many of them had been taken from the underground and how many had simply made the mistake of touching the "Request Assistance" button. This could have been him. Still more frightening, this could be Serena or Sierra someday.

Kevin waved the group forward. They walked through another door and down more corridors until they reached a hallway where cells flanked the middle, and there they stopped while Drew surveyed the situation.

Gaylen wondered why the prisoners didn't simply walk out of their cells, but sometimes he glimpsed a line of faintly gleaming light across the doorways, and he guessed that invisible barriers kept them inside. At some doors, he saw no light, and he realized that certain of the cells now stood open, their invisible walls disabled, though no one inside had yet noticed.

Drew picked a room and strode up to the man pacing inside. When she moved away from the group, she became invisible, but a shimmer in the air moved with her—presumably because she was moving so quickly. Now her instructions about moving slowly made more sense. The shimmer was obvious, even if no one could tell what caused it.

The shimmer moved closer to the man, a short fellow of Asian descent, and he frowned as he noticed it. Then the field enveloped him, and he disappeared, too. Next, a whirlwind of shimmering kicked up—and then settled out. Gaylen wished he could see.

Everyone waited. Soon Drew and the newcomer reappeared and joined the group. Drew signaled Kevin and another man, whom Gaylen had now overheard called Christian, to go to different cells. They repeated the process with two dozen other men, extracting each in seconds.

Men and women of every race, age, and description joined them. Kevin handed out stun guns. Most of the prisoners grinned broadly, and some kissed the weapons—their salvation.

The most striking of all the prisoners was a tall, muscular black man with both scars and tattoos curling along both sides of his face, which was broad and fierce. He was the only one to notice that the invisible walls had dropped, and he stepped out of his cell as the Lightbringers approached. As the shimmer drew nearer to him, he dropped back into a fighting stance. When Drew became visible, he reacted swiftly. Gaylen was close enough to see the man throw Drew onto her back and press her against the ground with a forearm to her throat.

Immediately, the other Lightbringers leaped into range.

The man looked around. The group outnumbered and outgunned him. He relaxed his grip on Drew. Kevin pressed his finger to his lips, and the bigger man sat back on his haunches.

Drew sat up with a brilliant smile on her face and whispered into his ear. She put her arms around him as she did so, as if he were a gentle kitten and not a hulking man.

After hearing her out, he shrugged and leaped to his feet as gracefully as a cat. He followed them out, but with a distrusting look on his face.

Drew stuck close to the man and smiled up at him while they walked out of the area, and Gaylen wondered why. Perhaps this was an old lover, he thought, someone from before she became the leader of a revolutionary cell. Yet the man wore no expression of recognition or welcome. For a moment, and for no good reason, Gaylen despised him.

They started hurrying out of the compound. Drew's movements were tense, urgent. The downed cell walls and the missing men could not go unnoticed for long. Gaylen guessed it was now a contest between revealing themselves through fast movement and delaying too long to get out.

He wondered how many DAA agents might be stationed at a Bureau of Provision prison. Probably a lot. He wondered if they would make it out if it came to a fight. He checked his weapon again, making sure the dial was set below the red line, to stun.

All went well as they went down the corridors with the racks of crops, but at the elevator banks three workers in coveralls stood around chatting. Drew held the group back, and they waited while crucial moments ticked by. She wore the focused expression of someone keeping count in her mind.

Just as Gaylen began to think that perhaps they could reach the left-most elevator door without getting within range, the workers shifted position. They blocked the elevators as effectively as if they'd been trying to.

All the revolutionaries and prisoners stayed still, everyone's eyes fixed on their leader. Gaylen's heart pounded. The wait was agonizing.

Drew seemed to reach a certain number in her mind, and she signaled some of the larger, stronger prisoners toward the workers. With little noise, they moved forward to bring their victims into cloaking range and then took them out with their weapons or hand-to-hand.

The rest of the group lunged forward, pushing the workers into the elevators and piling in after them. Gaylen ended up in an elevator with Drew and several others, but he'd lost track of Chloe. One of the other Lightbringers hit the elevator buttons frantically.

Chapter Eight

***Wayne Webster Watts, from his underground book,* 9 Lives:**

> *I never said I was happy. I'm* not *happy, but I'm alive. I'm strong. I take what I want. I make my own calls, and I can't be bothered with anybody who doesn't like it. What is happiness anyway? I'll tell you what happiness is: happiness is a hot babe and a strong drink.*

Moments before the Lightbringers and their recruits reached the ground floor, alarms sounded. Several of them cursed and gritted their teeth. The elevator doors opened to reveal security forces rushing around in confusion.

Time had run out, and it would be impossible for more than two dozen people to snake through the milling crowd without touching anyone.

Everyone looked at Drew. She called out, "Run for the doors! Stun as you go!"

The group obeyed. Anyone in their path who wasn't stunned was simply bowled over. There were startled shouts among the security forces, but no one could tell what was happening in all the confusion. To anyone outside of the cloaking shields, it must have looked as if the air itself had become possessed and was attacking them.

Gaylen strained to keep up and stay in range of the nearest shield without getting tripped up by the people the others were shoving aside. He had pulled out his weapon, but he couldn't pick out a safe target in all the chaos.

The group was pouring through the doors when the building itself started to emit a loud hum. Gaylen narrowly escaped as plates of metal slid out from the door frames and met in the center, blocking them off.

He looked back to see one of the prisoners caught half-way through as the plates snapped shut. The man's severed upper body fell in front of the doors, his eyes sightless.

On the streets, a change rippled across all the wallscreens mounted to the front of buildings: those facing out from the Bureau of Provision darkened, while those on the other side of the street all showed the face of a clown, who bellowed, "It's time for a Happiness Break! Come on, everyone, let's play some games!"

A shout went up from the people on the streets, and they stopped and dropped their shopping bags or purses to prepare to join in.

Gaylen had seen Happiness Breaks many times, but this was the first time he realized that they had a purpose. With everyone's faces turned in the other direction, no one was watching the building where the emergency was happening.

See only good, he remembered.

The revolutionaries and rescued prisoners followed Drew to an empty area near a wall, behind the crowds facing the wallscreens. They took a moment to regroup.

The clowns led the crowd in a rapidly-paced rendition of "Simon Says." Everyone, adults and children, joined in, laughing and giggling. Gaylen felt out of place, watching from back here instead of being in the thick of the crowd. On the other hand, he had always hated the Happiness Breaks.

In all the noise, Drew was able to call out so that most of them could hear her. "Don't attract any more attention. We can take our time going back out, so don't touch anything, don't move too fast, and don't make too much noise."

The group made the trip back into the abandoned area of the city quietly and slowly. It took at least thirty minutes.

And then, apparently, the big black man had had enough.

He casually reached over to Drew, as if he was going to put his hand on her shoulder, and wrenched her into a nearby wall, slamming her head against the bricks.

He pulled her into a headlock in front of him as he turned to face the rest of the group and pointed his weapon toward the others.

Her feet off the ground, Drew hung onto his arm for support, shock on her face. She tried to pull back far enough from his arm to breathe. Blood trickled from the side of her head.

The others stopped in their tracks. Former prisoners and revolutionaries alike pulled weapons. Some prisoners pointed their weapons at the revolutionaries, some at Drew's attacker, while the revolutionaries did the same in return.

Gaylen drew his weapon, too, but he was afraid to point it anywhere near Drew.

Kevin's hand, though, was steady, his gun level with the big man's head from a distance of about ten feet.

Each side eyed the other. The Lightbringers waited for orders, while the prisoners waited to see what the big man would do.

The man spoke in a low, slow, rumbling voice, his face impassive. He kept his weapon up, moving it deliberately from one Lightbringer to another.

"I call myself Mercy, because I'm used to hearing people beg for it. Consider that a warning. Now, this gorgeous little girl is going to stay right where she is, right where I'm in charge of things, until I get some idea of what the hell is going on."

Kevin spoke, his expression more intense than usual. "We're rescuing you, breaking you out. That's pretty obvious, isn't it?"

Mercy rumbled, "That is obvious, yes. But I don't think this was a random act of kindness. I think you want something, and I want to know what that something is before we go too far."

Drew strained through the choke hold to whisper, "'Mercy' is perfect for you."

He ignored her.

Kevin used his gun to gesture towards the man's captive. "Drew is our leader. She can explain this better than any of us."

"Well, she's my hostage, so she's not going to be explaining anything. Since you're the only one brave enough to speak up, you explain this to me."

Kevin paused for a moment. He didn't lower his weapon or take his eyes off the former prisoner. "We are the Lightbringers. We work against the government. We're on a mission, and we need backup. We rescued you hoping that some of you would join us."

"And I'd want to join you in your mission why?" Mercy asked.

Drew strained again to whisper, "Because we saved your lives, and because we are on the same—"

Mercy tightened his grip on her throat. She grimaced.

"Why would you people think that we are on the same side?" he said to Kevin.

Kevin was stock still for a moment, and then he slowly lowered his weapon. The rest of the revolutionaries followed suit. Mercy did not. Gaylen wanted to shout at them not to do that, not to leave them defenseless, but he just stood there.

Drew attempted to nod, apparently signaling approval. Tears leaked from her eyes.

Kevin said, "Because we both want to destroy the DAA and every bastard who has anything to do with them."

Mercy thought this over, his weapon still leveled at the revolutionaries. "So you're giving us another chance to strike back before we get dusted."

"Pretty much." Kevin looked around at the other former prisoners. "Some of you will die in the process. But you were going to die anyway. At least this way, by joining up with us, you've got another chance to do some real damage. And you'll die free men instead of dying in prison."

One by one, the prisoners lowered their weapons, and some put them back into their pockets.

Mercy's weapon was the last to come down. He dropped Drew to the ground and gave her a shove away from him, though not too roughly.

She allowed herself to fall to all fours, her head lowered, to rub her throat and catch her breath. Christian went to her side to help her up.

When Drew was standing again, she met Mercy's eyes with a wry smile.

He looked back without a word, his face stony.

She smiled bigger. "I forgive you," she said, her voice rough from being choked.

His expression only grew stonier.

Drew broke the eye contact first. She turned to the rest of the group. "It's all right that Mercy forced this conversation a little sooner than I'd planned. Now you all know what I was going to tell you. We're on the same side, we have the same agenda, and we all run the same risk of losing our lives in this fight.

"But for those of you who survive, I tell you now, I want you to stay. Your old friends failed you already, in that you were in those prisons at all. We offer you new friendship, and new resources.

"Perhaps even more important than that, though, we offer you new purpose. We hand-picked each one of you, because we knew that you were the ones who have been fighting back effectively and for the right reasons, but most of you have been trying to fulfill individual agendas. We offer you the chance to work within a large group that is organizing massive resistance. Striking a blow on a large scale. You'll be part of something here that matters.

"If you join us, you will be supplied and trained. If you survive long enough, you will also learn how to manage your emotions better, how to make decisions more wisely, and how to find meaning in your lives.

"And if you do not join us, you are free to go. You are free to go even now. I only *ask* you to stay, to help us, and to join us."

Some of the prisoners shifted, but no one spoke up or walked away.

Drew nodded. "Let's go."

Not much later that same night, John Oldman sat in front of his work screen in his office at the DAA headquarters and stared into space.

He'd talked to Nick about whatever the Lightbringers possessed that had allowed Chloe to disappear. Nick had claimed not to know anything about it, and John had told him to include the tech in whatever deal he made to ensnare Drew.

The crime statistics ticker scrolling past on the wall in front of John ticked up from 11 to 12 for October in the category of Terrorist Control. Another terrorist attack, then.

He pulled up the home page for the Terrorist Control division and read the announcement. There had just been a disturbance at the Bureau of Provision: criminals had been broken out, and the responsible group had not yet been identified. He frowned.

He both felt and heard a faint *buzz-buzz* and realized that his handscreen was ringing. He hurried to dig it out of his jacket pocket.

"Yes? . . . Yes, hello?"

"Is this . . . Goldfinger?" It was a girl's hesitant voice. It was Chloe.

He turned up the volume and closed his eyes tight to concentrate better on the sound of her voice. "Yes, it is."

"OK. Well, it turns out we are recruiting. In a big way, actually. So, Drew said it was all right to invite you to come join us."

If he had been younger and more optimistic, John would have thrown a fist in the air in celebration. As it was, he cracked a smile. "Good. Good, I'm . . . grateful."

"We do need somebody to vouch for you though. Somebody who was with FPU with you. Who can we call?"

"No problem." John recited a name and number from memory. He was glad he'd been able to keep his cover on that last assignment, even if everything else about it had gone to hell.

"Just a minute," Chloe said.

Waiting, the silence seemingly unending, John all but held his breath. Only a couple of minutes later, though, Chloe came back on the line and announced, "You're good." She gave him an address and a passcode and hung up.

He knew the area. The address placed the cell in the military housing on the defunct Fort Myer in Arlington, just across the river.

John took a deep breath. It was a breakthrough. Something he hadn't screwed up—yet.

He cast one last concerned look at the announcement about the terrorist attack and then turned off his work screen.

Back at the house with broken wallscreens, Gaylen sat against a wall in the living room, chilled and shaking with the aftermath of the mission. He kept remembering their final escape from the building and the man who had been cut in half by the doors. And then Mercy's attack and the stand-off they'd had. He wrapped his arms around himself in an attempt to calm his shaking body.

At the moment, Mercy leaned against the doorway, taking up most of the frame. He had found, borrowed, or stolen a patterned silver lighter, and he used it to light a cigarette. Mercy and Kevin had the same sort of inscrutability. Gaylen envied and resented their ability to seem perfectly calm no matter what happened.

Most of the others spread out into other rooms or the back yard. A few sat on the floor in here, mostly former prisoners who seemed to know each other already. One had found a deck of cards in the house somewhere, and they were playing some sort of game.

When they'd gotten back, Drew had told them that there would be a few hours before their next effort. She'd told them to grab some sleep while they could. But Gaylen knew he was too agitated to fall asleep.

Gaylen's body seemed to have taken on a permanent shiver. He felt he'd never be fully warm again. He stood up and went outside, his shoulders tight and hunched as if cast that way.

At first, he only saw that there were a lot of people out there in the darkness, illuminated only by moon and stars and the artificial lights of the city outside the base. People filled the two benches, and some were on the ground in clusters on the unkempt grass—all of them strangers to him.

He was about to go back inside when he noticed an unoccupied corner in the back. He went out there and sat on the cold grass and dirt, looking out into other, empty yards, shivering.

There, unhappy thoughts swirled through his mind in a cacophony, and he became more and more agitated. These people rejected President Martha's teachings, and they had gotten hurt as a result. Some of them had even gotten killed. Wasn't this proof that President Martha was right?

In fact, he found himself thinking, his whole life had been just fine, really, until he had gone into the underground. Every awful thing that had happened since then had been his fault, for abandoning what he had been taught all his life. Hadn't it?

Yes, their government was lying to them and hiding things from them, but without the underground, maybe they wouldn't have to. Maybe the underground was creating all the other problems by refusing to think correctly.

He had voiced this suspicion to both Nick and the Lightbringers, and they had both talked him out of it, but it kept coming back up. It matched everything. If there weren't all these people in rebellion, surely everything would be fine.

Soon, Gaylen had himself convinced that he would take the next opportunity to find his way back to civilization and resume a normal life. He would just try harder this time to keep his thinking perfect. He would fake it until the DAA let him go home, and then he would—

Then he remembered what might still happen to his family. Serena. His beautiful little girl.

His heart sank, and in that moment, he knew that he no longer believed in the law of attraction.

If he really believed that positive thinking would keep Sierra and Serena safe, he would be able to just leave them alone and let them go about their lives. But he knew that it wouldn't. The dread in the pit of his stomach told him that it wouldn't.

A few days ago, he had believed that everyone was always safe and always would be. He'd been wrong all along, and now he didn't even have the lie to make him feel better.

He put his head in his hands.

After some time, someone approached. He looked up quickly, apprehensive, but it was just Chloe. She sat down with him, a safe, quiet presence, and chewed on a dreadlock.

Words swam in his mind until they fought to come out, and in Chloe's silence he sensed an invitation to speak, and finally he did.

"I used to feel safe, sort of. I mean . . . Nothing bad ever happened, and nothing bad was ever going to happen. Everything was fine. I'm always healthy, I have work, I have food and clothes and a nice place to live, and I . . . had a family I loved . . . But, then, bad things were happening all the time, at the same time. Sort of. I mean, I wasn't . . . happy, even though I was supposed to be. I've never really been happy. Unless I was with Sierra . . . and Serena, at first, before things changed . . ."

The confessions spilled out of him, uncontrollable. "And I've done things that hurt people. And then Serena left me, and she took Sierra . . . But that was all my fault, because I couldn't think and feel the right way, right? But now, it turns out it's all a lie. Nothing is safe, after all."

His voice began to catch in his throat. "People get killed, they get sick, they die, they have horrible accidents, there's this secret police, prisons—life is bad, Chloe. And what am I supposed to do about it? I can't deal with this."

Tears spilled over. "And I can't even protect myself from it, because positive thinking doesn't—doesn't work—and I can't—I can't protect my—family—" He found himself sobbing the last words, and Chloe took him in her arms.

"I know," she whispered to him. "I know. I'm sorry."

He cried against her chest even as a part of him watched, uncomfortable, awkward with this. He hadn't allowed himself to cry in another person's presence since he was a child crying on his mother's lap.

"Go ahead and feel it," Chloe said softly." Make it even bigger. Let it kill you. I promise you won't die."

He took a deep breath and surrendered. The feelings overpowered him until his entire body shook, and then, just as he knew they would, the feelings passed like a tsunami crashing across him. Then he let them recede, his breath evening out, and he sat up, wiping his face with his sleeve.

He looked over at Chloe, tentative, worried about how she might see him now, and saw that tears streaked her face, too.

He couldn't remember the last time he had seen anyone else cry, besides his own daughter. In the past, even if he had seen such a thing, he never would have asked about it, but things were different here. Gently, he touched one of the tear tracks. "Why are you crying?"

She shook her head and wiped her face. "I just . . . I feel for you. That's all." She smiled wanly.

Gaylen sat back and took a deep breath. He didn't know what to think about it.

A few tears welled up in Gaylen's eyes again, and he wiped them away. He let the last traces of emotion bubble up and then fade away. As it had in his meditation with Drew, vulnerability assaulted him now that he had been seen in this state of weakness, and he had to bring that vulnerability to the light, too.

As it passed, he felt closer to Chloe than he had before. Her warmth soothed away the chill that had attached itself to him.

Time passed in silence and stillness, while Chloe glanced at him occasionally.

Finally, Gaylen said, "I really don't understand. New America was supposed to be safe, and perfect, and I don't see how . . ." It was hard to even find the words to explain the question. "The whole idea is just to be happy, right? We think positively so that we can feel good and keep our lives good. If that's all Martha ever wanted for us, then how could she end up killing people and lying and all of this . . . stuff?"

"I know," Chloe said. It wasn't an answer.

Gaylen sighed heavily.

After some time, Chloe put her hand on his shoulder and spoke softly. "It will get better. It doesn't ever really get easy, exactly, but it does get better."

"Do you promise?"

"I promise." She grinned a little, and he believed her.

They sat quietly for a while, and then Gaylen remembered the earlier kiss. She seemed to be a willing partner, and he needed comfort and distraction. For the first time, he was able to push aside his thoughts of Serena as he sat up, leaned in, and kissed Chloe gently.

For a moment, she accepted and returned the kiss, her lips soft and warm, and he heard her quick in-breath that signaled arousal, and then she pulled away. She looked up at him and shook her head sadly. "Not yet, Gaylen."

"Not yet?" He looked at her, his brow furrowed. He couldn't think of any reason to wait, and he didn't want to wait. "When? Tomorrow?"

She shook her head, smiling. "It's too complicated to explain right now, Gaylen, but . . . things are different in the Lightbringers world than they are in Martha's world. I want to take my time with you."

He didn't know what to say, so he didn't say anything. But he was glad that she couldn't see the rush of blood to his cheeks. Why was she rejecting him? She had kissed him before . . . it didn't make any sense.

She smiled again. "Thank you, though. For the compliment."

She got up and went inside.

Gaylen sat out on the grass for a while longer, trying to understand what might be different here—or what he had done wrong—but eventually he felt his eyelids growing too heavy to hold open, and he went in and found his bunk and collapsed into sleep alone.

An hour or so later—now in the early morning hours of Tuesday—John Oldman had his gold mask in place to hide his identity, plus a rucksack of basic belongings, and he knocked on the door of a rundown bungalow on the abandoned base. He felt alert and tired at the same time. He wasn't wearing his armor or carrying a weapon, because he would be undercover full-time now, with all the risks that entailed.

The door was opened by a black man who was the biggest man John had ever seen, wearing an unfriendly expression and pointing a gun right at John's face.

John flinched, just a little. Then he sighed, irritated with himself. "I was invited here by Chloe. She said the password was, 'Bring the light.'"

The guy's scowl didn't change. He opened the door and stepped back, waving John in with the gun.

John stepped cautiously into a room with half a dozen typical denizen types in it, all of whom had paused to look at him curiously. He glanced around. Nothing about the people or the place struck him as unusual for a temporary terrorist safe house. The room was empty other than the people, the walls were cracking and peeling, and the wallscreen was broken, of course.

A heavy-set Hispanic man with tattoos on his arms approached, studying his mask. "Don't tell me . . . I think I'm figuring it out . . . You're Goldfinger." His tone was dry.

John almost laughed, but he settled for nodding.

"I gotta scan you, man," the tattooed man said. "Plus, just so you know, only stun weapons are allowed around here."

John shrugged and raised his arms, surprised at the latter rule. Usually, groups like this let new recruits bring in whatever firepower they wanted.

However, it always made sense to scan for wires, implants, and the like. John hoped that the shielding around his subvocal communications implant would hold up. It was fairly new tech from the outside world.

A moment later, the scan was done. "Welcome, then," the other man said. He cast an appraising look at John, and then walked away.

John let out a slow breath, then turned back to the large man who'd answered the door. He was now cleaning his nails with a sharp knife. "Where can I find Chloe?" John asked.

The man gave him a look that said, *Not my problem*, and went back to cleaning his nails.

John turned back to the room. He glanced around, and a woman with thin cheekbones and dark curls said, "I think she's in the kitchen."

John nodded his thanks and headed toward the back of the house, to where he guessed the kitchen would be, given what he could see of the floor plan.

He guessed right, and in the kitchen he found Chloe talking to a pixie-like woman with short honey-blonde hair. He paused at the doorway.

Chloe saw him first and smiled. Then the other woman turned and looked at him—or, rather, she looked *into* him. Her green eyes were piercing, and they struck him with such intensity that he found himself taking a step backward. For a moment, he felt the urge to turn and run—a feeling that was foreign to him.

The woman took a couple of steps closer as she scrutinized him. Then she asked, "Can you turn that mask off?"

John flirted with the idea of lying, but he might not be able to do it well. She had him off balance. After a pause, he said, "I *can* . . ."

She stared directly into his eyes again. He wanted to tear his gaze away, but he waited, hardly breathing, hoping she would let him off the hook soon. Her gaze was so unsettling that he feared he would start babbling incoherently or confessing everything any minute.

In a tone of voice that made it clear that this was a gentle command, the woman said, "When you're ready, you'll turn it off." Then she walked past him.

John let out a breath. This had to be Drew, the leader of the Lightbringers. And now he understood why Nick, in particular, would hate her so much.

He stepped into the kitchen, where Chloe still stood. She grinned at him and tossed her purple dreadlocks over her shoulder. "That was Drew, our leader. Sorry, she can be kind of . . ."

"Wow," John said.

"Yeah."

John took a deep breath and refocused himself. "So, first, thank you."

She shrugged a little and grinned a little.

"So why the big recruiting drive?" he asked, trying to sound casual.

"There's a big mission coming up," she said, her eyes cast down. "But I don't really know anything about it yet—I mean, nobody does, not even Drew, I don't think. We've got some data to pick up first, but we're just waiting right now. Probably, we should all be asleep. Um, there aren't enough bunks anymore, but I'll show you where you can find a spot on the floor with some blankets."

The girl with the dreadlocks led him to a back bedroom. There were three bunk beds squeezed in there, but one ordinary-looking black guy slept in one bunk and backpacks staked out the others. Chloe pulled two blankets from under a bunk bed and laid them out for him along an empty wall.

John nodded his thanks. He decided that he had made plenty of progress for one night and should give the girl some space. He sat down heavily on the blankets, wishing his knees were younger. Chloe smiled at him and left.

He stared around the room. This was it: his chance at redemption. He was on the inside, and now it was up to him to drive this organization into the ground. He wished he had more energy for the task—he felt old.

Most of all, he wished he had some whiskey.

His communications implant sounded at a frequency only he could hear. He got up and headed back to the kitchen; he remembered seeing a back door there. He got outside before he answered the call. Even though subvocal speech couldn't easily be detected, John always worried that he might give something away with his facial expressions.

The call was from Nick.

"Good news," Nick said.

"What?"

"We've got Drew where you want her. Meet us in Constitution Below, under the Reflecting Pool, in an hour."

First, John had to settle out from the mental whiplash. He hated it when he had to jump from one persona to another. Then he had a moment of exhilaration. He had gotten into the Lightbringers and already Nick was going to give him his chance to capture Drew. If all went well, he would be able to work this from both sides—interrogating Drew for key information while simultaneously embedding himself deeper within the organization.

"I'll meet you," he said. "Why Constitution Below? That's not your territory."

"No kidding, it's not my territory. Do you think I'm stupid?"

John ignored that. "Did you make the deal for the invisibility tech?"

Nick started sounding pissy. "I did. I told you, I do what I promise I'll do."

"Good," John said. "Thanks." He ended the call, then prepared to call the DAA office to arrange the sting.

Just before he initiated the call, the reality of what he was about to do crashed in on him. A fair number of the people he'd just met were about to get dusted, and Drew was going to end up in a DAA holding cell for interrogation.

Just from their brief meeting, he had seen something about Drew that he didn't want to destroy, and Chloe was just a good kid gone down the wrong path.

He kicked himself mentally. This was the kind of thinking that had made him hesitate for too long with the FPU. He could not allow himself to make the same mistakes again. He made the call.

Almost as soon as John ended the call, the door opened behind him, and he turned around. The tattooed man who had scanned him earlier stood in the doorway. "Rounding everyone up for orders," he said and went back inside.

John took a deep breath, laboriously made the mental switch back to new recruit, and went in. He wished he'd gotten more sleep the previous night. It was going to be an all-nighter if they were just now getting started.

A few minutes later, dozens of people filled the living room—many more people than John had expected to see. The guy from the bunk room was there, looking sleepy and miserable. Probably a new recruit.

Drew stood before them, waiting, and the people soon gave her their full attention. John envied her natural charisma. The tattooed man stood next to her, an easy confidence in his stance, too, and John guessed that this was her second in command.

"OK, guys," Drew said. "I know it's late. I'll make this quick. All we have to do is pick up some data. I'm taking a small crew with me just in case something goes wrong. One piece of bad news right up front, though. Somehow, our contact knew about our cloaking devices. I don't know how our recruiting could have been connected to us already, but what's done is done."

John breathed slowly. Any guilty look or move here would ruin him. Instead, he looked around the room as if trying to see if anyone else looked guilty.

In the pause, Chloe shifted. Drew caught her eye, and Chloe said, "I used mine last night. I thought someone was following me. So, it might be my fault . . . sorry." She looked abashed. She did not look toward John.

John just kept breathing.

"Well, done is done," Drew said gently. "But we're having to give up one of the devices to get this data. So, we're paying the price. This is a good reminder that constant vigilance is necessary. Now, let's move on. Gaylen, you're coming on this mission. Kevin, you're my second. Mercy, you're our third."

The big man, who was leaning in the door frame and lighting a cigarette, raised an eyebrow.

Drew went on, "Six more, self-select. The rest of you, get back to sleep if you can. We'll have something for breakfast in the morning."

She waited a few moments for her team to sort itself out.

John went up to Kevin and volunteered himself. The man simply nodded. The others took no particular notice of him, except that one gave him a compliment on his mask.

He noted that introductions were being made within the team, and realized that many of these people were strangers to each other. He guessed that there were a lot of new recruits besides himself.

That was when he put two and two together: all these new recruits plus the breakout at the Bureau of Provision. He gritted his teeth. This group was more dangerous than he had thought.

Gaylen held back a yawn. The group was going down through the trap door in the laundry room. He rubbed his gritty eyes as the people in front of him descended the ladder. Mercy, Kevin, and Drew were on the team, plus Chloe, who had self-selected again. The other four self-selects were new recruits. One man had a gold mask tattooed across his face.

The group lit the way with flashlights as they walked through rough, dirt-walled underground corridors. It looked like someone had used a laser dozer to vaporize just enough earth for two people to walk side by side. The different flashlight beams played across the walls in a dizzying display.

Gaylen found himself next to Drew, who smiled at him, and he smiled back and took the opportunity to ask a question.

"Drew, what's it really like in the outside world?"

"I've never been there myself," Drew replied, "but I've talked to others who have. They say that Martha is both right and wrong. You know she says that it's chaos out there—total barbarism. She says civilization has collapsed. That part isn't true. The countries and governments and societies out there are perfectly functional. Now, yes, there is crime and war and sickness and accidents and old age and all of those imperfect realities of human life. But only because they don't cover it up there."

"How do people deal with it?" Gaylen asked.

"A lot of them find comfort in their religions. But mostly, people rely on one another. People help each other feel better when things go bad."

A day ago, that would have been an alien thought to Gaylen. Now he thought about how he had cried on Chloe's shoulder last night—how awkward and yet how comforting it had been. He wondered how his life might have been different if he had always had friends he could do that with.

At a T-intersection, the passageway opened up into a finished hallway with overhead lights. The group turned off their flashlights and turned right. After a few yards, they started encountering other denizens. For their part, the Lightbringers looked nonchalant as they walked along. Only Chloe still looked nervous. She popped her gum repeatedly.

Drew went on, "One really big difference is that the whole outside world is in contact, in communication. Even if someone moves to another city, their friends can still call them or message them. They can even visit. Almost everyone has friends and family outside of their own town. In fact, most people make friends with people who aren't local."

That sounded bizarre to Gaylen, but it also sounded nice. "Why don't we do that here?"

"The real reason? Because the DAA finds it a lot easier to cover up problems when people aren't in communication. We used to have the ability to travel and communicate freely between cities, too. The DAA locked down our communication technology and shut down our transportation systems and instituted checkpoints."

Gaylen had never even thought about trying to stay in touch with anyone who had moved away. He had intuited years ago that it just wasn't done. "How can people move away so often, then?"

Drew paused. "Most of them don't actually move away, Gaylen. That's the DAA covering up people being taken to prison."

Gaylen staggered, struck by the thought of Serena and Sierra. "How can you know whether they went to prison or actually left?" He couldn't breathe, suddenly.

"It's hard to know," Drew said, looking at him sympathetically. "But if they told you themselves, in person, or in a handwritten letter, it's probably true that they just left."

Relief washed over Gaylen, and he chose to stay silent for the rest of the walk. Again, he promised Serena and Sierra, *I will find you and tell you the truth. I will protect you.*

After a while, he noticed the fellow with the gold mask nearby. He glanced over, and the guy looked away. Gaylen felt sorry for him—he had an aura of age and defeat about him that inspired pity. It was a strange contrast to the shining, expressionless mask.

The other new recruit of note was a thuggish type he had overheard being called Erik. He looked like a good guy to have nearby in a fight.

Drew led them through a doorway and down another flight of steps and through another doorway into what appeared to be a utility conduit. The concrete tunnels were narrow and rounded instead of rectangular. There were no light sources, and large pipes ran along the tunnels in various configurations. The group broke out their flashlights again.

After some dozens of yards and many twists and turns, the tunnel opened up into a much larger area that looked relatively new and roughly carved out. Denizens must have created it. Can lights along the walls cast shadowy light, and a huge work of graffiti on the far wall read, "Welcome to Constitution Below. To reserve: See Jared."

A half-dozen or so denizens stood around the room. Gaylen's eyes widened as he recognized Nick at their center.

Drew stopped about a third of the way into the room, and the group stopped with her. Gaylen glanced over and saw that Drew was also staring at Nick, a thoughtful expression on her face.

Nick, for his part, displayed a sour look at the sight of the two of them. He recovered, however, and quickly had a big grin on his face. He crossed the room just to pat Gaylen clumsily on the shoulder, his gracious manner belied by the hateful look in his eyes when he glanced at Drew. "Gaylen! So glad you could make it! What are you doing running around with these losers? You're not letting them poison your mind, are you, buddy?"

Before Gaylen had a chance to speak, Nick laughed loudly and turned to Drew. "I'm just kidding around, of course," he said with a smile that came across more like a sneer. "You know I think the world of you, pretty lady."

He reached out to take her hand, but Drew just smiled at him with her hands still at her sides.

Nick flushed and said, "OK," with poor grace.

Gaylen heard Mercy snicker behind him, and he almost grinned.

Drew still smiled at Nick. It was an inscrutable smile that suggested that she saw straight through Nick and knew every thought that ran through his mind. It said that she knew every bad memory he'd buried and every fantasy he'd ever acted out. It made Nick take a step back and avert his eyes.

"Let's see the toy," Nick said, his expression and tone turning ugly. "And I got your boy with the data right over here. This is the boy you made the deal with, right? George?" He took a few steps toward a quiet young man in the corner and looked at him as if he distrusted his name and perhaps even his existence. The young man held up a data stick.

"Yes, that was my contact," Drew said levelly. "I didn't know he worked for you, Nick."

"Everybody works for me, didn't you know?" Nick said. "Everybody."

Drew pulled out her cloaking device and held it up so that Nick could see it. "Give me the data," she said to George.

Drew and George made slow underhand tosses of their respective items. George threw the stick clumsily and Mercy actually caught it. Meanwhile, Nick caught the ring.

"How does it work?" he asked.

"Put it on and press the gem," Drew said. Then, her tone casual, she added, "Lightbringers, get ready. We're about to be ambushed."

The revolutionaries drew weapons. Kevin and Mercy dropped back and looked for trouble.

Nick's scowl was the last part of him to disappear as the nanobots cascaded from the ring and surrounded him. Then, the telltale shimmer of rapid movement appeared where he had stood—and shouting and the whine of stun guns broke out behind the Lightbringers.

Chapter Nine

Wayne Webster Watts, from his underground book, 9 Lives:

> *Adrenaline, rage, lust, sadism, hatred—you'll never feel more alive than when you're indulging whatever makes your blood pump the hardest. And the ugliest, nastiest part of you is usually what makes you feel the most alive when you really dig deep into it and let it out. But you can't take my word for it—you gotta experience it yourself to know what I'm talking about. And that is what the underground is for.*

Nick's men started running at the same time that Nick did, without missing a beat, while DAA agents fired into the room from the other entrances. They quickly overwhelmed the Lightbringers at the wide doors and poured into the room.

The Lightbringers dropped to the floor and rolled to the sides of the room, even Chloe. Gaylen alone stood there for seemingly endless seconds before he dropped to the floor and scrambled to a wall.

His weapon out, Gaylen watched the fight from where he crouched. He flinched as hard blows landed and people dropped from stun shots. Things happened so quickly he couldn't track them. He couldn't keep track of who was winning, either, in all the confusion, though Mercy punched people like he carried lead weights in his fists, dropping one agent after another to the ground. Kevin also held his own.

One DAA agent hesitated near a doorway, clearly silhouetted, with no one near him. Gaylen aimed and fired. His eyebrows went up when the agent dropped, and he had a moment of exhilaration. It was his one opening. Everyone else stood too close to an ally.

Three DAA agents headed past him, half-dragging Drew toward the back exit. None of them seemed armed anymore, not even Drew. They held her arms behind her back, but she struggled fiercely, throwing herself back and forth and kicking out in all directions. He guessed the agents had dropped and not recovered their stun weapons, because this would be going a lot easier for them if Drew were unconscious.

He would have fired on them, but he risked hitting Drew. He glanced around for help. Mercy had disappeared. Erik was busy with other foes. The man with the gold mask crouched against a wall and fired his stun weapon at some agents who fired back at him from another doorway, although they all seemed to have pretty poor aim. Kevin and Chloe tag-teamed another agent.

Seeing no alternative, Gaylen ran toward the three men dragging Drew. As he reached them, Drew's struggles overbalanced the man at her back. They all stumbled over each other and one nearly fell. It was an opening.

Gaylen threw his tall, slender, untrained body at the nearest man—an attack made with desperation and no plan whatsoever. He managed to get his arms around the other man's neck and drag him half to the ground, and Drew exploded in a frenzy.

Something crashed into Gaylen's ribs and he nearly blacked out. He collapsed onto all fours, wheezing. Chaos erupted above him, but he couldn't track anything.

Moments later, Chloe and Kevin pulled him up and dragged him along the tunnels. He waited for the whine of dust guns behind them. Nothing. He got his own footing and drew breath again, painfully. He raised his head, but the dizzying flashlight beams revealed only nondescript tunnel walls.

He croaked, "Drew?"

Kevin said, "She's up ahead."

They kept running.

Mercy had seen it coming. He'd never met Nick before, but he recognized the type in a millisecond, and he knew the deal was going to go south. So, Mercy was ready to kick some ass the moment the DAA's dust guns started whining. First, he made mental note of the direction of the shimmer in the air Nick made when he ran through the large room. Then Mercy took a moment to put down a few of the DAA agents, to make sure the Lightbringers would win the fight, and then he took off.

Nick had betrayed Mercy's new allies, and probably the data he had provided was outdated, fake, or otherwise useless, and Mercy was going to punish him for it.

Mercy was a big, hulking man, but he was fast and graceful. He had always been an outstanding athlete back in school, and he'd kept himself in shape. Had to. Physical weakness was too much of a liability in a dog-eat-dog world.

He came up on Nick quickly, since the other man had stopped running long before, but because Nick didn't know the rule about moving slowly, he was moving too quickly, and the tell-tale shimmer was present.

Nick only had time for an astonished grunt as Mercy swept him bodily into a wall. Mercy threw him to the ground next, straddled him, and grabbed one of his hands. As Nick struggled, Mercy looked for the ring. By now, Nick was yelling, "Get the hell off me! You son of a—" His cheek was split open and bleeding from hitting the wall.

Mercy grabbed the other hand and found the ring this time. He wrenched Nick's fingers until he could get the ring off, while Nick writhed, furious, beneath him. The shimmering went away.

"Get the hell—"

Mercy stood up, the ring in his hand. He gave Nick a swift, vicious kick in the side, then another. He said nothing. Nick didn't need to be told what a worthless piece of shit he was.

Mercy was about to launch another kick when footsteps sounded. He looked up too late. DAA agents stepped quickly down the corridor, their arms extended, dust guns pointed at the two of them. Mercy's lower lip curled.

"Give it to us," the agent in the front said. "Now."

Mercy cocked his head back and contemplated the situation.

"Fuck you!" Nick shouted as he scrambled up from the floor. "That's mine!"

"Shut up!" the lead agent shouted at Nick. "Double-crossing piece of slime! You're just lucky we have orders not to kill you both."

Mercy took advantage of the agent's lapse in attention to slap aside his dust gun and punch him in the face, dropping him.

The agents behind the first one fired.

Nanobots swarmed Mercy's nervous system and interfered with the firing of synapses, bringing on a sudden exhaustion. The agents had set their guns to stun. If Mercy was a smaller man, he'd be unconscious already. Instead, he got to feel every moment of his body shutting down for a deep sleep.

Snarling, he launched himself at the second agent in line with a hard-hitting punch to the throat. The agent fell. The third agent shrieked and fired again and again.

Mercy's legs had turned to wood and the weight crept up his body to his arms. He felt like he was caught in quicksand. His vision started to darken as he fell.

The third agent stepped up as he fired at Mercy a fifth and a sixth time. Mercy's brain clung to consciousness, but by now he could no longer command his body.

The agent peered at his unmoving enemy cautiously. He nudged Mercy's arm with one foot to see if he was responsive.

Nick, meanwhile, huddled against a wall.

Mercy roared in fury, at least in his mind—all that came out was a low growl.

The agent snatched the ring out of Mercy's hand and then scurried back, wide-eyed.

Meanwhile, the other two agents had picked themselves up. Each of them clutched their injuries and swore, but both stayed well back from Mercy.

"Come on," one of the agents said to the third one. "We got the ring, we've gotta get back to the fight."

"We're supposed to take prisoners," the third one argued.

The other man's tone became querulous. "I can't drag that huge motherfucker, can you?"

They retreated, and the third agent fired once more at Mercy, as if for good measure, and finally Mercy went dark. The last thing he saw was Nick glaring at him.

The Lightbringers made it to an abandoned boiler room under a subway tunnel—the closest thing to a safe place they were likely to find. Everyone tumbled down onto the wet, dirty concrete and tried to catch their breath. Drew and Chloe went from person to person checking for injuries.

Gaylen had no idea where Mercy, Christian, or Erik were. Kevin and the man with the gold mask were still there, and so were the last two recruits, whose names Gaylen had never heard.

Gaylen's lower chest felt like knives were being driven into it. He had never felt pain like this before. He had no idea what might be wrong, because he had no knowledge of anatomy or physiology. The less one knew about one's own body, said President Martha, the less likely one was to imagine anything being wrong with it.

As soon as Chloe got to him, Gaylen said, "My chest hurts a lot. What if it's bad? What are we going to do?"

Chloe settled down on her haunches in front of him and lifted up the front of his shirt. She surveyed his chest while Gaylen stared at her, shocked that she seemed so comfortable with this. She pressed on his ribs in several places and on his breastbone, and the agony was immediate. He gasped and glared at her, both of which she ignored.

Chloe frowned. "A couple of your ribs are cracked, and you're bruising a lot. But there isn't much we can do for you. We can put ice on it back at the safe house. And I'll get you some painkillers." She jerked her head toward one of the new recruits lying down near a wall behind her. "He's a lot worse off—he's got a collapsed lung."

She pulled his shirt back down over his bruises. "You need to keep breathing deeply every so often, even though it hurts—that's important to prevent pneumonia. But don't worry. I don't think you're going to die."

Gaylen caught his breath enough to say, "You don't *think* I'm going to die? That's great, Chloe. Just great."

Chloe rolled her eyes. "It was a joke. You're not going to die. It will just hurt a whole lot for a long time. Broken ribs are awful that way." She looked at him sympathetically. "I'm sorry."

She got up and went to a backpack Gaylen hadn't noticed before, with a red plus symbol on it. She took out a small bottle and brought him two pills. "Here. Take these. They'll help."

While he swallowed the medicine, she gazed at him and tugged at one of her dreadlocks. "You know, I saw what you did back there, Gaylen. How you jumped in and tried to save Drew. You did help, you know. It was . . . brave." She smiled at him like she was trying to cheer him up.

Gaylen just leaned back against the wall, exhausted. He thought he had precious little to show for all his bravery. And he wasn't convinced that he wasn't going to die. He clutched his aching chest and wondered what death was going to be like. He'd never seen anyone die—never even heard about anyone dying. People just . . . went away.

It occurred to him again that he had not eaten enough or slept enough in the last couple of days. So much had happened since Wednesday morning, so many unwelcome things learned. He was so tired. And his chest throbbed.

He barely noticed when Chloe got up and walked away.

He did notice when Mercy returned. The man was walking slowly and unevenly, with a scowl that was far more ugly than normal.

And when he turned his head, Gaylen saw that where his left ear had been was only a raw, bleeding wound.

Chloe saw it at the same time that Gaylen did, and she went up to him with the red cross-marked backpack and gestured toward the side of his head. The big man scowled but sat down to let Chloe treat him.

Gaylen closed his eyes. He wanted with all his heart to go back to how things had been before, when he didn't have to think about dust guns and the DAA and broken ribs and missing ears.

A few minutes later, he heard Drew and Chloe conferring in hushed voices, and then Drew said, "We have to get this one out of here and to the doctor, he's the only one in real trouble at this point. Get him out of here. You're in charge of this."

Gaylen cracked his eyes open to see that they were talking about the recruit with the collapsed something. Chloe and Mercy—who now had a white piece of gauze taped over the side of his head—carefully picked him up and carried him away.

Drew watched them go, then turned to the rest of the team.

Only Gaylen, Kevin, the man with the gold mask, and the other new recruit remained. They were all bloodied, bruised, and exhausted.

Drew looked away, and her small body began to shake. "Dammit!" she yelled. Tears spilled down her face as she clenched her fists. "I'm sorry this happened," she said, her voice choking.

Drew wiped her face with her hands and took a deep breath, then began pacing. Kevin stood up and moved toward her, but she put up a hand to stop him. Everyone waited, all eyes on her.

She continued to pace as she composed herself. At long last, she said, "I promise you, I will get us back to the light. But for now, we will do what we must—we will walk through the darkness together. Let's go."

She came over to Gaylen and reached down to help him up.

He took her hand, which was still trembling and damp with tears, and he found himself smiling up at her. Her eyes met his for a long moment, and he put all the reassurance he could into his gaze, just as she had once done for him. For a moment, he forgot his own misery as he tried to alleviate hers.

And after a moment, she found a small grin of her own.

Gaylen let her help him to his feet, and they headed back to the safe house.

Their leader was only human, after all. Sometimes she needed help, too. Gaylen felt good knowing that he could be that source of help.

Back topside, the safe house held the stillness of early morning. A few of the new recruits and old hands were still awake or up early, sitting around in the living room and reading books or talking. They watched the few remaining team members come in. They dragged in, for the most part. Gaylen walked slowly and held his chest. The painkillers had only helped a little.

One of the former prisoners looked at the team askance. "It didn't go well, then, did it?" he asked.

No one said anything. The group settled on the floor to rest. Gaylen wrapped his arms around his ribs, as it seemed to help ease the pain a bit.

Eventually, Gaylen asked, "What are we going to do with the data we got?"

Drew shook her head. "Nothing."

Gaylen stared at her, confused.

She sighed. "Since Nick betrayed us to the DAA, there's no reason to think he didn't share the data with them as well. That means the DAA already knows our targets, and we can't use them anymore. We'll have to get new data, new targets. I'll go handle it in a few minutes."

No one said anything.

Drew got up and left the room and came back a few minutes later with what looked like granola bars. She handed them out to everyone, then nodded to Kevin. "Let's go update the book." They left. Gaylen had no idea what she was referring to.

Gaylen eyed his granola bar. It said, "ONE RATION" and advised one bar per hundred pounds of body weight, three times a day. It didn't list the ingredients, and it wasn't stamped "SAFE" by the Bureau of Safety. It said, in small print, "Made in Germany." He thought he had heard that word sometime, maybe back in school.

He opened it, sniffed it, discovered that it looked and smelled like chocolate, and wolfed it down. It was filling and delicious, and afterward he felt like he'd rested for hours and eaten a complete meal.

He glanced around to find someone to ask what they were. The only person familiar to him was the fellow with the gold mask sitting to his left.

"Hi," Gaylen said, trying to smile.

The man just looked at him for a moment before answering, "Hello."

"I'm Gaylen." He offered his hand, which the other man took after more hesitation.

"Goldfinger," the guy said. He pointed to the gold mask on his face.

Gaylen had no idea what that meant, so he ignored it. "What are these things?" he asked as he held up his empty wrapper.

The man paused again. He seemed to be a ponderous fellow. "Rations from the outside world. Very nutritious."

"Yeah," Gaylen said. He thought that over for a minute. It was still strange to him to imagine that the world outside their borders wasn't just wasteland and chaos. "What else do people in the underground get from the outside world?"

Again, a long pause. "A lot of useful things," Goldfinger said, sounding evasive, "and a lot that's not really useful. Banned books, music, and movies. Medical treatments. Drugs."

Drew and Kevin came back into the room and threw themselves on the floor near the rest. Drew looked exhausted.

"What about those cloaking devices?" Gaylen asked. "Are they from the outside world?"

Goldfinger looked to Drew.

"They are," Drew answered, sounding tired. "And our little recruiting expedition was the first time we've used them. We've had them for a while, but they're such good tech, we knew we had to save them for an important mission. We can only stay a step ahead of the government for so long. They eventually get their hands on our tech and find a way to work around it, and then we lose that advantage."

Goldfinger shifted his weight from one hip to the other and asked, "How long do you expect it to take before you can no longer use the cloaking devices?"

Drew shook her head. "Back in the old days, we could get away with new tech for years. New America stopped advancing in technology forty years ago, other than in DAA weapons, so there wasn't much they could do. But then the DAA started getting their counter-intelligence from the outside world, too. Now they can counter our tech within weeks, sometimes even days.

"The info could even be coming from the same group on the outside that's supplying us. It's not like we'd know. It would just be perfect if the same country was supplying both sides of the conflict."

At that moment, Chloe and Mercy came in without the injured recruit. Chloe sat down, and Drew handed her a ration bar, which she tore open and began to devour. Mercy took up his usual position in the doorway.

"What news?" Drew asked Chloe gently.

Chloe shook her head. "We were too late." Tears filled her eyes, then spilled over, but she wiped them away and took another bite of her ration bar.

They all sat in silence for a few moments.

Then Chloe asked, her voice trembling, "What were you guys talking about?" It sounded like she wanted a distraction from her thoughts.

Touched, Gaylen supplied it. "Counter-intelligence from the outside world helping the DAA."

Chloe sniffed and wiped her face with the back of her hand. "Yeah, that's been a big problem for us."

Goldfinger asked, "Do you think the conflict between the underground and the government will ever break out into open warfare?"

Drew shook her head. "They don't want it to, and they won't let it if they can stop it. The whole premise of New America is that everything is perfect, so they've got to cover up anything that's not perfect. And if it breaks out into open warfare, they can't hide that. That's the problem with perfectionism—perfection isn't attainable, and the illusion can't be maintained forever. Eventually, it will become obvious that there are things outside Martha's control."

For a moment, Gaylen wished Goldfinger didn't have that gold mask. He thought Goldfinger had reacted oddly to what Drew had said, but the metallic oval obscured his expression.

Chloe added, "We don't want it to go to open warfare, either, simply because of the loss of lives. We believe in protecting life." Her chin trembled again.

Gaylen shook his head in confusion. "I thought no action was dark unless it came out of the darkness, or something, like you said, Drew."

Drew nodded. "Yes, but there are some actions that none of us can even contemplate without feeling the darkness rise up. We can't say that there's no one with the spiritual strength to commit these acts, but none of us have it."

Gaylen thought this over. It made a certain kind of sense.

"What about you, Gaylen?" Drew asked. "Could you imagine finding a place of light that would allow you to press a button that killed a million people?"

Gaylen thought for a moment, his eyes downcast. He said, "I'm not sure I even know what the light is yet."

Drew smiled. She visibly lit up at the chance to be in teacher mode. "That was good clarity, Gaylen. Consider this. You've felt the darkness fully now—you've embraced it under my guidance and instruction in the meditation we did together. For now, simply know that the light is the opposite of that darkness, in every way."

Still in the doorway, Mercy flicked the top of his silver lighter open and closed over and over, listening, but with apparent disinterest.

Drew looked over the small group. "In fact, this is a good time for you to learn the lesson, and the rest of us need it, too, even if it's just a reminder. Let's step into the light."

The seasoned revolutionaries nodded as if they understood this and sat down cross-legged. The newer recruits followed along, except for Mercy, who stayed in the doorway and eyed all of them with suspicion.

"You're welcome to join us," Drew said to him. When he said nothing, she held his gaze for a long moment before giving her attention back to the group.

"Close your eyes," she began. "Let yourself feel the grief and exhaustion of the last couple of days. We have lost some of our friends—again. We have suffered betrayal—again. We have learned things we did not want to know. We are exhausted. Let yourself feel it."

The room settled into silence and stillness as everyone followed her directions.

Gaylen's feelings rose up so strongly, in such a rush, that his body swayed in response.

"Be aware of your feelings. Give them labels—grief, despair, sadness, anger, hostility, rage, fear, terror, horror."

Gaylen didn't know most of those words, because talk of negative emotions was forbidden in New America, but he got the general idea.

"Add to this every despairing or broken thought you have ever had—remember every time you have ever felt lost, hopeless, helpless, or out of control. Add it in. Let it strengthen. You know it can't hurt you."

Gaylen could hardly bear any more, but it was effortless to summon up the feelings that had always come to him every time he could not stop his ugly thoughts—it was second nature to feel those. They swarmed inside him like huge ugly flies.

"Imagine now that where you are sitting, you are sitting in shadow. The darkness represents the dark emotions that surround you now. See the shadow as dark as your emotions are strong."

Gaylen's shadow was black as pitch. He felt alone in it, and Drew's voice began to sound far away.

"Imagine how you might act if that darkness were to take you over. Imagine the thoughts you would think, the words you would say, the things you would do, if you simply gave in to it."

Gaylen's mind filled with a chaotic rampage of destruction. He wanted to rage, to hit people, to throw himself to the ground and scream like a two-year-old. He wanted to get himself killed, and he wanted to take others with him. He wanted to hit everyone around him. At the same time, he wanted none of these things.

"Now, become aware that there is a line on the floor in front of you, and on the other side of that line, a few feet away from you, there is light. It is brilliant; it is glowing; it is alive the way sunlight is alive.

"Stay in your own darkness, but merely watch what is over there in the light. What is there? What people, what colors, what sounds? Don't go over there, just watch it. Discover what is there."

It took a few moments, but then Gaylen saw images taking shape in the light that was just out of his reach. He remembered images from childhood—the way his father had pushed him in the tire swing in the front yard, how his family had made lemonade together in the summer. He saw the colors of flowers there in the light, a whole flower garden unfolding before him. He saw Serena's smile, and he heard Sierra's laughter. It was lovely over there. And simultaneously, the shadow covered him like a chill that made his bones ache. It was desolate, vast, imprisoning.

"Now, simply make a decision that you will go into the light. You will choose to leave behind the shadow, and you will envelop yourself in the light. Don't do it yet . . . just know that you will do it."

Gaylen decided, and every part of his spirit came alive with anticipation.

"And now, in your mind, stand up and walk into the light. Let it embrace you fully as you do; let it effortlessly wash away the shadow, instantaneously, a complete transformation. Feel and enjoy what it feels like to be in the light. Then turn around and sit down in the light, looking back at the darkness you were once in."

In his mind, it was, indeed, effortless. In his imagination, Gaylen stood and crossed the boundary between shadow and light. His body felt warmer from the outside, as if sun touched his skin, and the chaotic swirl of dark voices and dark emotions dropped away, left behind. In his mind now there was stillness. Inside his spirit, the buzzing of flies was gone—a sense of wholeness replaced it. Sierra's giggles seemed louder, and now he also heard the sound of trees rustling in the wind. He was a small child again and running into the warm embrace of his mother or father. Everything was all right. This was home; this was where he belonged.

He looked back across the line and into the darkness. He had imagined that it would be roiling and raging like a black tornado over there. But to his surprise, it was only dark and empty, nothing more. He sat down and looked, and as he observed, he realized that the shadow simply had nothing to it. It was an illusion. As long as he stayed within it, he was subject to its power, but as soon as he stepped outside of it, it was nothing. Over here in the light was the only reality, and the only power.

A smile came to his face, both in his imagination and in real life.

"Bask in the light for a while," Drew said. Her voice had the sound of a smile in it, as well. "Enjoy it. Let it feed you, sustain you, and strengthen you."

Gaylen did, and he felt so filled up with warmth and joy and the relief of his discovery that he thought that soon he would explode.

"The light will always be here for you. Always."

How long they sat there then, he did not know, but when Chloe nestled up behind him, it was perfect. She put her arms around him carefully, so as not to hurt his injured ribs, and he put his arms on hers. She held him gently, her chest pressed against his back, her head resting on his neck. Eyes still closed, they said nothing. They were two beings sharing in the light, and it was enough.

Chapter Ten

Wayne Webster Watts, from his underground book, 9 Lives:

> *Everything's really about power. That's the whole deal. Martha is a control freak. She's got all the power, and she'll never let it go. She preaches about taking responsibility, but did you ever notice that the actual instructions she gives you just make you more passive and more under her control? The day I broke out of that B.S. was the day I got some power of my own.*

John Oldman got to his feet as soon as he could after the meditation ended and headed outside, trying to be quick and at the same time not draw attention to himself. He barely made it into the moonlit back yard before he fell apart.

He leaned against the wall and cried, his eyes squeezed shut but leaking tears anyway. The "stepping into the light" meditation had done a number on him. He had experienced peace of mind for perhaps the first time in his life.

The group he'd infiltrated previously, FPU, had had a charismatic leader full of surprising and impactful words, too—cults and terrorist cells always did—but this was different. Drew's truth was *truer*, somehow.

Wiping away the tears, he tried to pull himself together. He was such a mess, he feared that if Drew or Chloe stepped outside, he would confess everything.

He pressed his hands to his temples. "All is good and right with the world," he recited. "All is good and right with the world. All is good . . ." He stopped. The words made him nauseated.

He sat down on a nearby bench and tried to complete his daily visualization. Something in him rebelled, and the images fell into fragments, leaving him even more lost than when he'd started.

He struggled to gather his thoughts.

In the moments surrounding the DAA attack, he'd figured out that Nick was leaving with the cloaking device and wasn't planning on handing it over. John had managed to trail behind the Lightbringers just long enough to give a few quick commands to the DAA agents: catch Nick and confiscate the device. But that might be a challenge, with Nick going invisible at will.

But Nick's theft was a tangential issue. The main thing was that John had underestimated the revolutionaries, the sting had failed, and Drew had gotten away. But his cover was intact, so he had another chance.

It was another chance that, at this precise moment, he didn't even want.

He had never liked his job, truth be told. A hundred times he had asked himself why he hadn't become a taxi driver or opened a bakery instead. He was a feeler, after all.

He paced the yard and tried to calm down before someone came outside and found him in this state. He still had a job to do. This one experience didn't—couldn't—change anything, not really.

He used his subvocal communications implant to call his office. A weary-sounding agent answered. John had forgotten that it was four in the morning. Trying to sound casual, he asked about their efforts to find Nick. There were no results yet. Then he left his brief daily report with Wallace by voice mail.

By then, calm had returned, but exhaustion had also settled on him, and he still couldn't bear to think about the experience he'd just had. He did his best to simply shut off his mind as he went into the house and found a corner to sleep in.

Nick Aglaeca zoomed down the narrow, sporadically lit corridors of the underground on his Widowmaker C47 motorcycle, tires squealing as he put the bike through ninety-degree turns too fast. There was no easy way to travel D.C.'s miles of tunnels, but a bike was the best of the choices. Plus, it was fun.

Nick sped through the tunnels with no regard for pedestrians or the likelihood of destroying himself and his bike if he hit someone. As usual, though, the roar of the bike echoing through the tunnels was enough to warn people to flatten themselves against the walls. And he was a tough guy, so he'd walk away from even a nasty accident OK, and the other person would almost certainly be worse off. It'd be worth it just for the fun.

He was heading home after picking up weed and blow from greasy low-life suppliers. Today, he'd gotten to put bullets in a man— a somewhat rare pleasure. The guy had said he'd decided to stop dealing to Nick's area. Moron. Nick had put six bullets in one leg, and the guy had changed his tune. Plus, he would never go another day without knowing if it was raining topside, and he'd think of Nick every time. Knowing that made Nick smile.

He smelled the smoke from blocks away from home. It grew thicker and more foul the closer he got to his area. He gunned it.

Moments later, he pulled up to where thick black smoke billowed out of the room where he usually kept his C47. Flames licked out of the door. Large, clumsily painted letters on the nearest wall said, "NO MERCY."

Nick's lip curled and his breath came faster. His head pounded with the rush of blood. His ulcer stabbed at him.

A few of his men and a few other people from his area were working a bucket brigade that was hardly making a dent in the flames. Naturally, they redoubled their efforts when they caught sight of him.

He revved the engine and sped down to his main offices around the corner.

It was the same story there. The rooms where he kept most of his drugs and valuables roared with flames. More men were here, with more buckets, but he could tell that it wasn't going to matter.

He sat on his bike and lit a cigarette with trembling hands and watched fire devour most of the little empire he'd spent thirty years building up from nothing.

The Lightbringers had done this to him in retaliation. He was sure of it. If not the whole group, then that big man whose ear he'd taken.

He'd make them pay for this.

"Time for breakfast," Drew said gently as she shook Gaylen's shoulder.

He looked up to discover morning light peeking through the sheets taped up on the windows. He and Chloe had ended up asleep on the cold wood floor together, which had been bad for his injured ribs. He grimaced as he gingerly pulled away from Chloe. Plus, he needed to empty his bladder. He got up, fending off Chloe's well-meaning help, and staggered to the bathroom in a fog of misery.

When he got back, Chloe was gone. Drew was leaning against Mercy with her arm around him, smiling up at him, while Mercy, as far as Gaylen could tell, ignored her completely. Gaylen ground his teeth and glared at them both. Why did Drew seem to like Mercy so damn much? Nothing about the women in this group made any sense.

Meanwhile, the revolutionaries settled into small groups, and now Kevin and another Lightbringer passed out their first hot meal in days—packaged, pre-cooked scrambled eggs and canned sausage heated over Sterno cans. Chloe came up to hand Gaylen more painkillers and then sat down with another group to eat her breakfast. Gaylen wolfed down his food. It was almost delicious, but he was in too much pain to enjoy it.

When only a few people were still eating, Drew stood up and raised a hand. The group gradually fell silent.

Drew began, "Most of you are new to our group, and most of you didn't come out with us last night, so you have had very little time to get to know us. So I want to give you all a few words about what our group is really about, before we take you into additional danger."

She paused for a moment. "All of you are former denizens, so you know the truth about the world. You know that the law of attraction is nonsense. You know that Martha is a fanatic. And you know that New America is not a perfect place."

"Damn straight," somebody in the crowd said.

Drew smiled and paused before going on. "You know that the DAA is our—"

At the mention of the government organization, hisses and boos and colorful curses erupted. Gaylen noticed that they came only from the escaped prisoners, not from the Lightbringers, who remained quiet.

Drew simply smiled again. After a moment, she raised her hand again, and again the room fell quiet.

"You know that the DAA is our enemy. And our group, the Lightbringers, works against the DAA, in hopes of bringing it down entirely and overthrowing President Martha and the government."

"Yeah!" someone said.

Another person yelled, her tone derisive, "How the hell do you think you're gonna do that?"

Drew paused briefly. The effect was that everyone got quiet, eager to hear her answer. Then she spoke with her tone low and serious. "Stay with us for just a few more days, and you may see it happen."

The group was mostly quiet, other than a few mutters and whispers. Gaylen half-expected sarcastic retorts, but Drew's tone had been too serious to easily dismiss.

Drew went on, her voice level, "Our goal is to overthrow Martha and her cult. It is to destroy the DAA and end its crimes against New American citizens. We want this to be a country like any other—a place where people can say and feel whatever they want, where they have freedom of movement and freedom of communication and freedom of thought. We want to tear down the walls at our borders and rejoin the rest of the world."

There were a few scattered cheers and some nodding of heads.

"But there is something else that we want. It's not just about freedom." Her voice became quieter, and the room became perfectly still. "In the end, we want to bring life back into the citizens of this country. The sleepers are stagnant, weak, helpless, locked into superstition."

"Screw 'em," someone said. Some of the others laughed.

Drew remained still, her gaze downcast, until the room was quiet again. When she spoke, her voice was level. "And the denizens are filled with hate, out of control, indulging their worst selves like children throwing tantrums, and physically and emotionally sick as a result."

The room was silent now. Gaylen marveled at her ability to rein in the crowd.

"We will not rest until every person has come back to life. Until we all have rediscovered true passion, learned who we are as free and fulfilled individuals, experienced reconnection to one another, relearned compassion, rediscovered what it feels like to contribute meaningfully to a greater whole. Because what is the point of freedom if everyone is still angry and miserable and lashing out in violence and hate?"

Gaylen glanced around. Some of the freed prisoners looked thoughtful, though some had blank expressions and others frowned. The experienced Lightbringers either nodded or just listened.

"In the missions that will happen in coming days, I will trust every one of you as if you had already been a Lightbringer for years. I have no choice, because I need you, and I don't have time to train you."

Slowly and with utter confidence, she stated, "I will place my trust in you. And you will not let me down." She surveyed the room, and serious faces looked back at her. "You will fight hard, but not cruelly. You will preserve life when you can. And in your spare moments, you will start to think about the kind of life you want to have when this is all over. The kind of person you want to be when there is no enemy left but yourself.

"I will teach you in every spare moment I can find, and you will apply those lessons every time you can remember to do so. The experienced Lightbringers will help and will answer your questions."

Her voice became warm, her eyes shining. She radiated compassion. "You have been people without homes. And we will give you a home. And you will find strength and peace with us."

Gaylen found himself smiling. Something about her just made him feel good.

When she wasn't draped all over Mercy, anyway.

He let his gaze linger, enjoying the way she moved as she knelt to speak to a Lightbringer. Then he felt someone else's gaze on him. It was Chloe, with something unhappy in her expression, but she looked away again.

John Oldman leaned against a wall in the living room. He was throwing a pair of dice over and over, just observing what numbers came up, so lost in his thoughts about what Drew had said that he was startled to hear the voice.

"You look like you're having about as much fun as I am."

He looked up. It was Gaylen. The lean black man gingerly sat down next to him, his arm wrapped around his ribs.

John shrugged and picked up his dice. Speaking would have been too much effort, and anyway, his thoughts weren't ones he could share. Again, Drew had done a number on him. That woman inspired loyalty, which she had no damn right to do. She was a criminal, after all.

"Here," John said, handing Gaylen the dice. "We take turns throwing, and anyone who gets doubles scores a point, unless it's double ones. And double sixes are two points."

A few minutes went by while they passed the dice back and forth. No one scored anything and neither of them looked at the other or spoke, and then both of them sighed almost in unison. John glanced at Gaylen, who now looked back at him, and they both chuckled.

"What day is it anymore?" Gaylen asked. He threw the dice again.

"Tuesday," John said. That much he could say. He picked up the dice and tossed them. Double sixes. Two points. Both men let the dice lay there for a moment.

"That means . . . three days ago, I had a normal life. Three days." Gaylen rubbed his hands over his face.

"You went from being a sleeper to being here?"

"Yeah. Just like that." He sighed again. "Well, I had about half a day as a . . . what is it called—denizen? I went underground . . . but immediately—and I mean, within hours—there was a DAA attack, and then Drew rescued me from that. And here I am."

John said nothing. He still didn't trust himself to choose his words wisely in this moment.

Gaylen picked up the dice and rolled them around in his hand. He seemed to take John's silence as encouragement to go on. Tentatively, without looking at John, Gaylen said, "My wife . . . had left me. And took my daughter with her. I wasn't . . . handling it very well."

John looked down at his hands. He could identify with that, more than he wanted to admit.

Gaylen said, "I still can't really believe that any of this happened. That I'm here." He threw the dice. A one and a five.

Me, either, John thought.

The two of them sat in silence for a bit. Then Gaylen spoke again. "Drew promised that the Lightbringers would help me find my family after this. My ex-wife and my daughter. I want to warn them. Now that I know what happens to people . . . They might request assistance someday. Sierra—my daughter—she might not be able to think properly all her life."

John didn't know what to say. How many people went to prison every week? How many got dusted every day? Gaylen's fears were justified.

He also noticed that the other man had made rapid progress with the Lightbringers, if he had only been here a couple of days. This level of emotional disclosure would never happen topside.

"I have a daughter, too," John admitted. He picked up the dice, but just held them. "In her twenties, by now. I worry about her, too." He had told both his kids over and over, from early childhood, that they must never request assistance. But they might not listen. He hadn't been able to tell them why.

"I wish there was some way to know," Gaylen said. "Right now, I mean. Drew said it's only a few days before they can help, but . . ."

John looked away. *But that might be too late.*

John could find out about all of their family members easily enough. His clearance level gave him access to the databases. But he had never even been able to bring himself to look up his own children, or his father.

"What if they were locked up?" John asked. "Would the Lightbringers break them out for you?"

"Maybe. I don't know. They probably wouldn't be able to until after the mission anyway, but I'd still want to know now." Gaylen sighed. "I want to know that they're OK. And if they're not . . . I'd still want to know."

John said nothing for a while. He understood what Gaylen was saying, but he didn't share those feelings. John didn't want to know. He was quite clear about that.

Finally, he said, "Probably they're OK."

Gaylen rubbed his hands over his face. "Yeah. I guess so. Probably."

They both stared at nothing.

Drew had stepped out of the room a few minutes ago and conversation had resumed, hesitant at first, and then more spirited. Mercy sat in his usual spot at the door, playing with his silver lighter and ignoring the persistent throbbing of his missing ear.

He was seriously pissed off about the ear. It wasn't about the deformity itself—he was already tattooed and scarred, and he was indifferent to his own appearance anyway. But the missing ear damaged his hearing on that side, which reduced his effectiveness in a fight. That was a handicap he didn't want and couldn't afford. More importantly, an enemy had left a permanent mark that he could never forget. For the rest of his life, he'd think of Nick on what was likely to be a daily basis, every time he noticed it again.

The only way to buy off that kind of mark, psychologically, was vengeance that topped the original wrong.

Mercy heard a woman's voice near him saying, "Come with me." He glanced up. Drew held out a flashlight to him. "I need to pick up the replacement data and I need a bodyguard."

Mercy nodded grudging assent and stood up and took the flashlight. Together, they went down the trap door in the laundry room and started through the tunnels. Their flashlights illuminated their paths. He stayed one step behind and to the side of her, since he figured she knew where they were going.

As they walked, he remained mute and listened carefully. He wanted to figure out exactly where his hearing was weakest, so that he could learn to compensate.

Drew glanced back at him from time to time. At length, she asked, "So, who do you want to be when all this is over?"

He scowled. Her pretty words earlier hadn't impressed him. He rumbled, "This will never be over."

She said nothing, and they continued walking through the tunnels.

Finally, she said, "You don't talk unless you have something to say."

He cast her a glance intended to say *No shit*. He kept his focus on their environment and his hearing. He wanted to make sure there were no ambushes waiting for them this time.

Drew seemed to be focused on the ground in front of her. In time, she said, slowly and thoughtfully, "I want you to tell me your story,

Mercy. The story of your life. Not right now, but someday. Because you have a story, even though you think you don't. And it's a tragic one, even though you don't think it is. It's heartbreaking, actually."

She'd caught his attention. He stared at her.

She went on without looking at him. "And you need to tell it, even though you don't think you do. And it will help, even though you think it won't."

He stopped walking, and so did she. "And I want to be the first one to hear it." She looked him in the eye. "Right now, you won't let me. Someday, I hope you will."

They were silent, unsmiling, their gazes intense. The darkness and quiet of the tunnel pressed in on them.

Mercy agreed with about half of what she'd said: that he didn't have a story, that it didn't matter, and that it didn't need telling. He didn't understand what she was getting at, and he didn't trust her. Allies they were, but friends they weren't. Finally, he said, "Why?"

A ghost of a smile crossed Drew's face. "I'm a good listener."

"Bullshit. What do you want from me?"

Her eyes widened. Then she looked thoughtful. "No, it's true. I want to hear your story because you need someone who will know how to hear it." She thought for a moment longer. "But also . . . yes, I . . . do . . . like you." She gazed up at him, her green eyes seeming to glow. "I think you're beautiful. I think you're the most beautiful person I've ever seen. You have a purity I've never encountered in anyone. A single-mindedness. A . . . perfection, in all your imperfection."

They stared at each other a moment longer.

Mercy snorted. He'd figured it out. This little girl was into him. Well, she was gorgeous, but she wasn't his type.

He tapped his chest and rumbled, "There is nothing here for you. We're allies." He bent down to look her straight in the eye. "Until one of us dies. And because I'm protecting you, I'll die first. That's it." He watched her face fall by degrees. "I do my job. You do yours." His gaze bored into hers, unrelenting.

Drew looked away. "Of course," she murmured, sounding both happy and sad. "You wouldn't be you if you didn't answer that way."

She resumed walking, and he took up his place one step behind her. He refocused his attention on their environment. Keeping her alive was important to him. He'd made that agreement within himself, that he'd protect the members of this new group. So he would.

And after he escorted her back to the safe house, he had a little something to take care of. A little something called Nick Aglaeca.

Mercy took no joy in the fires he'd set at Nick's place last night. And he took no joy in his plans to finish Nick off. It was simply the law of the underground, and something he needed to do to feel right with himself. Betrayal for betrayal. No mercy.

Back at the safe house, a new recruit, one of the freed NCPs, had caught John's attention. After Drew's departure, the thin man with deep-set, shadowed eyes had come out into the backyard and paced with agitation in his movements. Within a few minutes, he started talking to himself in a whispery, reedy voice. Over the next few minutes, the man's volume went up, bit by bit, but still not enough for John to understand.

He caught John's eye and yelled, "What are you looking at?"

John shrugged away the question and looked elsewhere. Not his business, not his problem.

A few minutes later, Kevin gathered experienced Lightbringers and new recruits alike into the living room. The thin man was among them, quiet for the moment, as everyone else took seats on the floor. But as soon as Kevin took his place at the front of the room, leaning against a bare desk, the thin man waved his arms to catch his attention.

"What's happening now?" he demanded in the same aggressive tone he'd used with John.

Kevin seemed to take him in at a glance. "I have a few things to tell you. Then some weapons practice."

"What's our first mission or—whatever?" The man's breath was coming faster and harder.

"I don't have any information about that right now."

Everyone, John included, stared at the two, the thin man intense and erratic, Kevin collected.

"The hell you don't—you know what we're doing next and I—I want you to tell us. I'm not about to just keep—doing what you all are telling us to do. I'm not going to just—obey. If I was going to obey, I'd be topside. With goddamned Martha, OK? I'm not doing this like this anymore. I want to know what's going on."

"It doesn't work that way." Kevin's tone remained calm. "I can tell that you're not happy about it, and I'm sorry about that. But we're a revolutionary cell. Everything is need-to-know only."

"I already said, I'm not just going to—do what you tell me to. OK? I'm not. I'm not goddamn obeying any goddamn—"

"OK," Kevin said with finality. "That's fine. No one is required to be here or to be part of this—not now, not ever. So you can leave. But I can't let you go right now because you could reveal the location of this safe house. So once we're ready to move, in a day or two, I'll set you free in the underground. Unharmed. My word on it." He glanced at a couple of Lightbringers. "Wayne, Alyssa, escort this guy to a room."

John looked around. The two Lightbringers stood and moved toward the thin man, who staggered as if his knees were buckling. He advanced on Kevin, his voice going up. "I—No, no, that's not right. You can't hold me. You can't tell me what I'm going to do ..."

Kevin raised an eyebrow. Without flinching, he let the man advance aggressively on him. He kept his arms folded and his posture relaxed.

The thin man punched him.

Kevin let the blow glance off his cheekbone as he twisted to the side, and the man's weight overbalanced him and he crashed to the floor.

Kevin pulled his stun gun and pointed it at the man as he clambered back to his feet.

"Friend," Kevin said, "you've got a choice here."

Some of the other new recruits recoiled or leapt to their feet. Some pulled their own weapons.

"Stay cool," Kevin said to the room, his tone quietly authoritative. "My gun's on stun. Friend, you want to go conscious or unconscious? I don't care which."

The man shifted from foot to foot, then his face twisted and he lunged toward Kevin a second time.

Kevin fired. The other man fell heavily to the floor.

One of the nearby new recruits scrambled over to check on him, making sure that Kevin's gun had indeed been set to stun. "He's fine," he said to the others.

Everyone who had pulled a weapon holstered it again. Wayne and Alyssa picked the man up and carried him away while Kevin put his own gun away and leaned on the desk again.

John discovered that he had been holding his breath, and let it out again.

"It's that simple," Kevin said. "You can leave any time you want. You just have to wait till we shift safe houses, which is every couple of days. You get stunned if you're going to freak out. You'll be held in a room until we're ready to move. You get food, water, and basic consideration in the meantime. It's not a problem. Does anybody else want to leave now?"

The room was quiet. The people who had stood up took their seats again.

"All right, then let me get on with it."

Everyone was quiet. The tattooed man had won their full attention.

Kevin took a moment to close his eyes, collecting his thoughts, his expression unchanging. Then, for about twenty minutes, he talked quietly and conversationally about the importance of the work they were doing. "We're not terrorists and we're not regular denizens. We are revolutionaries," he said. "We're out to change the whole country fundamentally and make it a better place to live even than anywhere on the outside."

He talked, as well, about the importance of each one of them to the other Lightbringers once they committed to being a part of the Lightbringers family. Then he held up an antique-style leather-bound book.

"One of the things that bothers Drew the most about New America is how no one is remembered once they're gone. How many people have you known who moved to some other city and you never heard of them again? How many people die or get dusted and no one even knows? Nobody misses them? You're not supposed to miss them. You're not even supposed to remember them. You even get rid of the evidence when they leave. Nobody's really supposed to matter too much because then it hurts when they leave.

"But people are supposed to matter. It's supposed to hurt when they leave. It's part of human nature for us to need connection. It's OK for people to have strong unhappy feelings because that's the only way to feel the joy of love. You can't have one without the other.

"The outside world has memorials. Stone walls where people's names are chiseled to last hundreds of years. There are biographies written about people so that we can learn about them long after they're dead. Important buildings are named after people. We can't do any of that here and now, but we have our own equivalent. We have this book."

He told them that the book had a page for every Lightbringer in the Washington cell—living and dead—since Drew had taken over a few years ago. It had names, signatures, portraits, personal facts, and comments from other people. The Lightbringers protected it with their lives. It was always at the current safe house. Kevin digitized and backed up its pages, also, just in case.

He told them that the same practice had spread to all the other Lightbringer cells in other cities in New America. "This is how you are known. And when the Lightbringers have won, all of these books will be published to the world. You will be remembered forever for your part in saving this country. This is how we can promise you that you will be remembered. That your life mattered."

A little while later, John sat outside in the back yard with Chloe near him, the Lightbringers book in her hands. She was sketching John's portrait, complete with gold mask, on his new page. He felt unexpectedly torn about putting his name in the book, but Kevin had told everyone that creating a page wasn't optional: "Either you make a page today, or you leave the Lightbringers. Your choice."

Chloe had been drawing in silence, glancing rapidly back and forth from John's face to the page in front of her. After a bit, she said, "You know, I think you kinda remind me of my dad."

It seemed like a compliment. And the ages were about right. "That makes sense." John thought of Suzy. "You're about the age of my daughter."

"Oh. That's nice." She erased a line she'd just made. "Do you see her often?"

John shook his head sadly. "No, not for a long time, now." He was about to tell her more about his family, and he had to remind himself again that these were terrorists, whether they called themselves revolutionaries or goddamn Barbie dolls.

Silence continued. Chloe tucked the end of one purple dreadlock into her mouth so that she could chew on it while she drew.

Finally, John had to say something, anything. "Why are you here? Part of this? In the Lightbringers?"

Chloe shrugged a little. She swiped the dreadlock out of her mouth and spoke while keeping her attention on her drawing. "I was brought to the underground when I was young. My little sister . . . she killed herself when she was eleven." She frowned at the drawing again and moved the book away from her face to get a better view of it. Then she erased and redrew a line. "My whole family was going to be taken by the DAA and put on ice. But my dad's friend was a tourist. He was with my dad when he found the body, and he knew what to do."

She squinted at him. It was odd, having someone look so intently at just the surface of his face, no attention paid to what his eyes or expression might communicate.

She went on, "We got separated down there. My mom and dad and me. And I never found them again. I guess they got killed. So I grew up by myself down there. And I . . . started doing drugs pretty early, I guess."

John knew all the things she was leaving unsaid. There were no pleasant or easy ways for a teenage girl to stay alive alone in the underground. And he couldn't help but think that it could have been his Suzy, just as easily.

"And Drew rescued me. She always rescues someone when she goes down into the underground. And it was me that day." She glanced up at him and frowned at something in the vicinity of his eyebrows. "Drew is a really good person. And the Lightbringers . . . they're not wrong, you know? The whole country is fucked up, both above and below. The Lightbringers are the only thing that makes any sense."

The back door opened and Kevin came outside. He lit up a cigarette while stepping behind Chloe to look at the drawing. "Not bad," he said as he glanced from the drawing to John and back again. "Nice mask."

"Thanks," John said. "Nice job with that crazy guy."

Kevin waved off the compliment.

"Your style is a lot different from Drew's," John observed. "She's . . . really emotional. I thought maybe that was a Lightbringer thing. But you're not like that."

"Nah," Kevin said, his tone dry. "It's not a part of the philosophy. Emotions don't have to be all out there. Drew only expresses hers so openly because it's so important for new recruits to know that emotions aren't anything to be ashamed of."

Her attention still on her drawing and her tone absent, Chloe asked Kevin, "Then why do you keep yours hidden all the time?"

A muscle twitched on Kevin's face, and he was quiet for so long that John thought he wasn't going to answer. Then Chloe seemed to catch up to what she'd said, and she lowered her pencil and looked up just as Kevin said, "Maybe I'm still ashamed of them."

John didn't know what to say, so he didn't say anything. Neither did Chloe. After a moment, she resumed drawing.

Kevin didn't say anything else, either. After he put out his cigarette, he said, "Thanks for the insight." And then he went inside.

Chloe kept drawing, though just the hint of a grin turned up the corners of her mouth.

John was more touched than he would have expected.

He realized that he was going to have to find some emotional defenses if he had any hope of succeeding in this mission. No matter how interesting or enticing these people were, they were the enemy. They were dangerous and crazy. Or, at least, they were breaking the law. And that was supposed to be good enough for him.

While he waited for Chloe to finish the drawing, he worked hard on assembling an emotional wall. He resolved that he simply wouldn't let himself think or feel anything anymore. He would just do his job.

Nick pulled up to his offices again. He had a good number of men there working on the place. They'd been dragging out the trash and putting it in wheelbarrows and taking it away.

More interesting to Nick was the large biker gang near his offices. All of them had sport bikes and wore leathers and helmets ornamented with neon colors. Most of them sported Mohawks in neon colors, and even from twenty feet away, the bright neon inserts permanently implanted in their irises were visible. Even without the neon, he would have recognized the Double Double gang, an anarchist group. They were from a neighboring area, but he'd known them for a while.

Their leader, Mikey, a short, wiry guy, came up when Nick got off his bike. His iris implants were a bright neon lime-green. They were highly distracting. His eyes were surrounded with black tattoos that gave him a raccoon-like look.

Nick nodded at him. They exchanged a series of gang handshakes and briefly embraced. Then Nick punched Mikey on the shoulder. "What's been going on?"

"Nothin', man. Heard about this." Mikey waved at Nick's offices. "Couldn't believe it, had to come see it for myself."

"Yeah," Nick said bitterly. "They'll pay." His ulcer stabbed at him.

"Who did it?"

"Fucking Lightbringers." He spat.

"They did this?" Mikey's eyebrows went up. "Doesn't seem like their style."

"Yeah, well, I pissed them off."

"Looks like."

They stood for a moment, taking in what remained of Nick's space. Nick took out a smoke for himself and gave one to Mikey, and they both lit up.

Mikey asked, "You out?"

"Hell, no," Nick snapped. "You kidding me? I'm not that easy."

Mikey nodded, his facial tattoos and neon eyes so distracting it was hard to read his expression. "That's what I told 'em. I told 'em, no way is Nick going down that easy. I know you, bro."

Appeased, Nick nodded. They both smoked in silence for a moment.

Mikey asked, "So, what's the plan?"

Nick had been wondering that himself, but the big picture was simple enough. "They think they shut me down. They just bought themselves a war."

"This is why I love you, bro."

Nick grunted. "Thing is, I need more men."

"I got men."

"This ain't your fight, Mikey. And I can't pay."

"Come on, Nick. I'm your friend. Besides, it'll be fun."

Nick shrugged. He didn't want to look too eager.

The biker glanced at him before saying, "Hey, the Lightbringers piss me off, too. They're just denizens like us, but they think they're better than us. For no reason that I can see."

Nick couldn't argue. That was exactly what he hated so much about them. Drew, especially. He remembered how she'd ignored his hand, back in Constitution Below, and looked at him like she knew him.

If she could really see into him, she'd have blinked. That was for sure.

Nick shook his head and dropped his cigarette, stomped it out on the concrete. "So what's your cut, Mikey?"

Mikey grinned, tilting his head, and his neon eyes flashed at Nick. "I gotta get evasive with you, Nick, so far as the exact reason for it, but I need some money in a hurry. You take your revenge, I take all their cash and valuables. That fair?"

Nick pondered for a moment, then nodded. "That's fair."

Mikey smiled. The raccoon-style tattoos gave him a mischievous look. "Then let's do this, buddy."

Not long after, John and the rest of the Lightbringers waited in the living room for more instructions from Drew, who had returned from her mission in an unusually subdued mood.

"I have the new data. We'll break into four teams. Let's do six to eight people on each team, so we need everyone on this run. Team leaders are myself, Kevin, Chris, and Shannon. Break out and pick your teams. Team leads, choose your seconds. Gaylen, Chloe, you're with me. Mercy will meet up with us on the way."

John stepped up to join Drew's group, along with a couple of other revolutionaries who were strangers to him. They silently watched the rest of the Lightbringers sort themselves out. Once John knew that his place in the group was assured, he excused himself to go to the restroom.

The door securely locked, he activated his communications implant and sent a code to Wallace's handscreen. This pre-arranged signal would have the DAA lock on to his implant's location and send agents to intercept them. With Drew away from the safe house in a small group, this was going to be a good time to try again to capture her.

If the DAA had wanted to kill everyone in this cell of the Lightbringers, they would have just sent a dust team to the safe house. But John's purpose was to infiltrate and learn more about the national structure of the Lightbringers—the number of cells, the leadership, the goals—and take down the entire organization.

John sent the code on autopilot, his mind and emotions a deliberate blank. But he found himself grinding his teeth as he stepped back out into the living room.

This time, when Drew started them off, Gaylen was ready to finish the sentence along with the more experienced revolutionaries: "Let's bring the light."

Moments later, Drew led Gaylen's group into the underground via the trapdoor they'd used before, in the laundry room. It proved to be a lengthy journey this time. Everyone remained quiet as they made their way through the rat's maze of hallways, rooms, stairs, ladders, trapdoors, subway tunnels, and sewer systems that made up the underground. Drew always seemed to know just where she was going, though. She glanced back from time to time, usually to cast a smile at Mercy, who, as always, appeared unmoved. Again, Gaylen found himself irritated by their interaction.

He caught Chloe looking at him a couple of times, her expression unreadable, and he didn't know what to think of that, either.

At long last, Drew called a halt. They had just climbed stairs into a finished room and now faced a door to the outside world—Gaylen could tell from the natural light that outlined the doorway.

Drew took out a cloaking device and activated it, bringing all of them into the shimmer that would hide them.

"OK, team," she said. "We are here to pull off a kidnapping. We're bringing in a former government worker who will be able to help us with the next phase of our plan. The target should have no reason to anticipate our arrival and no unusual security. It should be an easy snatch-and-grab from a residence."

Goldfinger straightened and asked in his usual slow manner, "Are the other teams doing likewise?"

"Yes," Drew said. "Now, we'll be spending some time outside getting to the right house. Remember the rules. Move slowly, as any rapid movement will give away your presence. Stay within three feet of one another at all times, or you'll lose the shield. And stay quiet, because this device does nothing about sound."

After making sure everyone had their stun weapons, Drew opened the door, and they stepped into the outside world, from the back side of a small building of corporate suites. From this side, Gaylen saw a parking lot and then a residential area.

The group moved slowly onto the sidewalk, everyone matching Drew's careful pace and slow movements.

Their efforts seemed somewhat pointless at first, since the streets were nearly deserted on a Tuesday afternoon, but they did eventually see a couple of cars moving slowly down the street, and then a young mother and her small children walking out to their car from their home.

For a moment, Gaylen could not handle the contrast. They were revolutionaries about to kidnap a government worker in order to help bring down a corrupt government. But the world was so beautiful and peaceful. He breathed in the fresh, clean air and tried to forget everything but what he was seeing in front of him.

After a few hundred yards, they drew up to a certain house and Drew signaled a stop. She turned toward the group and said, so softly that they all drew closer to hear her, "This is our destination. We're going to make it simple. We'll go in through the back door, cloaked. We'll move through the house until we find him. We should be out and gone in no time, even if someone else in the house requests assistance through a wallscreen. Any questions?"

There were none, and Drew led them toward the back door of the house via the driveway and carport. An old Buick sat in the carport. A chain-link fence stood between the carport and the house, but the gate in the fence had no lock.

The backyard held children's toys and a colorful plastic slide. Gaylen winced as he realized that this man was either a father or a grandfather. He wondered what the Lightbringers were going to do to this man after they'd taken him. So far, the Lightbringers had been humane, and he could only trust that they would continue to be that way.

A small fenced-in patio wrapped around the back door, and a wallscreen chattered on the outside wall. It was the one o'clock Good News update. According to the perky brunette on the screen, the weather was fifteen percent more pleasant this year than it had been at this time last year.

They moved to the back door. It wasn't locked. No one in New America needed to lock their doors. The normalcy of that soothed Gaylen, until he realized how vulnerable it made this house, not only to the Lightbringers, but to denizens and—though this last thought was slow to occur to him—to the DAA.

Drew stepped to the front and pulled out her stun gun, and the others followed suit. She nudged the door open. It creaked just slightly. They could hear the wallscreens inside, all of them broadcasting the perky brunette in cheerful unison.

They moved quietly through the kitchen, then a hallway. Gaylen could see a small part of the living room, a grey-haired head at the back of the sofa. Presumably, this was their target.

All of them edged up, closer and closer. Someone's footstep was a bit too loud, and the man sat up straighter to look around. But Drew simply moved forward, bringing her stun gun to bear, and then fired at him even as he looked right through her.

The man dropped onto his side on the sofa. Mercy moved around and picked him up. All else was quiet in the house. The group retraced their steps to the back door.

Gaylen caught a fleeting movement out of the corner of his eye, through the window. He thought about saying something, but they were still supposed to stay quiet.

Drew opened the back door and they started moving through it to the back yard. Gaylen followed her, with Mercy and the others behind them both.

And then a rushing noise erupted from their left as slender lances of fire struck out at them. Gaylen barely caught sight of men wearing goggles and holding large weapons before all he could be aware of was the searing agony coursing down his left side and the sudden weakness in his body. Drew screamed.

Things went black for Gaylen for a moment, then they got confusing, though it was clear that something had gone wrong. Someone had dragged him back into the house. He heard shouting and running feet and cursing and those weapons being fired again outside, along with the whine of stun weapons. Then someone was dragging him again. He caught glimpses of the clear blue sky, and the sun's blinding warmth, and the green grass beneath him.

Someone picked him up—Mercy's scowl flashed above him—and threw him into the backseat of a car. The door slammed. Drew lay partly beneath him. The car's engine came to life. Outside, there were screams and shouts, and a bright red light and a roar washed over the windows, bringing heat with it. Perhaps there was fire outside.

He looked down at Drew and then at what he could see of himself. He lay partly on his right side. The flesh along his left hip and along the lower left part of his abdomen was charred and cauterized. That part of his abdomen had a big cavity in it, and it seemed curiously empty. Maybe he had lost pieces from in there that he needed. He thought he could see more charred bits of things that might be trying to fall out. He wanted to press his hands there to hold them in, but it didn't seem right to touch parts that weren't even supposed to be on the outside. He saw no blood and felt no pain.

He looked at Drew. Most of her left arm was dangling by skin and muscle, her elbow all but charred away. She used her other hand to cling to the upper arm as if it, too, were in danger of falling off. The flesh along her left side was charred and her left breast was gone.

Her eyes were closed, her face was white, and her lips hardly moved as she whispered something. He watched her lips, transfixed, until he could discern what she was saying.

"Though I am surrounded by darkness, within me there is only light," she whispered over and over. Gaylen picked up the mantra in his mind, though it was too much trouble to move his own lips.

The car moved violently and erratically. He wished they would stop doing that. There were shouts from the front seat.

Pain set in around the edges of his burns, unstoppable, like an ocean wave. He started shaking. He got cold all over. Nausea swept over him.

He tried to keep watching Drew. She was so beautiful, even when she was so unnaturally pale. But he couldn't focus his eyes anymore.

He kept trying to recite the mantra in his mind. "Though I am surrounded by darkness . . . surrounded by darkness . . ." He couldn't remember the words.

The pain got worse. His flesh felt like it was being torn from his bones. He screamed and screamed.

Chapter Eleven

Drew Ashling, Lightbringer:

Perfectionism leads to stagnation. It means being entirely focused on the end goal, the desired state. Then, once you're there, you've got to keep it frozen exactly as it is. It can't change. This is why our technology has stopped advancing, why our culture is barren. I've read literature and seen art from the outside world, and there's no comparison. Because they haven't stopped living and breathing out there.

Mercy drove as if he were behind the wheel of a tank outfitted with turbo boost instead of the rusty old Buick that had been in the carport. Pursued by a half-dozen DAA agents in two black, unmarked SUVs, he flew down the center of the road, overtook and sideswiped a compact car, then skidded across sidewalks and curbs to cut the corner off a block. He plowed down a mailbox as he turned onto the next road in search of the nearest freeway.

All the while, one image recurred in Mercy's mind—something that he was sure he alone, out of the Lightbringers, had seen. Just as they'd come out of the back door and the fire weapons had activated, Goldfinger had stepped out and thrown out his hands toward the DAA agents as if to say *No, stop.* And one of the agents had shaken his head in response and then fired at a different one of the Lightbringers, not at Goldfinger.

Now, Goldfinger was in the back seat with Gaylen and Drew. Chloe was next to Mercy in the front seat, having hotwired the car and then scrambled over so that he could drive. She hung onto the seatbelt with both hands, her jaw clenched. Mercy looked into the back seat using the rear-view mirror. Goldfinger had his hands over his face as if he couldn't bear to look. The five of them were the only survivors of the team.

A major intersection was coming up. Traffic was going across it—against him—but he had a good view to both sides. He floored the accelerator while he looked for an opening in the traffic.

One black SUV was right behind him. The other one lagged by a block.

He didn't have time to glance at the speedometer, nor did it matter, but he was confident that he was going around eighty mph by the time he reached the intersection.

Out of the corner of his eye, he saw Chloe brace herself as he hit the brakes hard, then the accelerator again. They slipped through the intersection between a green truck heading left and three sedans heading right.

An impossibly loud crunch sounded behind them as the closer SUV missed the same opening. He glanced in the rear-view mirror and saw it flipping end-over-end.

He glanced forward again in time to recognize road construction cones and heavy equipment in front of them. He swerved hard, braked harder, but the traffic had slowed down to merge. He took them onto the raised median—they sideswiped young trees—the back end of the Buick swung out into the oncoming traffic—

The impact spun the Buick back the other way and threw it onto its side, with Mercy on the ground side. They slid with a screech of metal and the shattering of glass. They came to a stop, teetering but still on their side.

Mercy looked behind them to see the remaining SUV catching up.

The car was still running.

Mercy took off his seatbelt. Chloe hung from hers, her eyes wide. She was pale but looked unharmed. He twisted and looked into the back seat. Goldfinger, Gaylen, and Drew lay in a heap back there, Goldfinger on the bottom. He was still alive, pale, no visible injuries. Gaylen was unconscious. Drew's eyelids fluttered and she moaned.

"Gun," Mercy ordered. Goldfinger hastily handed it over. Mercy pulled himself up and whispered directly into Chloe's ear, "Goldfinger is one of the DAA." He lowered himself to the ground and crawled out of the shattered window.

The SUV slowed to a stop. All around them, cars stopped and sleepers hesitantly got out, faces pale and serious. One called, "Are you all right?"

The DAA would have a hard time covering this up.

Mercy sprinted away from the Buick, then turned around and ran back toward it as vigorously as he could run. He used all of his massive strength to throw his immense weight against the highest point of the car. It teetered, then dropped back to all four tires.

The car was still running.

He looked in the window. "Drive," he said.

Pale, Chloe nodded and unbuckled her seat belt so she could move over to the driver's side.

Mercy turned back and took out his two guns. The DAA faced off with him. Three agents tried to handle the crowd and four others took aim at him.

They still carried the fire weapons.

He took the first lance of fire, and his left arm was gone.

He fired rapidly with his right hand and took out two agents immediately.

The Buick's tires squealed as Chloe took the others away to safety.

Another lance seared his shoulder. Then his side.

He wasn't going to get to kill Nick after all.

Walking tall and silent and strong, firing relentlessly, he dropped two more.

Another bolt struck him, then another.

Cold and nausea set in. His legs went weak. And then the darkness came.

Some time passed in darkness and then someone was dragging Gaylen down a hallway by one leg. It hurt too much to endure, and he started crying out again. He tried to pick himself up while he begged for the person dragging him to stop. They didn't. Soon, things went dark again.

Later, he woke up in light so bright that it hurt his eyes even though they were tightly closed. Something agonizing was happening to his abdomen and his legs.

The pain intensified beyond any point he could imagine, until he began screaming, and then got even worse. It became so great that he floated away from his body. He felt only a mild interest about what was going on, though his body screamed and begged for the pain to stop. It tried to writhe and kick, too, but he was restrained in some way.

He couldn't make his body quiet down, but screaming and begging seemed to be the thing to do.

Eventually, he went to sleep again.

John Oldman squatted, his back up against a wall, and stared into space. The dented plaster on the bare wall beside him and the bruises on his knuckles bore mute testimony to the anger he'd been unable to control. Punching the wall hadn't helped.

One of the socios that staffed the DAA—quite possibly Russell Wallace himself—had to have authorized the fire weapons. But Martha would never have sanctioned such weapons, and everyone at the DAA knew it. That meant someone had given orders in direct contradiction to the first two rules of the DAA: "Protect criminals from their own fear and pain; Cause no additional fear or pain."

As soon as he had the opportunity, he would report it and trigger an audit. It was foolhardy for a feeler to report a socio, and he would almost certainly lose his job, if not his freedom or his life, but he was too angry to care.

Chloe walked in. "The doc thinks they'll make it," she said, her face drawn. "He had to blast out the wounds to clear out the dead tissue and then blast them again with an antibiotic treatment. He told me that the painkillers they have in stock were not very good, and he was out of sedatives." Anger made her words clipped, and her jaw was set in an uncharacteristic way.

John closed his eyes, let out a slow breath. He could only imagine what Gaylen and Drew had suffered, and he didn't want to—especially since it was his fault.

Chloe leaned against a wall, facing away from him. "The tech they have is really good. Gaylen's organs and skin will be regrown in a matter of hours."

"Can they fix Drew, too?"

"Yes."

John shook his head. "They are ridiculously lucky that someone has bio-regrowth technology here in the D.C. underground and that we got here in time. By all rights, they should be dead."

"Yes, they are lucky, you're right about that." She folded her arms and tossed her dreadlocks over her shoulder.

"What now?" he asked.

Chloe shrugged. "We won't stop. We'll never stop. We'll just wait for Drew to wake up and tell us what to do next." She looked at him for the first time, unsmiling, and then walked out.

She was more upset and angry than he had ever seen her. But he couldn't blame her.

CHAPTER TWELVE

Drew Ashling, Lightbringer:

Human beings can't do perfect. We aren't perfect. We have a shadow side that has a voice that must be heard. Martha's mistake is in thinking that ignoring it makes it irrelevant. It's still there, and the more it is ignored, the more violent it becomes. That is why we have this damned underground at all. New America's shadow is expressing itself violently because Martha will not allow it to express itself peacefully.

John Oldman walked wearily toward the kitchen of the abandoned low-rise condominium—their newest safe house—hoping against hope to find coffee there. When alcohol wasn't available, enough caffeine helped.

The other teams had joined them at the doctor's office, and they'd all helped transport Gaylen and Drew to this new safe house, along with their kidnapped captives. All of that had gone well, and everyone had had a few hours to rest, but John was still reeling from the day's events.

Drew stepped out of a door at the other end of the hallway so quietly as to spook him.

He silently cursed himself for jumping. Then he looked her over with concern. She looked tired, pale, and drawn.

She approached, and he tried to decide what to do. Smiling and speaking to her seemed dangerous, but keeping his eyes down and avoiding her would telegraph guilt. He elected to keep his head up but say nothing.

She stopped in front of him and gazed up into his eyes. He found himself noticing again how small she was, and yet what a strong presence she had.

Expressionless, but with a sarcastic tone, she said, "I'm guessing you aren't ready to turn off the mask."

John hesitated, trying to figure out what she was getting at.

She said, "Tell me your name."

He thought about that for a moment, and he decided he could safely reveal his first name, which was common. And he still had his disguise intact. "John," he said.

"John," Drew asked, "if you were to bring the light into your life completely, what kinds of darkness would depart from it?"

He could not tell if it was a rhetorical question or not, but he found himself pondering the answer anyway.

He looked into her eyes, and suddenly an odd feeling swept over him. He felt that her eyes carried the light and that simply looking at them opened doors and uncovered cobwebs that had been undisturbed for decades. It almost made him dizzy.

He could imagine that, from her perspective, letting in the light would mean abandoning the DAA and leaving his topside life. It would surely mean joining the Lightbringers for real. It would probably also mean somehow letting go of all the guilt he carried for his drinking, for his wife and family leaving him, for the massacre of the FPU.

Drew laid one hand upon his shoulder. She said, "John, I made a mistake with you. I saw your potential, and I allowed it to cloud my perception of your present reality."

John's breath caught and his heart beat faster. He tried to decipher her words.

"We cannot have you among us now. Go do what you must, and when you are ready to take off the mask and let in the light, come back to us."

His mind raced. Did she know what he had done, who he was? Was she letting him go anyway? "I don't understand."

"I trust you," she said. "That is, I trust the part of you that means well. And I trust the person you will become, the person who will return to us. But until you are him, I cannot have you here. Go now."

He found himself speechless. Questions raced through his mind. He needed to know if she knew what he had done and who he really was, but he couldn't ask without revealing it all himself. Surely she didn't. Surely, if she knew, she wouldn't let him leave. She couldn't.

Drew turned and walked away.

He stared after her. She wasn't even having him escorted out. She had just left him here. She trusted him to show himself to the door—trusted that he was utterly harmless to them all.

He found himself picking up his backpack and walking toward the door. Every step of the way, her words resounded in his mind. *"I trust the person you will become, the person who will return to us."*

She wasn't wrong about him, he realized. He was showing himself to the door just as she had known he would. He had capitulated without argument or additional lies. She had known that he would. *"I trust the part of you that means well."*

She wasn't wrong about him.

The idea shook him. If she was right about him, and if she was so sure that he would return . . .

He went outside and closed the door carefully behind himself and walked, oblivious to his surroundings, until he found himself in a beautiful city park. The sun had set and it was getting chilly. A handful of New Americans were still there—mostly college students staying warm by throwing a Frisbee or playing football—but even they were packing up to leave as the autumn night set in. He stared at them without really seeing them.

He had devoted his life to protecting these people until the new society could reach its inevitable state of perfection. Was it possible that trying to do so had been an act of darkness all along?

How could Drew know with such certainty that he would join a terrorist group devoted to undoing all of it?

He had never been so challenged before.

He had never been tempted to believe in the FPU's principles. The Free People United had been an anarcho-hedonist group; all they wanted was . . . to do whatever they wanted. Even if he did come to appreciate many of its members, the philosophy itself was childish and didn't appeal to him. What was so great about freedom? Why work so hard for the ability to do stupid, destructive things? Why not just be grateful for the perfect society they had been born into?

But this was different. The Lightbringers had something meaningful to offer. And Drew had turned everything he thought he knew on its head.

He sat down heavily on a park bench. His knees and back ached. He didn't want to think anymore. He wanted to go find a warm, cheerful underground pub that would serve him enough alcohol to get him blitzed.

Gradually, it dawned on him that he had failed in his latest assignment. He was going to have to go to Wallace and admit that the Lightbringers suspected him and had kicked him out. He hadn't even made it three days.

He sighed as the weight of defeat came down on him. It was crushing, and for a while he just sat there, paralyzed by his long list of failures. He didn't know if he had the will to go back to the DAA, to sit through that conversation with Wallace.

For a long time, he thought about disappearing alone into the underground forever—no Lightbringers, no DAA, just anonymity and alcohol.

He also toyed briefly with the idea of joining the Lightbringers for real . . . but joining the other side was too alien a thought, no matter how certain Drew was.

Then he thought about throwing himself in front of a fast-moving car, or off an overpass. He remembered his mother and the bathtub of blood. It had been a way out for her, he understood that.

He understood the desire to stop, to be done, to have no more of the endless struggle.

He thought of how his father had slipped into depression before he had moved to Florida.

If he had moved to Florida.

For a moment, John was lost in despair, deep enough to contemplate, for the first time, the possibility that the DAA had taken his father. If they had, then by now they would have disintegrated him.

The next time Gaylen awakened, Chloe sat by his side, staring into space and biting her lip. He lay on a pallet in a room he recognized as being in the underground by the graffiti and dirt and lack of wallscreens. His head was clear. He looked down and saw new, paler skin through the holes in his burned clothing.

As he stirred, Chloe grinned and gave him a big kiss on the cheek. Her dreadlocks bumped his shoulder. "You're awake!" she declared. "Come on, try getting up."

He looked at her like she was crazy. He remembered the hole in his stomach, the agonizing pain from earlier. Surely he was in no condition to move at all. But she held out a hand and nodded at him. "You're fine," she said.

He placed one hand in hers and used her weight to brace himself as he rolled over a little. That went OK, so he finished rolling over onto his side, then let Chloe help him into a sitting position. He kept expecting to feel agony or some wrongness in his injured areas, but he didn't. The skin was tight, maybe. He got to his feet and looked at Chloe.

"Medical tech from the outside world," she explained. "We re-grew your skin and organs and fixed your ribs, too." Her happy expression fell. "I'm sorry it hurt."

He remembered the unstoppable screaming and decided not to think about it.

Then his heart skipped as he remembered Drew's injuries. "Is Drew OK?" he asked.

Chloe's face tightened, but she nodded. "She's fine, too. Come on, we need to get moving to the new safe house and join the rest of the group."

They were quiet as she led the way. Gaylen wondered what had happened to the group, and why they had been attacked, but Chloe seemed to be preoccupied and he couldn't bring himself to break into her thoughts. Also, he wasn't really sure he wanted to know what had happened. Not yet. He had nearly died—perhaps, *should* have died.

After they had walked for a while, his thoughts returned briefly to the night that Chloe had rejected him, but after all that they'd just experienced, he thought it would seem hopelessly childish to bring it up now.

Minutes later, his thoughts had turned back to Drew. Soon, he would see her again. As they walked, he daydreamed about her. He hoped that she would be glad to see him.

Chloe took him into a broken-down, abandoned condominium building. They climbed the stairs to the third floor, entered a vacant condo, and there found the rest of the Lightbringers sitting cross-legged in meditation in a large, empty living room, Drew at their front.

Her eyes flickered open when the door opened, and she smiled warmly at them. She looked paler than he had expected, but healthy. Whole. Gaylen returned her smile, and she closed her eyes again.

Gaylen and Chloe joined the group on the floor. They sat in silence for a few minutes. Gaylen guessed that Drew had been giving the rest of them some sort of training, and he decided to use the time to go through the "stepping into the light" meditation.

He was just beginning to bask in the warm glow of the light when Drew spoke.

"Our mission is still a go," she said. "Despite the betrayal and failure of my team, the rest of the teams succeeded, and we should get enough information from our captives to proceed.

"Now that we are approaching the final phases of our mission, Don has revealed our ultimate aim to me and has given me permission to reveal it to you. You will see that this is by far our most ambitious plan to date, and I hope you will share my excitement."

There were slight stirrings of anticipation around the room.

"From our captives, who are all former government workers in the Bureau of Entertainment, we have already found the key to our objective: the weakest link in the wallscreen broadcasting system used throughout New America.

"None of us even knew that this weak link existed. It is old tech, a network called the Emergency Broadcasting System. Before the borders closed, it was used to notify people of earthquakes, hurricanes, and other disasters. It could broadcast locally or nationwide.

"Of course, President Martha ultimately decided that it was better to cover up natural disasters than to warn people of them, since if people were thinking correctly, no disasters could happen . . . Wouldn't *that* be nice?" She grinned wryly.

People around the room shook their heads and cursed or laughed bitterly.

Drew went on, "The Emergency Broadcasting System is the only communication system that the government can bring online at a single location to deliver information nationwide while being almost uninterruptable, even in a variety of emergency situations. And so the DAA decided to keep it and keep it functional, just in case it was ever needed. And those qualities make it our best way to get into the system and control it."

There were slow nods around the room.

"So, even as I speak, we are learning the information necessary to break into the Emergency Broadcasting System. We will get in, hijack every wallscreen in the nation, and broadcast a message of truth to every person in this country."

She paused a moment to let this sink in. The long-term Lightbringers nodded and exchanged glances. They looked excited.

"We anticipate that the message will be shut down fairly quickly and that new security measures will be put into place soon after. But while we control the airwaves, we will bring more light into the dark corners of this country than it has seen since the borders were closed.

"We will bring the light into the darkness, and the darkness will be lifted, to some degree. No one in this room can foresee exactly what will come of it. But the light is always good, and what arises from the light is always light."

One of the Lightbringers raised his hand and asked, "When does all this happen?"

"Tonight," Drew said. "In a few hours. The DAA knows that we're in motion, so we have to act fast. We have only a little information yet to get from our captives, and then we begin."

Enthusiastic shouts went up around the room.

"Right now, we have a hot dinner coming to us from some of our denizen friends. So let's enjoy our meal, and we'll pick back up with the planning afterward."

The Lightbringers broke into conversation among themselves while the hot food was brought in. It was a simple beef stew with rolls, but it tasted delicious, as if it were Gaylen's first meal in days, and he wolfed it down.

After his appetite had subsided, he turned to Chloe, who sat next to him. He asked, "So, how are they getting the information from the captives?"

"Outer world tech again," she said. She kept her gaze on her food. "It's a mental digital imaging process, or something like that. I don't really know what that means, but I guess they can take their thoughts and make them into pictures. They just have to make them think about the right things, which isn't real hard, since they don't realize that their thoughts are being watched." Her voice grew thoughtful. "You know, it's really lucky that the government doesn't have this yet. They would use it to see what people were really thinking and then no one would be safe."

Gaylen shuddered. Then a different unnerving thought occurred to him. "Could . . . does Drew . . . does she watch our minds?"

Chloe chuckled, then broke into laughter, and Gaylen blushed. "No, silly," she said. "They have to hook you up to computers and stuff. They can't just . . . do it." She chuckled some more.

Gaylen kept his head down and ate his last few bites. He eventually worked up the courage to ask another question. "All this technology from the outside world . . . If it's so easy to get it all, and it's so powerful, why haven't we overrun the government here a long time ago? Couldn't we have done a whole lot with all this technology before now?"

Chloe shook her head vigorously and her dreadlocks whipped around her face. At least this time she didn't laugh at him. "It isn't easy to get this stuff. Drew told me it's taken years to get it together to do this one mission. The mental imaging part is really important, because nobody here is willing to torture people for information, and that has been a big limitation for us. No, it's really a big deal to have all this stuff right now. You just happened to show up at the right time. You're getting to see all the toys in action."

Gaylen nodded. *Lucky me.*

After the meal, Gaylen found a quiet corner to relax in. Well-fed, rested, mostly healed, and given time to himself, he felt better than he had in days. He also had the luxury to really think about what had been happening to him.

He realized that his mind had not been full of the same old horrible thoughts since he had first come to the underground. He guessed that wasn't too surprising, since it had been full of new grievances. But there was something else going on—something different.

Before, he would feel bad, and then he would wonder what was wrong with him, and then he would beat himself up and try to chase away the bad thoughts, and that would only make him feel worse and make the thoughts stronger. His thoughts and feelings would spiral out of control until he felt certain they would drive him mad.

Now, knowing that he felt grief because people had died, fear because he was in danger, rage because he had been hurt, and shock because his world had been turned upside down, he could stop right there. The emotions didn't feed upon themselves. And if he took the time to step into the light, he could take a break even from those feelings.

Wryly, he wondered whether there would have been some better way to stop his insanity than going through such great trauma. Drew knew a lot of useful tricks. Perhaps he could have learned a new way of being just by studying with her. Perhaps he could still have that, sometime in the future, once this mission was over.

Again, he found himself daydreaming about her. His imagination supplied him with a vision of sitting peacefully with Drew, her hands in his, her warm smile directed his way. She would teach him some great wisdom, and then embrace him, her body warm against his body . . . then her lips would find his lips . . .

Someone approached. He glanced up to see Drew, and he was glad she couldn't see the warm flush that came to his cheeks.

Her expression was grim. She extended her hand to him. "Come on," she said. "I have something to share with you."

He got up and went along with her. He worried about what to expect, but he enjoyed the fact that she kept her hand in his as she guided him to another room.

There, they sat together on some cushions laid out on the floor. Drew pulled close a box of tissues, the cheerful blue flowers on the box in stark contrast to the bare, ugly room.

"I need to talk and to grieve," Drew said. "And it will be instructional for you. I want you to watch. You don't have to do anything, you don't have to say anything, just watch."

Gaylen took a long, slow breath and nodded. The old Gaylen would have been acutely uncomfortable. But he simply waited for Drew to do whatever she needed to.

"I guess the first thing to tell you is that Mercy is dead," she began, and already her face began to contort.

Gaylen realized with a shock of shame that he had given no thought at all to the big man's absence.

"He died saving us. He got us into the car and he held off the DAA until Chloe got us away. And they burned him to death." Her eyes filled with tears and then overflowed. "I'm so outraged and angry and heartbroken. I really liked Mercy, I really did," she said, her voice cracking. Her small body shook. "He's gone now, and he died because of me, because of my mission and my team, and he died for us, to save us." Her voice rose unsteadily. Tears ran down her face. She wrapped her arms around herself, as if to try to hold on.

Gaylen witnessed silently, in sympathy. All selfish thoughts and anger toward Mercy had disappeared.

Drew sobbed quietly for a moment.

"I think I was falling in love with him," she said, her voice straining. She straightened up and grabbed tissues to wipe her face.

"He was beautiful," she said. She made a sound that was between a sob and a laugh. "He was noble. He was good. He'd lost his way to darkness but he wanted to get out of it, I could see it in him. I wish he'd—" She stopped and covered her face in her hands. "I told him I liked him and he rejected me. It hurt. But I couldn't stop thinking, maybe, maybe he'll change his mind . . ."

She caught her breath again. "Why did I have to meet him and love him just to lose him?" she wailed. "Why?" She asked no one in particular, with the tone of voice of someone who already knows that there is no answer. She cried hard for a while.

In this moment, she was so delicate, so frail. Gaylen wished he could bundle her into his arms and protect her. Yet he also knew that she didn't need him. She was doing fine by herself.

He knew that she was giving the emotions full sway, just as she had taught him, until they lost their power and diminished. He could see the moment that the storm passed. She sat up and wiped her face again. She took a deep breath and let it out slowly, then did it again, and again.

Then she sat still for several minutes, her eyes closed, her chin trembling from time to time, her face weary.

"This is grieving," she said. "And it's hard." She laughed a little and wiped her nose again. "It's some of the strongest emotion you'll ever have, and you have to trust that it won't kill you, because it really feels like it will."

She stopped and breathed slowly and deeply again for a moment.

"You have to let it come up fully, like I taught you for embracing the darkness, but you have to express it, too. You have to cry and you might even have to scream, because that's how the poison of grief gets out of your body.

"I'm not done grieving now, of course. But if you do this consciously each time the grief comes up, the grief will only last a short while. But if you don't get the poison out, the grief will consume you for months or years and turn you bitter. It is important to fully go into the pain and really feel it."

Gaylen nodded. He understood, and he knew that he could do it himself if he had to.

"Now I'm going to step into the light and then hear what it has to say to me. Just as the darkness is a part of you trying to tell you something, the light always has a message as well, if you can get quiet enough to hear it."

Gaylen nodded, but Drew had already closed her eyes.

He watched her face as she went through the process. She had done it many times, so it was rapid for her. He watched the redness fade from her nose and forehead as time passed. Her lips twitched at times, and her forehead wrinkled in concentration.

He could *see* the moment when she stepped into the light—her body swayed and her face relaxed and her smile seemed to light up the room.

She tilted her head to the side a little, as if listening to something far away.

She nodded slowly, and her smile deepened. "Love is always perfect," she murmured, and her eyes fluttered open. They were filled with tears that overflowed as she looked at Gaylen. "Love is always perfect," she repeated, her voice stronger, and she wiped away the tears. "It doesn't matter whether it's received, doesn't matter whether the person who's loved even knows about it. It doesn't matter how good they are or whether they deserve it. It doesn't matter what obscures it or confuses it. With love, the point is the love. And it's always beautiful and good and right." Her tone was jubilant.

Gaylen grinned, caught up in her joy.

Drew laughed and took more tissues to wipe her face again. "Love is always perfect," she repeated again, thoughtfully. She looked at Gaylen, who was thinking that perhaps it was OK, then, that he loved Drew. Because he had just realized that he did.

He recognized it now only because of this conversation; otherwise, it might have taken him weeks. It was so new, this love, it was like a tiny dandelion peeking out of a crack in the sidewalk, reaching toward the sun. Perhaps it didn't even deserve the name *love* yet, but in this moment of clarity, Gaylen could see its whole lifespan, the entire arc of it, from youthful infatuation to long-standing commitment. Maybe it would be more accurate to say that he was *going* to love her, but in knowing it, he found himself surrendering to it now.

Drew leaned forward to hug him, and Gaylen hugged her back unselfconsciously. He felt the rightness of Drew's words in his own soul. It *was* good, to love her. What came after that didn't really matter. As long as he didn't let the darkness poison it, it was just good. It was of the light.

It was the same for Serena. He had loved her, and she had loved him, once, too. Then she had stopped. And his own love had changed—he knew that now, too, in this moment of clarity. He could not love her in the same way now that she was no longer the Serena who had loved him. But whatever it was—everything it was—was perfect.

They both took deep breaths.

Drew said, "I wanted you to see, Gaylen, because I want you to understand that this journey is never finished. I'm one of the strongest among us. But that doesn't mean I'm never lost in darkness. Life is just hard that way." She laughed a little, wryly.

"Remember, Gaylen—and I repeat this only because it is so important for you to understand it—the darkness will never go away entirely, and the harder you try to banish it, the more power you give it. The more you fight it, the more you fear it—and the more strength your fear gives it. Martha's teachings make the darkness stronger, not weaker.

"The darkness cannot be ignored and there are times that life demands that you must go into it, as I have just done. Just, never for long. You go there to hear it, to respect it, to learn from it, and to see *through* it . . . and then you go back into the light. Always, back into the light."

Gaylen nodded. He felt the weight of knowing that he could not be permanently free of pain, coupled with the strength of knowing that he could deal with it. And for the first time in his life, he thought that maybe that was OK.

"I want to teach you our central and most important recitation," Drew said.

Line by line, she said the recitation and had him repeat it back to her until he had it by heart. He recognized the first line from yesterday, when they had lain jumbled together in the back seat of the old Buick, being driven toward safety and healing:

> Though I am surrounded by darkness, within me
> there is only light. And as I walk into darkness,
> may I never forget that it has no power over me
> that I have not given it. As I go out into the world
> of darkness, may I act out of the light that I carry
> within me. And if that candle should go out, may
> I find it alight again from the flames of the others
> who carry it within.

Chapter Thirteen

Drew Ashling, Lightbringer:

The really big problem with Martha's philosophy is that it doesn't work. Even if you never think of violence, you might still get mugged. But by telling us that our circumstances result from our thinking, everything we experience becomes our fault, and now it's not only bad, but also a source of shame, because we brought it on ourselves. The positive thinking dogma is a way of controlling people. If you believe it's your fault, you won't look to anyone else.

Nick opened his eyes to find himself in a basement in restraints—each wrist in a manacle and the manacles attached to a ring in the ceiling, at a height that had him on his knees, his hands up over his head.

The last thing he remembered was approaching the underground entrance to a house that Mikey said was the current safe house for the Lightbringers cell—then, a sudden blow to the head.

He scrambled to his feet. He saw two men in the basement with him, both wearing the distinctive garb and iris implants of the Double Double Gang. They got up when they saw him awake. Immediately, one of the men—a skinny black man with a tall Mohawk—kicked his legs out from under him, taking him back down to his knees. "Well, let's do this," he said to his partner, who was a bald white guy with vivid orange iris implants.

By now, Nick knew about half of what was going on. Mikey had betrayed him; the gang had been sent to hurt him. The only question was who was behind it. Surely not Drew—Miss Goody Two-Shoes herself.

"That goddamn big black man?" Nick asked, his voice hoarse with rage. "He set this up?"

"No talking," the bald guy said. The skinny guy went over to where a crowbar and a baseball bat leaned against a wall.

Nick had little time, but he knew what to do. He closed his eyes and summoned the wolf within him. Helpless he might be, but no one was going to break him—not ever again. He breathed harder and faster than he needed to, until he panted, to kick up his adrenaline, a natural painkiller.

The skinny guy noticed his heavy breathing and gave him an odd look as he stepped back.

The wolf inside Nick called up the memory of every vile act he'd ever committed—every rape, every beating, every moment of torture—and wrapped it up into a big ugly ball of sickness.

The bald guy picked up the crowbar and his friend picked up the baseball bat and then they both turned toward him, their mouths in firm lines.

Nick let his sickness explode outward at his captors in screaming hysterics. His whole body shook as he screamed. Spittle flew from his mouth. "Hurt me!" He threw himself forward and backward against his chains.

The men hastily stepped back, their jaws dropping. "What the hell?" the bald guy said. They stared at their convulsing captive.

"Come on! Don't be fucking pussies!" Nick's eyes bulged out at them. "Do your jobs! Beat me!" The wolf inside him laughed and laughed.

They stared at him.

Nick writhed within his chains and giggled.

The skinny man raised his eyebrows. "What? This seem messed up to you?" he asked his friend.

"Yeah. But Mikey said to hurt him." The other guy hesitated, but he took a firmer grip on his crowbar, raised it, and struck a vicious blow to Nick's chest.

It hurt. Nick howled and flailed. He hurled his reaction at them like a weapon, his eyes fixed on them.

"Again! Again!" he screamed. "More!"

Both men stared at him with disgust on their faces.

He didn't look away. He took in their abhorrence and relished it. He *was* revolting. He was full of a kind of sickness they couldn't imagine. They thought they were bad guys, but they had lines they wouldn't cross. The wolf within him didn't.

The bald guy took another swing, then another, while the skinny guy just stood there. He weighed his baseball bat in his hands but he was afraid to use it, Nick could see that.

Nick laughed when he wasn't choking and gagging from the pain of his ribs cracking. He threw himself toward his attacker with his arms open wide, to expose as much of his chest to the blows as he could. He howled and writhed as if in ecstasy.

Apparently, the bald guy had had enough. He turned on his heel and flung the crowbar away. "Jesus."

"Yeah," the other guy said. "What the fuck?"

"This is sick. I'm not doing this shit."

"Maybe it's an act."

The two men turned and looked at Nick, who laughed again. He knew that he had just won a psychological victory. He was worse than they were.

He was also dizzy from hyperventilating, which made the scene all the more surreal.

He bit his tongue open and spat blood at them. They backed up again. He screamed at them wordlessly, his voice raw. He felt out of control and in control at the same time. It was a state he had cultivated.

The men turned away again.

"I don't care if it's an act or not," the bald guy said.

"What are we gonna do?"

"I'm done. We did enough. I don't want to look at him for another second."

"Fine with me, man. Fine with me."

The men left without a backward glance.

Nick laughed hysterically. He threw himself against his chains and howled at the walls until he was able to come down from the adrenaline high. Then he sat still, chuckling sometimes, until the dizziness subsided.

This was what fully indulging the wolf inside got you. The strength to endure anything. An unbreakable will. Dominion over others. Winning even when other people thought you were losing.

He knew that the pain was going to get much worse as he cooled down and got stiff and the adrenaline wore off. It was nothing new to him. He settled down to wait out the rest of his captivity.

"Goldfinger?"

John's head snapped up at the sound of the soft voice. It was Chloe. He stood up hastily, not sure how to react. He had disabled his mask when he went topside, so she could see his real face for the first time. It was too late now, or he'd turn it back on.

Then he really thought about where they were. "Chloe . . . you shouldn't be topside." He gestured toward her eyebrow piercing, her purple dreadlocks.

She shrugged one shoulder. "The exit I used is really close to here. Anyway, I'm safe, aren't I? I'm with you, right?" Her tone of voice was half smile, half accusation, and her look was knowing.

She sat down on the bench and stared up at him until he sat down as well.

His heart had stopped, it seemed. He had to look away. His mind felt like a line of dominoes toppling over one at a time. *Chloe knows. But she's here. I don't understand.*

They both sat in silence for a bit. Then Chloe sighed deeply and spoke. "So, yeah, everyone knows now."

John couldn't speak.

"I was really, really mad at you, at first." She spoke shyly, while playing with the end of a dreadlock.

It was hard to imagine Chloe being angry at anyone, and it reminded John of being chastised by his own sweet mother. And somehow it seemed perfectly natural when he found himself apologizing to the denizen it was his job to bring in or dust. "I'm sorry. I really am. For what happened." He turned toward her. "I didn't request those fire weapons. I never would have done that."

"I know. I believe you." She looked at him calmly. "And on all the rest of it—you were just doing your job. And it's not your fault, really. You believe what you believe about the world. If I was you, if I had grown up the way you did, if I felt the way you feel, I would be on your side, too."

It could have been condescending, and if anyone else had said it, it might have been. But Chloe's tone was matter-of-fact.

"Drew said that there aren't any bad guys," Chloe went on. "Just confused or ignorant or wounded or broken people. People who wouldn't be confused or ignorant or any of those things if they had a choice, if they could fix it. And a lot of the time, they can't. But she thinks you probably can."

John waited. For the first time, he found himself entirely in the perspective of the Lightbringers, and he looked at himself through that lens. From here, it was clear that he was in the wrong, that the side he worked for was the wrong side. It was so jarring as to be dizzying, to feel his perspective swing a hundred eighty degrees.

"I think you're one of the honest ones, aren't you?" Chloe's voice was suddenly hesitant.

John didn't know what she meant. He tried to parse her question, but it fell apart in his mind. "One of the honest whats?" he asked.

Chloe just nodded once. She sighed and resumed chewing on her dreadlock. "I thought you probably didn't know. And I thought you should. I think you deserve to know."

Tension rose in him. He waited.

She turned toward him, and John saw that she was ready to break it to him gently—whatever it was.

"A lot of the DAA is corrupt," she said, her tone kind. "They take money from the underground bosses in exchange for not taking them to prison. A lot of DAA agents aren't really trying, you see? They're just pretending." She paused, searching his face for a reaction.

John didn't see.

Taking bribes to overlook underground behavior was, of course, forbidden. And Martha had designed the audits, which other government workers ran like clockwork, to catch exactly this kind of corruption. John had heard rumors of corruption and bribery from time to time, but the auditors always either cleared or dusted the subjects of those rumors soon enough.

Or so he had thought.

For the first time, he wondered what it really meant when someone was "cleared" during an audit.

He took a deep breath. He felt impossibly naive. "How much . . ." He had to stop and clear his throat. "How much of the DAA is corrupt?" For one excruciating moment, he feared that he was the only idiot in the entire agency actually trying to do his job.

Chloe shrugged. "I don't know. A lot of it, is all I know."

John looked at the ground. Thoughts tumbled through his mind too swiftly to manage. He knew his expression was forlorn, and he didn't have the energy to try to change it.

Then he felt white-hot anger flare. He had been lied to, misled, used. He had tried so hard to do what was right, and it hadn't meant anything to anyone. Decades of his life wasted trying to do the impossible and pointless.

He was so dismayed that he simply stood up and walked away.

John, the ever obedient. John, the fool.

He let his feet choose his path. He was blind with anger and embarrassment. For the moment, those hot emotions chased away the despair.

Maybe he would have known if he hadn't worked in isolation and undercover for so long. He'd had partners, before, but even then it was just the two of them working together. They'd reported in to their manager, and the rest of the time they'd spent undercover.

And yet . . . the denizens and tourists of the underground had talked of the DAA many times in his presence, and always with anger, frustration, fear, disgust, or hatred. The DAA was the enemy. That was certain.

As he walked, he convinced himself that not all of the DAA could be corrupt—not if they were consistently known as the bogeymen of the underground. But if Chloe was telling the truth—and John thought she was—then there were DAA agents who were above the law. Just not the ones John had worked with.

He wondered whether he had dealt only with the lowest level of the underground—the scum. He tried to imagine what the shape of it looked like. What percentage of the denizens were in bed with the DAA? Was it the majority, or the minority?

Had he been given assignments designed to keep him from noticing the corruption? He was a feeler, after all . . .

The whole thing sickened him. The fear that he had spent his entire life in a futile effort—manipulated and misdirected—weighed on his chest, so heavy as to be suffocating.

Then it dawned on him that he had just walked away from Chloe, who had gone to this trouble to find him and tell him the truth, and he stopped still. Now it was too late to go back and apologize—she would have left again.

He couldn't even sigh. His body was locked up too tightly.

He resumed walking, his mind a blank.

"Dammit!" Gaylen paced, his fists clenched. "I can't believe it. I can't."

Drew sat with her back against a wall, looking as calm as ever. "Gaylen, I'm telling you this because I think you need to know that there are no bad guys."

"No bad guys?" Gaylen stared at her incredulously. "They used fire on us. John's people. He lied to us. He burned you! Me! They killed Mercy!"

Drew closed her eyes for a moment. "I'm not saying they didn't make an evil choice. What they did was inhumane. But you have to be careful about writing people off as 'bad.' When you do that, you stop seeing them as human. And then anything you want to do to them becomes acceptable. That's when you start committing evil acts of your own."

"Aren't you angry with them for what they did?"

"Sometimes, yes. Mostly, I feel sorry for them. They're in a dark place. They don't know what they're doing. They're trapped by their own blind spots, by the things they don't understand about themselves and the world.

"It's important to know that they can't help it. They have found themselves where they are because of their personalities, their past experiences, their capacities for thought and conscience, their education. If you had all the same factors, you'd believe the same things. You'd make the same choices."

"I would not. In the same circumstances, I would choose something different."

"No, if you were the same person as them, with the same personality, you would choose the same things."

"Well . . . yes, I guess so. If I were literally them, I guess I would do what they're doing, since . . . that's what they're doing." Gaylen stopped pacing and sat down. "How is this useful? Isn't it their personality that makes them bad? So saying I'd be bad if I were them is really just saying that they're bad. Which is where I started."

Drew chuckled. After a second, Gaylen did, too.

Drew went on, "No, I didn't say that their personality makes them bad. Their personality makes them choose the way they do. But they can't help it, because they can't help who they are. Not yet.

"No one chooses things that he believes are evil, unless he has himself convinced that the evil is for a good purpose. Everyone aims for the good. They're just confused sometimes about what the good is or what acceptable tactics are."

"What about the socios?"

Drew nodded. "Fair enough. Some socios embrace evil deliberately, though most of them just rationalize their behavior. Either way, it still isn't helpful to think of them as bad. They have grown up psychologically disabled. It isn't their fault that they are the way they are.

"If a person has the energy and the motivation and the conscience and the knowledge to choose what's good, then of course, they do. In other words, to put it in our terms, if they're in the light, their actions will be of the light. But if they lack conscience or the right kind of motivation or the right knowledge, that doesn't make them bad—it makes them disabled or wounded or ignorant or unwise. It means they're in darkness. If you can bring them to the light, they'll start making different choices."

Gaylen let this sink in. He suddenly remembered Chandi of the dark brown eyes, the old girlfriend he had hurt. He had always felt so bad about that. Now he tried to see it according to Drew's words.

He hadn't meant to hurt her. He had just wanted what he'd wanted, and he'd ignored her reactions.

He shook his head. "I did something bad once. And I knew better. At least, I should have. But I ignored what I knew. Doesn't that make me bad?" His throat was tight as he said it.

"It means you weren't in touch with your conscience. If you had been, you would have done differently. Now that you're in touch with your conscience, you've never done it again, correct?"

He nodded.

"You weren't bad. You were just unwise. You lacked awareness. You were in darkness. Now that you've corrected that, you're no more or less bad than you were. You're just in a different place. Didn't you ignore what you knew because you wanted something that seemed good at the time?"

He thought about that. "Yes." It was a reluctant admission.

"So now you know better. You're the same person, still seeking what's good, but now with more clarity and wisdom. And that's preferable to the rest of us, of course."

It seemed too easy. Slowly, he said, "You don't understand, Drew. What I did was bad. I mean, it really was bad."

She shifted a bit, sat up straighter. She leaned forward. "Tell me about it."

He looked away, his heart beating faster, his hands going clammy. "I don't want to."

"Look at me."

He forced his gaze back to hers.

"I can feel that you're ashamed. And the only way to undo the shame is to bring this to the light. So bring it out, Gaylen. Expose it to the light of truth. It will melt away."

"I—I can't." He looked away again.

She reached out and touched his face, guiding his gaze back to her own. "Tell me." Her voice was soft.

He contemplated starting the story, but he couldn't bring himself to confess this, the most awful thing he had ever done. "I can't, Drew, please, don't make me."

She stroked his face. Her words were both gentle and commanding. "Tell me."

He took a deep breath. Tears started even before the first words came out. "She was my girlfriend. We were really young. I was twenty, she was eighteen. She started it. She said she wanted me. She took off my clothes. And I wanted her so bad."

Drew's gaze was unflinching.

"And when I started . . . when I . . . entered her . . . she went all tense, she said it hurt. It must have been her first time. And I should have stopped. I should have stopped, Drew."

Drew said nothing. She didn't blink.

"But I kept going because I . . . wanted it so . . ." His voice gave out and he couldn't speak. He turned away.

Drew reached out again and brought his gaze back to hers. Her face was gentle, her eyes filled with compassion. "Tell me."

"She closed her eyes, she turned away . . . her hands were clenched into fists, she was so stiff, and then she started crying . . . I mean, just a few tears . . . and I . . . just kept going until I . . . finished. And she didn't say anything. She got up and went into the bathroom for a long time and then she left, took a cab home. And then she wrote me a letter. She said—I remember every word—she said, 'I hate you. You make me sick. I hope no one ever loves you.'" Gaylen's stomach was in knots, his face contorted.

Drew put her hands on his shoulders. "If you had known better, would you have done it?"

"I did know! I saw her get tense. I heard her say it hurt. I saw her crying. I knew I was hurting her."

"Did you really know at the time, at that moment, or did you only know in retrospect?"

Gaylen closed his eyes, focusing intently. He forced himself to remember.

"No," he said at last. "I saw that something might be wrong, might be bad. I wasn't sure. I thought maybe she would be OK when she relaxed a little. I did go more gently. I did slow down. I hoped it would be enough." He looked at her. "But I was stupid, Drew. I should have stopped, told her we didn't have to keep going. I was older. I had experience. She didn't."

"Now that you have seen it in retrospect, now that you understand, now that you know better, would you do the same thing again?"

"Never."

"Then you aren't a bad person. It was a mistake. Good people make mistakes. You were blinded by desire and by ignorance. You were selfish at the time, because that's who you were back then. You couldn't have chosen anything else in that moment. You were in darkness and you acted from darkness.

"Please understand, I agree that it's awful. It probably wounded her more deeply than you have even imagined. And you deserve to feel guilty for it, Gaylen. Guilt is the appropriate reaction to making a mistake.

"But what you shouldn't feel is shame. Shame is the feeling that you *are* bad, deep down. Listen to me, Gaylen, you are not bad." She looked him in the eyes. "You just screwed up. You're just human. That's all."

Gaylen wiped away tears. He wasn't sure if they were tears of relief or misery. Maybe both.

"If you ever see her again, you must apologize to her, and you must try to find a way to make amends. In fact, you should try to find her so that you can. Do you understand? That's how you pay for your mistake."

Gaylen nodded.

"But let go of the shame. You don't deserve that. Use the methods I've taught you to let it go. Bring it to the light."

Gaylen nodded and put his feelings through the process. It took much longer than anything he had done before. One emotion would break over him and ebb away, only to be replaced by a fresh wave of a different emotion. But he took away the layers one at a time until they were gone.

Finally, he came to the cold, hard feeling of guilt, like a stone slab, that told him that he had done something wrong, something that could never be undone. He realized that the guilt could not be released, but he could accept that. He deserved it. The guilt would remind him to be more careful with the feelings of others in the future.

Even with the weight of that knowledge deep in his heart, when he had finished, he felt like a man released from decades of imprisonment.

He looked up at Drew and she took him into her arms and caressed his face. He relaxed into her lap and soaked up the warmth and compassion that she emanated as if it were the sunlight on a cold day. She held him for a long while.

He had never known such peace before.

"Thank you," he said.

She smiled. "Now the hard part is for you to apply this to John and to all the others. Remember, there are no bad guys. Whatever happens from here on out. There are just people lost in the darkness."

Some time later, John realized that his feet had, ironically, brought him into the Bureau of Safety and down the hallway to his office at the DAA. He stopped walking.

The overhead lights were off, since it was past working hours. The wallscreens every few feet were the only source of light. They played a cheerful cartoon music video starring animated cats and dogs that strutted and jumped around while they sang. John stared at them without comprehension. They might as well have been aliens.

He trudged to his desk and sat down with a bone-jarring thud. For the moment, his entire plan was to go to sleep on his desk and face the world some other time. For now, he wanted an Off button. He would have found solace in booze, but he was, frankly, too exhausted to make it to a bar now. He cursed his feet for not taking him to a place that had alcohol.

On his wallscreen, the ticker went by. All categories had ticked up. Personal Control violations for October were up to 148. He resisted the urge to throw something at the marquee, to shut it up forever.

A thought crept into his mind. It was an errant thought, but it called to him the way whiskey usually did. It asked him, what really did happen to Gaylen's wife and daughter?

He could find out easily enough.

In fact, he could easily find out what had really happened to his father. And whether his own family was still safe.

Gaylen's words echoed in his mind. *"I want to know that they're OK. And if they're not . . . I'd still want to know."*

John began to look them up. One methodical keypress after another, the information came closer and closer, all while his mind protested vigorously. He didn't want to know. It was true. He didn't. But he couldn't seem to stop himself.

The screen flickered in response to his query.

Bob Oldman. Detected in randomized home review. Taken into custody July 25, 2041. Rehabilitation unsuccessful. Reduced on November 29, 2041.

He refused to process the words, not yet. His heart thudding slowly, John hit more keys to look up his ex-wife and his two kids.

Rebecca Leigh Lawrence. No record.

His ex-wife was OK. He typed in his daughter's name.

Suzanne Mary Lawrence. Health issue discovered during Wellness Confirmation. Taken into custody January 11, 2074. Rehabilitation unsuccessful. Reduced on April 29, 2074.

He typed in his son's name.

John Robert Oldman, Jr. Requested assistance due to disappearance of sister. Taken into custody February 1, 2074. Rehabilitation unsuccessful. Reduced on May 1, 2074.

He kept up the emotional wall that protected him from feeling this. He pulled up Gaylen's profile, then looked for his family connections.

Serena Anne Tate. Watch list. Checks every five days until November 31, 2079.

Gaylen's wife was still free.

Sierra Tate Andrews. Requested assistance due to missing her absent father. Taken into custody September 03, 2079. Rehabilitation unsuccessful. Scheduled for reduction.

John fell back into his chair. Moments passed as his emotional wall began to crumble under the onslaught of information he had never wanted to know.

The agency he had dedicated his life to had been lying to him all along. It had killed his father years ago. It had killed his two children. And now it was about to kill a five-year-old girl whose only crime was missing her daddy.

His face contorted as if he would cry, but his eyes were dry.

Inexplicably, the feeler mantra worked its way into his mind. *There is only good and right in the world*, he heard in a cheerful, vacuous wallscreen voice. *There is only good and right in the world.*

He started screaming. He swept everything off his desk indiscriminately, some items hitting the walls and everything crashing to the floor, with no regard to whether they might be watching his wallscreen right now. He picked up his chair and threw it at a corner of the room and stood there still hyperventilating. He tried to settle his breathing, but he couldn't. He threw over his entire desk, yelling, "No!" as if it would make any difference.

He fell to the ground in the midst of the mess and tried to cry. He couldn't. Adrenaline pumped too hard through his system. This wasn't grief, he realized then. It was rage. Pure, fervent rage.

His mind fixated on Sierra. She was still alive.

He picked himself up off the floor, breathing hard.

He was going to save Gaylen's daughter.

It was decades too late for his father and years too late for his own children, but whatever it took, whatever it cost him, they would not kill this little girl.

Chapter Fourteen

Drew Ashling, Lightbringer:

Let me be clear: The light is not perfection. And it is not a goal. It is not some bliss to aim at achieving and then staying in forever. Looked at that way, the light is just as much a trap as Martha's positive thinking. The light is a tool—and so is the darkness. We must use them both. We travel between the two, listening to both, delving deeply into both, transcending attachment to either one of them. The Lightbringers emphasize the light now only because our society does not know it at all. Someday, we will find balance.

Gaylen leaned on the kitchen's island at the abandoned condo, where a number of Lightbringers had gathered informally, Drew at their center. Chloe leaned on the island, too, a few steps away.

"What will be the team breakout?" Kevin asked.

"Alpha team goes in to gain access to the Emergency Broadcasting System," Drew answered. "Beta team will back up Alpha team from the outside. It will take some time for the DAA to show up, and Beta team will hold them off long enough to try to get Alpha team back out.

"Gamma team sets up to broadcast. Delta team guards Gamma team and keeps the escape route clear all the way to the underground.

We need all hands to cover all the teams. Assignments will be on a volunteer basis. I'll be on Gamma team, live on camera."

People around the room nodded, their faces serious. Chloe chewed on a dreadlock, her expression pensive.

"When do we go?" Kevin asked.

"We're still waiting to get a way onto the floor of the Bureau of Entertainment that has the Emergency Broadcasting System. The BoE isn't secured in general, since it's mostly staffed by sleepers, but the DAA manages that one floor and they keep it locked down. We got a picture of a DAA worker who has the passcodes or badge or whatever's needed, but it's taking some research to find out exactly who he is and where to find him."

Gaylen thought about his job for the first time in days. He wondered what Tommy had thought when he had failed to show up at the office.

"Drew?" Gaylen said.

Faces turned toward him, including Drew's.

"I don't know if this is helpful, but . . . I worked at the Bureau of Entertainment before I came here. And my old boss, Spider . . . He's a tourist. Maybe he would know something useful?"

Drew nodded. "Yes. He might. Good idea, Gaylen. He's trustworthy?"

Gaylen had to think about that. "I'm not a hundred percent sure, but I don't think he's the type to turn traitor on us. Not like Nick."

"Bastard," Chloe added. Then she glanced at Drew. "Sorry." She grinned.

Drew turned back to Gaylen. "Can you reach him on short notice?"

"I think so," Gaylen answered. He had been to Spider's—or, rather, Tommy's—house a few times for barbeques. He checked his watch. Tommy should be home from work already.

"Take a cloaking device," Drew said. "Be careful. And come back as quickly as you can."

"Understood," Gaylen said.

"Go with the light," Drew called after him.

He smiled.

Twenty minutes later, Gaylen sat in the back corner of a subway car like a statue. A child was horsing around on this section of the train, and that made Gaylen nervous. It would be funny, but not helpful, for the kid to run full-tilt into his invisible body.

He was surprised that he wasn't more nervous in general. He had been through so much already, he thought he should be jumping at every shadow. But while he was alert, he was also strangely calm. He wondered if it was because of all that Drew had taught him. And the fact that, so far, he'd survived. And, maybe most potent of all, that he'd already come so close to death that he knew what it was going to be like. It would be sudden, shocking, horrible, and painful—certainly—but then it would be over. Endless sleep.

New Americans had no belief in an afterlife. This world was supposed to be so good, so full and rich and happy, that no one needed to believe in anything else.

Not too much later, after scanning the street to be sure no one was paying attention, Gaylen rang the doorbell of Tommy Hiyashi's house.

Tommy opened the door with a cheerfully expectant expression that had just started to shift to confusion when the nanoparticles swarmed him and Gaylen appeared. Tommy blinked a few times, then, apparently recognizing Gaylen, pulled him inside the house and shut the door.

"Hey, what the hell was that?"

"Listen, we can't talk in here. Let's take a walk."

"Something weird just happened out there." Tommy had a stubborn set to his jaw.

"OK, I'll show you. Then we need to go out to talk. Take five steps back."

Tommy stepped back. His eyes got comically wide as he saw Gaylen disappear.

"Now come back," Gaylen said.

Tommy stepped forward slowly while staring at the place where Gaylen should be standing, until he could see him again. His mouth hung open. "Holy *shit,*" he said.

"You're invisible, too, as long as you're near me. Now let's go." Gaylen gestured at Tommy's wallscreen. They went outside and moved into a busy area where it would be harder for the wallscreens to pick up their voices.

"So what the hell are you into?" Tommy asked. "What's going on? I got the postcard. Did you go underground? And what the hell is that tech you've got and where the hell did you get it?"

Gaylen took a deep breath. He knew Tommy was a tourist in the underground, but he was unsure as to where Tommy's loyalties lay.

"I'll be straight with you, Tommy, I need help because I'm up to no good. At least by our society's rules. Things have changed a lot for me since I went underground. You wouldn't believe . . ." He shook his head. "You wouldn't believe what I've learned, what I've seen."

Tommy laughed. "Are you trying to scare me, man? You should see what I've seen underground. Go on, fill me in."

Gaylen described the Lightbringers' plan in brief.

Tommy's eyes and smirk got wider and wider as he listened. "That's fantastic," he said. "I've never heard of your Lightbringers, but if their goal is to release the truth—it's going to be nuts out there. It's going to be unbelievable."

"So can you help me get in?" Gaylen asked.

Tommy thought for a moment. "No, but I know someone who can. I know one of the DAA agents who works the secured floor, and he owes me a favor." He winked at Gaylen. "When is this going down?"

"Tonight. As soon as possible. I'm talking hours, max. An hour from now would be great."

Tommy nodded. "An hour it is. I will have your way clear, man. And congratulations. Welcome to the real world."

A short time later, Gaylen reported his news to Drew and the assembled Lightbringers. There were high-fives all around, and then Drew dove into the plan.

"All right, we need multiple teams. Alpha, Beta, Gamma, Delta. Who's taking what teams?"

To his surprise, Gaylen found himself volunteering for Alpha team. He felt a sense of ownership over this. He knew the building; he knew Tommy.

Also to his surprise, no one argued. Drew even smiled at him, and he felt a surge of pride—not an emotion he was used to.

Drew said, "Alpha team can be quite small. All you're doing is taking in a laptop and following some pretty simple instructions. Beta team will be the muscle. So, Gaylen, just take one other person with you inside."

Gaylen knew exactly whom he wanted. "Chloe, come with me?" he asked.

She hesitated and wouldn't meet his eyes, but she nodded.

Moments later, they were on their way.

John Oldman let himself into the DAA armory only minutes after his resolution to free Sierra. Though he had no reason to think that she would be executed tonight, he was taking no chances.

First, he slipped on full-body stun armor, leaving his head bare so that he wouldn't draw too much attention. He put on two over-the-shoulder holsters and slid in one old-school revolver and one stun gun. He added a second stun gun tucked into his waistband. Over that he put on his dingy gray trench coat. Next, he threw a stun rifle over his shoulder. All the while, the wallscreens played an animated family program: the family's pink poodle could talk, and she was full of one-liners that prompted raucous laughter from the laugh track.

John left the door open and ignored the equipment sign-out sheet. As he walked out, he cast a resolute look at the wallscreens. This was only the beginning. He knew that no matter happened next, he would not be able to return to his old life. But it seemed as if everything that had happened until now had prepared him for this moment—had made it inevitable.

He went to the DAA impound area, a room that was always staffed. The clerk behind the counter was younger than himself, but no greenhorn. Luckily, they were strangers to each other.

As he walked up to the counter, he summoned up all his strength and his best acting skills. Not giving the clerk a chance to speak, John demanded, "I need an item that was impounded this morning. Let me in."

The clerk pulled out a clipboard with a sign-out sheet on it and pushed it toward John on the counter. "Who's the authorizer?"

"I am," John said, getting louder. He leaned over the counter as far as he could and stared the guy in the eyes. "And I don't need to sign a damn clipboard. Let me in." He was doing his best to impersonate a socio and not to reveal a trace of feeler tendencies. Desperation and determination gave his voice a hard edge that he hoped was compelling.

The clerk's face tensed. The look he gave John was dismissive and angry. "Everybody signs the clipboard. It's my job."

John shoved the clipboard back at him. It hit the clerk in the chest and bounced to the floor. "And if you want to keep your job, you moron, you will not stand in my way. There's an audit going on right this minute, remember? Are you sure you have enough friends, if you get reported for something you shouldn't have done?"

The clerk picked the clipboard up off the floor without a word, his expression stony.

John recognized by the other man's behavior that he was a feeler, too. That was lucky, because John might not have been able to fool a socio. And it made him hate himself at the same time. DAA workers feared the audits above all. Every report was taken seriously, the word of socios was taken over that of feelers, and failing an audit got you dusted. What he was doing was unfair to this man, but freeing Sierra was more important.

Without speaking, the staff person hit a button under his desk, and the buzzer at the door to the impound room sounded.

John bit back an automatic "thank you" and went in. A few minutes later, he came back out with the cloaking device impounded from Nick Aglaeca.

His final stop was the Bureau of Provision, where criminals were kept before they were dusted.

As he trudged through the streets to the Bureau, he didn't let himself reflect on his actions. Grim determination settled like a cloak over his shoulders, forming a barrier against every other thought and emotion.

Cloaked, he walked into the Bureau and roamed the hallways floor by floor until he found a central room filled with banks of wallscreens showing hundreds of criminals in their cells. A DAA agent was eating a microwave dinner and messaging his friends via wallscreen. John knew that that an agent in this position would be a socio. He would not be able to intimidate the man, nor would it be wise to let himself be seen, in any case.

John backtracked down a few hallways and picked out a random wallscreen. He pulled on it and worked it back and forth until the mounting bracket came out of the wall. Then he threw it downward, a couple of wires yanking out. He hurried back toward the security room.

Sure enough, the disconnection of the wallscreen had triggered an alarm, and the DAA agent walked briskly down the hallway with a deep frown. John had to press himself into a corner. Even though he was confident that the cloaking device was working, it was hard to stay still and wait for the man to walk right past him.

John hurried back to the security room. He knew he had a couple of minutes at the most.

He threw himself toward the nearest screen and spent agonizingly long seconds figuring out where and how to search by criminal name. His fingers trembled as he tapped the screen. He found Sierra Tate Andrews, looked for her cell number, found the cell's location on a facility map—and then read the words, *"Scheduled for reduction on Oct. 10."*

He dropped his head into his hands. October 10 was *today.*

He looked for more information but found nothing. He didn't have time to figure out how to turn on the camera to her cell, so he could only hope that she hadn't already been transported somewhere else in preparation for the execution.

The security agent came back in, his brow furrowed, his handscreen to his ear, and headed right toward John.

John silently dodged back several steps and froze, not moving or breathing until the guy passed by him, nearly close enough to intercept the cloaking field. The agent sat down heavily.

"Yeah, it fell right off the damn wall," he said. He pushed the remains of his dinner aside. "Well, how should I know? Your guys are lazy. They put it up wrong. Go fix it."

It had been a long shot to hope the agent would see it as a random break and not an act of vandalism. John would have thought luck was with him, were it not for the news he had just learned about Sierra.

John slipped out of the open door and ran like hell toward Sierra's cell, wincing at every step at the pain in his knees, ignoring the stitch that formed in his side. Eventually, someone would figure out that the wallscreen had been deliberately ripped off the wall, and then the alarms would sound and the entire building would be locked down.

A chilling question occurred to him as he ran up a flight of stairs, panting. How often did the reductions happen, and on what schedule? He checked his watch. It was 7:42 pm. Did they happen at 8:00? Surely not. Odds were too far against it. His luck wasn't running that bad.

John found the right corridor, then a door that wouldn't open. He rushed the other way. He checked his watch. 7:46.

Surely, he told himself, surely the reductions weren't at 8 pm. There were no personnel around. Surely personnel would be needed to run the reductions.

These thoughts, reasonable though they were, didn't quell his panic. He might still be too late.

His heart was beating so hard and his breath coming so fast that he thought he might die. But he couldn't. He wasn't allowed to die until he saved her.

He came to a skidding stop in front of a door that said "Authorized Personnel Only." He peeked through. Ahead was a long corridor lined with cells on either side. He'd found the right area.

7:49.

He moved smoothly into the corridor and jogged down it while he looked for cell 3126, Sierra's cell.

He was at 2955 when voices echoed down a cross-corridor. It was the idle chatter of DAA agents doing their job on a dull day. He mouthed a curse as they stepped out into his row and then turned the same direction he had been going—closer to Sierra.

John took a deep breath and followed from a safe distance, hoping that this was a coincidence and that they were merely making their rounds or just passing through.

His heart sank when they stopped in front of Sierra's cell.

"Hey, sweetheart," one of the men cooed. "We're here to take you to another place, OK?" The other one pressed the button to open the door.

John heard no sound from inside.

He pulled out one of his stun guns and trained it on the first of the two agents.

"Is this the last one?" the guard asked the other.

"Yup. This is lucky number thirty-three."

God damn it. John lowered his gun. He hadn't even been thinking of the others who were slated to die today. Of course he wouldn't have—his job was to dust denizens or bring them in to get dusted, after all. But something in his mind had shifted now. These were thirty-three fathers and mothers, sons and daughters, exactly like Sierra.

The first guard turned back to the cell. "Come on, sweetheart. Move it. This way."

John let out a slow breath. It would be a significant risk to let Sierra go with them, but if he took them out now, he wouldn't know where to go to find the other condemned NCPs.

Now Sierra was stepping out of her cell—a too-skinny black girl, her braided head bowed. John's heart broke. She was tiny, delicate.

The two men flanked her and they walked down the hallway.

John followed, his heart hammering in anxiety. He checked his watch. 7:54.

Minutes passed as they traveled through corridors and doorways. John prayed that they would not take an elevator. He would have no way of following them if they did. An elevator wouldn't give him enough room to keep up the cloaking field.

He learned nothing else from the guards' chatter, and the girl never made a sound.

The men went through a door and in the next hallway, a huge doorway gaped open. "Go in there, sweetheart," the first guard said. "Through the big door. There are people in there to see you."

Sierra stepped through the door, and the two guards began to walk away.

John froze.

If he followed Sierra, he ran the risk of being trapped in the execution chamber himself, but he was terrified to leave her there.

He took a step toward Sierra, then a step toward the guards, then a step toward Sierra . . . then he cursed to himself and dashed after the departing guards. He couldn't help anyone if he died alongside Sierra.

A dozen or so yards down, another door was marked, "Authorized Personnel Only." One of the guards rapped on the door, opened it a crack, and called in, "Got 'em all, boss." Then he slammed the door and they moved on.

John stopped, waited an agonizingly long count of five, then opened the door a crack and peeked through.

There were two personnel inside wearing white coats. They stood in front of a screen mounted on a table, and through a large window above the panel, John could see dozens of people crowded into a bare room. One of the DAA workers was saying something, gesturing toward one of the NCPs, and the other man laughed. They both tapped buttons on the screen. The sound of a large door closing rang through the walls.

Then, from somewhere, John heard the whirring of large machines start up. The people in the room looked up and around, looking for the source of the sound. As they shifted, John saw her: the tiny, brown-skinned girl with the braids, looking upward with wide eyes.

John screamed, "No!" as he leaped into the room and fired his gun.

He brought down both men.

He threw himself at the screen and hit the "ABORT" button.

The screen flashed, "AUTHORIZATION REQUIRED." A badge reader to the right of the panel blinked red.

The sound of machines was growing louder, the people in the room crouching low, as if it would protect them to do so, as they look-ed up fearfully. Seconds remained, surely, before they began to disintegrate and swirl away into dust.

John grabbed the badge from one of the two men he had stunned, tapped the badge reader, and hit the "ABORT" button again.

The screen flashed, "OPERATION TERMINATED."

The whirring abated.

The people in the room looked around nervously. They were still OK.

John slid to the ground against the panel, dizzy, his hands over his thumping heart. He really thought he was going to die this time.

As soon as his vision had cleared, he climbed to his knees and looked for a button that would open the chamber door. He found it and tapped it.

Inside, the people shifted about and began to move away from the window John was looking through.

He ran from the room and back down the hallway, where the large door stood open again and the thirty-three people moved through, looking confused and apprehensive but eager to leave the room that had frightened them. John knew that all of these people would still die, dusted by DAA security forces, unless he got them out of there.

He turned off the cloaking device, took a deep breath, and bellowed, "Citizens, your attention, please." He stepped forward.

Accustomed to obedience, the crowd stopped and looked at him.

"Thank you for your attention. Good news: I'm here to get you out of this place."

There were smiles and sighs of relief from many of the NCPs, and looks of suspicion from men and women John recognized as denizen types. He made mental note of who they were.

"First, I have a message for one of you. Is Sierra Tate Andrews among you? Sierra?" He looked for her anxiously, afraid that somehow she had gotten lost in the confusion.

There was a ripple of movement among the people, and then the crowd parted, and Sierra stepped cautiously forward, her eyes glistening with frightened tears.

Ignoring his aching knees, John crouched down. "Hi, Sierra. It's OK. Your mommy and daddy sent me to get you, OK?"

Her eyes widened, and she lit up. "Daddy sent you?"

"Yes. They sent me to get you and take you to them, OK?"

"OK."

That was all it took. She threw her little arms around him and let him pick her up. She felt like a songbird trembling in his arms.

Tears came to John's eyes, and for a moment, he fought down a desire to punch something. That his government, his own agency, would have harmed this child—

He had known that small children were taken—were sometimes casualties—but it had never struck home to him in this way before this moment.

He forced himself to refocus, and he addressed the crowd again. "We're all going to leave the building in an orderly fashion. But there's construction on some of the floors, so we can't take the usual routes out. We'll be taking some side passages and little-used stairwells. I apologize for the inconvenience."

There were knowing grins from a couple of the denizen types, then. He spoke to them next. "You, there, woman with the tattoos. You, boy with the green hair. Come with me, please. I need to speak with you regarding your appearances."

He set Sierra down next to an older woman with a kind face. "Stay with this nice lady for a minute, OK, Sierra?"

Sierra nodded, and the woman smiled at her and engaged her in a game of patty-cake.

Once John had taken the denizens aside, he whispered to them, "I need you to help me get these people out. I hadn't planned on so many. Can either of you hack a wallscreen?"

"Yeah," the woman said. "I can."

John closed his eyes in relief. Then he went on, "Find us a map of the building and a little-used route out, maybe through service areas, and then disable the wallscreens along the route."

She nodded and ran off, and John turned to the green-haired boy, a mere teenager. "Can you scout ahead as we move through the building?" The kid nodded. John handed him the cloaking ring and explained briefly how to operate it. "I'll take up the rear, guarding the group. The woman will be with you, giving directions. Clear?"

"Yeah," the boy said. He grinned. Here was a kid still young enough to think that all of this was exciting, even the fact that he had just almost died. John envied him.

"Then let's save these people."

They soon got the thirty-three people down the hallway to a stairwell, got them down the four flights of stairs, and brought them to the door that led to the lobby.

John handed his two stun pistols to the green-haired kid and readied his stun rifle. Then he instructed the rest of the NCPs: "I know this doesn't make any sense to you, but I'm going to need you to run out of this building in a minute, and then through the streets to another building, and then we're going to go down into the basement. Trust me, it will all be fine in a few minutes."

They all nodded or said, "Yes, sir," and as he turned back to the lobby, he mentally thanked President Martha for giving him such cooperative citizens.

He signaled the kid and then threw open the door.

At this hour, there were only three DAA agents passing through and two on guard. John brought down the guards while the green-haired kid took out the rest. Then they were all running.

Only after they were all clear of the building, John heard the sirens, and then a Happiness Break flashed across the wallscreens.

He let the green-haired kid lead the rest while he let himself fall back, watching, his weapon at the ready.

They weren't followed. The DAA knew better than to have an armed pursuit on foot.

They were going to make it.

Nick waited in the basement. It had been just long enough for his body to stiffen up when the two men returned. Unspeaking, they unchained him. They dragged him up the basement stairs and through a hallway with an elaborate rug, past a kitchen and dining room that were fully furnished and more beautiful than anything Nick had seen in decades.

As they went, Nick caught sight of a few Double Double Gang members in some of the rooms, talking and smoking. In the living room, a frightened-looking middle-aged couple sat on their sofa hand-in-hand, under guard. No Mikey. His former friend didn't even have the courage to face him.

Then the two men did something unexpected: they dragged him through the entryway and out of the front door of the house.

Chills ran down Nick's spine. He kicked and fought, but it was too late. While he tried and failed to think up a better plan, they carried him down the driveway and through a gate and then threw him out into a street. The *public* street.

The pain of his broken ribs sent stars through his vision as he hit the pavement, but he ignored it. What mattered was that he was topside in the early evening.

He struggled to his feet, looking around to find his bearings. The gate was already shut behind him and the two men were locking it with a chain.

He spotted several sleepers walking their dogs or jogging, and he cursed his luck. A beautiful woman a few yards away shrieked. She stared at him, her manicured hand at her lips. He knew it was his blood-spattered black clothes, overweight body, and goatee. He was probably the ugliest thing any of these sleepers had ever seen. All the beautiful New Americans stopped to stare in horror or moved faster to get away while they stared wide-eyed over their shoulders at him.

His heart raced. He had not been in the outside world in public in years. He didn't recognize any landmarks. He didn't know where the nearest entrance to the underground was. They had taken his handscreen.

Then he saw a girl break for the nearest wallscreen and touch the "Request Assistance" button.

"Shit," he said, his voice cracking.

He ran on shaking legs, his arms wrapped around his torso to protect his ribs. He had to find a place to hide.

CHAPTER FIFTEEN

Drew Ashling, Lightbringer:

Experiencing and expressing your emotions doesn't hurt other people if you do it in the right way. Other people can and will help you with how you feel, and when you let them, you build a precious bond with them. The key is to tell them what you need from them. To just helplessly whine all the time—yes, that'll bring others down. But to ask for the kind of help you need, when you need it—that is simply sharing in being human.

Gaylen and Chloe got into the Bureau of Entertainment without event, both of them focused on their mission, Chloe chewing on her purple dreadlocks. They left Beta team outside: a dozen men who would defend them against the inevitable attack of the DAA. Gaylen carried the laptop Drew had given him, as well as a brief list of instructions.

Drew had kept the explanations simple, since Gaylen was not an IT person. They had said that the laptop would take over from the existing broadcasting servers and confuse the machines that were monitoring things, to delay their discovery for as long as possible. They called it a Man-in-the-Middle computer, "MITM" for short. Gaylen didn't really understand any of it, but he was confident that he could follow the instructions.

When the elevator doors opened on the eighteenth floor, a shadowy figure stood in the lobby and watched the elevators closely. Gaylen froze at the sight.

The figure chuckled and said, "Hey, man," to the apparently empty elevator car.

It was Tommy.

Gaylen groaned. The adrenaline rush had hit and his heart pounded.

They moved up until they were close enough for Tommy to see them. "You scared the hell out of me," Gaylen said. "What are you doing here?"

Tommy laughed. "Are you kidding me? I wouldn't stay away if you paid me a million bucks. I want to help. This is going to be freaking fantastic."

Gaylen shook his head. "All right. So how do we get in?"

They stood in a hallway. The doors at either end had badge readers, which meant that they were secured.

Tommy grinned as he walked over to one of the doors and pulled it open with a dramatic gesture. "After you, my friends. My contact disabled the security on the doors for the evening." He sounded proud of himself. Gaylen had to grin.

The trio crept into the darkened offices.

"I gotta tell you, man, the denizens are freaking the fuck out," Tommy stage-whispered with a broad smile.

They quickly determined that there was no office door labeled "Emergency Broadcasting System," so they started checking individual offices.

"I only told a few people—I couldn't help myself—but the word has spread like crazy, and it's not stopping," Tommy continued. "The denizens have plans now, man."

Chloe had just opened a door that revealed an unusually small, bare office with computers that looked like they were of a much older vintage. They went in to look at the machines more closely.

"What kind of plans?" Chloe asked.

"Dude. The minute the broadcast goes out, they're coming topside. They're breaking cover, and they're going to fucking riot."

Chloe put one hand over her face and groaned. "Oh, great."

"What does 'riot' mean?" Gaylen asked.

"Rioting means, you know, breaking stuff," Tommy said. "Looting, breaking into places, knocking over cars. Rioting."

"Why would they do that?" Gaylen asked.

Looking at a computer sitting on the floor, Chloe said, "This is it. There's a label on this one that says EBS1."

Gaylen checked his watch again, even though he already knew that they had mere minutes remaining until the scheduled time. He pulled out the laptop with cold, trembling hands.

"Because this is the perfect moment," Tommy said. "Picture perfect."

Gaylen looked at the first instruction.

> **Step One:** Plug the laptop into the network with the blue cable, boot up the laptop, then run the "MITM" script.

"The whole damn country is going to hear the truth all at once, according to you," Tommy went on. "What better time would there be to come out guns blazing? This is exactly the time for a revolution. The riots will draw out the DAA, and we'll have a pitched battle. A war. The war we've all been waiting for."

Gaylen's eyebrows went up, and he looked at Chloe. "Drew wouldn't want that. People will get hurt. Didn't we say we didn't want all-out war?"

Chloe nodded her head.

Hesitant now, unsure whether he should continue and unsure what other choices he might have, he plugged in the laptop. They all watched the wallscreen in the room to see what happened. So far, the evening programming—the late evening Good News report—was still running uninterrupted, as it should.

He found the icon labeled "MITM" and double-clicked it. A small black window appeared and white text ran by too quickly for him to read. He could only assume that was the expected response.

He breathed deeply, trying to calm his racing heart. "Tommy, if the denizens all come topside and riot . . . how many are there?"

"Nobody knows, not even the DAA," Tommy answered, "but nationwide, it's definitely in the millions. And—"

"Millions?" Gaylen echoed, shocked. "Really?"

"Dude, there's been an underground since the twenty-twenties. Tens of thousands of people went underground before the borders were even closed, and it's been almost fifty years since then. We've got almost as many people defecting to the underground every week as getting dusted. So, yeah, at least a few million. And a lot of them are coming up tonight. Not everybody in the whole damn country, of course. But a lot. If we pull off this broadcast, it's going to go nuts out there."

Gaylen's heart skipped beats. He continued his work mechanically, not sure what else to do.

> **Step Two:** Turn on the EBS machine, slot the badge into the badge reader, and log in with the attached password.

> **Step Three:** Run the EBS software.

He took the steps, his mind going in a hundred directions at once. Then he looked at his watch. It was almost time.

"How many will die if it comes to war?" Gaylen asked.

"I don't know. A bunch of denizens, then the DAA—there's hundreds of thousands of them nationwide. Then all the sleepers caught in the crossfire. Millions? Who knows?"

Gaylen rubbed his face with his hands.

He looked down at the instructions. He was almost done.

Step Four: Click "Interrupt" button in EBS software. Wallscreens should show introductory EBS message.

Final step: Go to the laptop and run the New-Feed script. Lightbringers broadcast will begin on wallscreens.

"Depends on how long it lasts," Tommy said. "And how it ends. Does the DAA win? Or do the denizens? And if the DAA wins, how many more die? Because they will kill every damn person who can't pretend it never fucking happened. Doesn't matter if that's half the freaking population."

Gaylen's stomach turned. "They would really do that?"

Tommy shrugged. The two men stared at each other.

Chloe shifted uneasily, tugging on her dreadlocks. "Drew knows about that . . . That's how she ended up the underground. They killed every single person in a football stadium, including her family. About twenty thousand people."

Tommy nodded knowingly. "Experiments in crowd control. Why do you think they never broadcast large events live? Their biggest worry is crowd control. They spend all their time working on it. They have a ton of ways to kill a lot of people at once."

The room was quiet for a moment. Gaylen's chest tightened up so he could hardly breathe.

Tommy laughed. "You know what, it's going to drive them freaking crazy that they'll never be able to completely clean it up. Whatever happens tonight, even if we lose—they can never take it back. Every single person will know, even though they'll all pretend they don't. The DAA is going to lose their minds trying to figure out what to do about that."

"I can't believe they would kill that many people," Gaylen said.

"Have you ever talked to Deadly Shining Martha? I have, once. She's not human. She'll do whatever it takes to have her perfect society. Oh, man"—Tommy's tone was exuberant—"I wish I could see her face when she sees the broadcast. No one's ever done this before, you know. This is a coup. It's going to be amazing."

Gaylen's mouse pointer hovered over the button that read "Interrupt." If he clicked this button, the wallscreens would cease their broadcast for the first time in decades. Then one more click would allow the Lightbringers to start broadcasting their own message.

He looked down, confounded.

Tommy caught his hesitation. "What, you're worried about all those people dying? They don't matter. They're sleepers, or DAA, or else they're the denizens who are freaking starting it. They all deserve it, one way or another. And anyway, maybe we'll win. Maybe this will break the back of Martha's tyranny. A new freaking world. Just what your group wants, right?"

Gaylen glanced from desktop monitor to laptop screen, staring at the two icons that would set all this off. He remembered something Drew had once said to him: *"Could you imagine finding a place of light that would allow you to push a button that would kill a million people?"* His hands were shaking.

It seemed like a terrible idea. He couldn't go through with this, not if it would provoke war and then maybe a massacre.

But if he did nothing, then things would remain the same. His people would have died for nothing. The Lightbringers waiting in the warehouse would wait for nothing, their moment of hope extinguished.

If Gaylen clicked these two buttons, a thousand things would move into motion—beyond his control, but toward change. Toward death and brutality, maybe, but change. There was hope in change.

How many people was he willing to kill for that hope?

Certain he looked as lost as he felt, he turned to Chloe. "What should I do?"

She looked at him wide-eyed and slowly shook her head, her dreadlocks swinging back and forth. "I don't know . . . Everyone's path is their own, Drew says. I don't think I can decide for you."

"Would you do it?"

"I don't know. I wouldn't know unless I was you, and I'm not you, and . . . and I won't be you unless you die and I have to take your place."

Gaylen looked back at the computers.

"Come on," Tommy said. He sounded alarmed that Gaylen might not do it. "Come on, do it! What are you waiting for?"

Gaylen closed his eyes and went inward.

A myriad of images coursed through his mind. He remembered faces, voices, and images from the denizens, the prisoners they had freed, and the Lightbringers. What Nick had first told him in the underground. Drew's words, flowing over him like water. Memories of over thirty years of nonstop wallscreen viewings—the interminable Good News reports, the vacuous family shows, the morning messages from President Martha. What Tommy had just said about talking to her in person echoed through his mind. And then a simple but shocking thought occurred to him.

Enthralled by the possibility he had found, he turned toward Tommy and said slowly, "The DAA won't fight if President Martha tells them not to."

Tommy blinked at him. The wheels turning in his head were practically visible. "What are you saying?"

"Has anyone ever tried to get to President Martha herself before?"

"I don't know," Tommy said. "Probably. Are you insane? Surely they have her guarded. The whole place guarded. It's the White House!"

"We're *invisible*," Gaylen said. "Drew said they won't have found a way around the cloaking devices yet. We can walk right in and carry her out with us, bring her to our live feed, force her to make a statement, keep the DAA in check. Maybe, together, we can even convince the denizens not to riot at all. Maybe we can come to some other kind of agreement." Chills went up his spine.

Tommy shook his head. "I don't know, man. Look, I can help you from here, but . . . dude, you've lost your mind. You're on your own."

Gaylen nodded. "All right," he said. He swallowed hard.

Chloe's eyes were wide again.

"Chloe, I won't ask you to come with me," Gaylen said. "Tommy's right—it's insane. But I can't do this"—he gestured at the computer screens in front of them—"if it just gets all those people killed. Tommy, stay here, finish the process when I call, OK?"

The other man nodded.

"Chloe, you go back, report to Drew what I'm doing. Tell her what we learned. Tell her it will be an hour or two before I bring Martha back. And . . . if she thinks I made the wrong call, then tell her I'm sorry. Tell her I thought I was doing the right thing."

Nick scuttled along, low to the ground, like a cockroach racing away from fluorescent light. He had no money cards, no handscreen, and none of his thugs to help. He was injured and lost. And he was topside, with beautiful New Americans hitting "Request Assistance" buttons everywhere he looked. He knew he only had a matter of minutes before the DAA showed up.

He was confident that these houses were unlocked, but he hated the idea of taking cover in a house. Without an entrance to the underground, he'd feel like a cornered rabbit. But he didn't know where the nearest entrance to the underground was. He ran down the sidewalk, hoping to see a side street with no pedestrians.

Nick was an adrenaline junkie, and there was adrenaline in fear, but it didn't feel good. Fear was unfamiliar and awful. He spent most of his waking hours making sure that he never had a goddamn thing to be afraid of. Now, his heart was racing, and he felt like he couldn't breathe, not even considering his broken ribs. He kept looking behind him. His face was twisted and he couldn't smooth it out.

He guessed at which way to go, and turned left at the next stop sign, knowing that any decision he made could be the one that got him killed or imprisoned. He passed a young woman who was jogging with headphones on. When she saw him, she stopped running so suddenly that she nearly fell over her own feet. He snarled at her and kept going. He looked behind him again. Still, only confused and upset people were in his wake. No one followed him purposefully.

He ran straight for three more blocks. By then, he was so breathless and in so much pain that he could hardly keep moving. He'd been in lousy shape to begin with. Black spots danced in his peripheral vision, and his ulcer stabbed at him.

He forced himself to keep moving, despite the risk of passing out. He turned right at an intersection and nearly ran over an older couple. They broke apart and stared after him with shock on their faces.

Finally, a side street without people. He turned and ran hard another block, making sure no one was watching, and then ran up to the nearest house. The doorknob turned in his hand. He opened the door and lurched inside. He slammed the door behind him. Two middle-aged women—a redhead and brunette—sat on a sofa in the living room, watching the wallscreen. They saw Nick at the same time. Their eyes widened and their jaws dropped almost in sync. The redhead started to rise.

Nick grabbed them each by an arm, pulled them off the sofa, and threw them into a corner near the wallscreen, out of its viewing range. He pressed them against the wall and slapped them both. Both cried out. "Get on the wallscreen!" he screamed. "Bring up a map. Now!"

Both women looked shocked. Likely, no one had ever spoken so harshly to them in all their lives. They had probably never been hit before. The redhead recovered first and moved to the wallscreen. Her hands shook, but she pulled up the menu and then the local map.

The brunette was sobbing, and Nick slapped her again. "Shut up!" he yelled.

Her face expressionless, the redhead looked at Nick for instructions. Nick edged close enough to the viewing angle of the screen to see where he was. "Zoom out," he demanded. The woman did so.

After a few moments, Nick figured out exactly where he was in the city and knew he could make it to the nearest entrance to the underground—if he was lucky. He ducked toward the window and peered through the blinds as he clutched his ribs. He cursed. A handful of nondescript men walked purposefully down the street.

He had to hope that they weren't watching the wallscreens in the houses on this street yet. He grabbed the brunette's arm and forced her at a run into the hall closet—there were no wallscreens in small closets—where he joined her and threw her to the floor. He turned back to the redhead, who still stood in front of the wallscreen. "You tell them you haven't seen anything. You make it believable or I'll kill you and rape your corpse."

She nodded, her face blank.

Nick shut the closet door and slapped his hand over the brunette's mouth to stifle her sobs. He tried to catch his breath, as he was in such pain and his heart pounded so hard that he felt close to passing out. He wrapped his other arm around his chest.

He had made it just in time; the wallscreen interrupted its evening broadcast.

"Good evening!" a chipper male voice said. "President Martha likes for us to check in on folks every so often just to make sure everyone is as happy as can be. How are you doing? Is everything great?"

The redhead answered smoothly. "Oh, yes, everything's great." She sounded just a little breathless. Nick imagined her smoothing down her hair and smiling at the man on the screen as she sat down on the sofa. "It's so nice of you to check in."

"Did you have work or school today?" the wallscreen voice asked.

"Oh, I had work," she said. "It was a nice day at the Bureau of Entertainment. I've been packaging baby toys—such a pleasant job!"

"Of course," the voice agreed. "Where are your roommates?"

"Sarah's—she's just changing clothes," the woman said. Nick caught the hesitation in the lie, but he thought it was smooth enough that the wallscreen operator probably hadn't. "She just had an early bath."

"That's nice." The voice sounded approving and happy.

Meanwhile, the brunette looked at Nick with wide eyes. She was listening to the exchange in the living room. Gradually, she took on the look of someone who was about to try something stupid. Nick had seen that look enough times to recognize it anywhere.

He started throttling her. People who are suffocating don't do stupid things. She kicked and flailed, making a couple of slight banging noises against the walls and door. Once he had adjusted his position to where his body was pressing down all of her limbs, he choked her harder.

The conversation stopped in the other room and the wallscreen resumed its normal programming. But Nick didn't trust them not to still be watching and listening. To her credit, the redhead stayed on the couch and kept watching the evening Good News report, awaiting further instruction.

Nick let the woman under him pass out. It was easier to deal with her that way.

He tried to calm down. His hands were shaking. His whole body was shaking. He wanted a cigarette about like a junkie wanted heroin. The pain was unrelenting. He needed pills.

When he couldn't stand to wait any longer, he opened the closet door. "Go check outside," he snapped at the redhead.

She got up and looked through the blinds. "I don't see anyone."

"Good," Nick said.

He ducked back into the living room, into the corner, out of the wallscreen's range. He glanced back. The brunette was half-spilling out of the closet. She looked dead, though Nick knew she wasn't. Now the redhead was looking at her roommate, her hands over her mouth.

Nick spat out the few words that would ensure that the redhead never reported this: "Just remember this is all your fault. You must have wanted this on some level, or you wouldn't have attracted it into your life."

She stared at him, her hands still over her mouth. Nick loved this part of New America. Victims who blamed themselves—it was the perfect world for criminals.

"If you hit the 'Request Assistance' button, that's what they're gonna tell you, too, and you know it. So you better forget about me, or I might be back someday, and that'll be your fault, too."

The woman lowered her hands. "I'm a tourist," she said, her voice strained.

"What?" Nick was taken aback. "Oh, well, *la dee* fucking *dah*."

"It means I know better," she said, her voice taking on a harder edge.

This one had some backbone. He got in her face. "So what? You turn me in and I will *kill you*."

"No, because you'll be in a DAA meat locker," she said, her voice flat.

Nick slapped her hard, the movement sending pain shooting through his whole chest.

She took the blow in stride and smiled. Her jaw was set.

Damn.

"Now get out of my house," she said. Her eyes were intense and cold.

This wasn't like it had been in the basement earlier, where he could relax and let go and use the pain to his advantage. He had to keep thinking and planning, keep on top of things, move fast, and the pain and fear was getting in his way. He couldn't think straight anymore. For the life of him, he couldn't figure out what to do with this damned woman, and he couldn't risk wasting any more time with her.

He snarled at her and then ran out of the house.

By the time he made it to the nearest underground entrance, he was trying to shake two teams of DAA agents. But once he was there, it was easy. He'd spent his life avoiding the DAA underground.

Once he'd found a corner to hide in and the DAA was well out of his way, he sank to the ground. He had come too close to being captured—closer than he had ever come. He was still shaking. He still couldn't breathe properly. He realized, with shock, that he was close to tears.

He left his corner and stalked the hallways in search of drugs. He grabbed every low-life denizen he encountered and screamed at them for drugs, until one scrawny kid with a shaved head yelled, "OK, OK, I got some in my bag!"

The kid knelt to open his backpack and pulled out an assortment of plastic bags. "What do you need, man?" He looked scared, but he had evidently seen enough junkies in withdrawal to know that this was just part of the cost of doing business.

"Something for pain," Nick said, his voice rasping.

The kid dug through the bags until he found the right one and shook out a handful of small purple pills. Nick recognized them. They were strong, and he'd only have some disorientation and dizziness. He swallowed the whole handful, which was difficult—his tongue was still torn up from when he'd bitten it open earlier. He shoved the kid to the ground and staggered away.

He paced the hallways at random while he waited for the medicine to kick in.

He had not been so humiliated in years. He had never had a woman throw him out of her space. He could not believe that that big bastard had come out victorious. That Mikey had betrayed him. They had made him afraid. They had made him run. He would never forget that. Never.

The tears threatened to come back, and that made it worse.

As he regained control, the wolf inside began to return to him, more fierce and bloodthirsty than he had ever known it. Only the pain pills took the edge off enough that he didn't start attacking everyone he ran across in the hallways. As it was, the tourists and denizens he passed gave him a wide berth, as if they could see the predator inside him snapping its teeth. Hungry for vengeance, the wolf propelled him onward.

He resolved to find the Lightbringers, to find that big bastard and make him pay back every drop of blood and sweat. He knew it would be wiser to wait until he had healed up, but he could not wait. The wolf would not wait.

Chapter Sixteen

Drew Ashling, Lightbringer:

*When Martha tells you not to indulge yourself in your nega-
tive emotions, she's telling you the right thing. But then she
doesn't tell you what the alternative is—she doesn't tell you
how to deal with those emotions. She just wants you to cover
them up. And that doesn't work. She did us all a serious
injustice when she made certain emotions wrong, but then
didn't tell us what to do with them.*

It was 9:45 in the evening when Gaylen finally stepped, cloaked, into the large master bedroom of the White House.

He was tired and his muscles trembled from the tension of creeping silently through hallways and stairways. Gaylen had under-estimated the size of the White House considerably. He guessed that there were over a hundred rooms, and he felt like he had found most of them before he finally found the president's residential rooms. He had been surprised and amused to discover a one-lane bowling alley along the way.

There were a lot of household staff and a large number of busy people whose purposes Gaylen could not easily identify, and he'd had to move quietly and carefully. The whole process had been far more taxing and time-consuming than he had naively expected.

In the end, however, he had found his quarry. She sat on an overstuffed chair, wearing a chestnut-brown dressing gown that matched her eyes and hair, reading a novel on her handscreen with a glass of red wine nearby.

Her face was not quite as perfect in person as it appeared on the wallscreens. She looked slightly older as well.

She looked up when her door opened, and her eyes narrowed when she did not see a person enter, though the door closed again.

Gaylen approached quietly. He took a moment to look her over while he thought about what he knew of her. Given all that he had learned in the past week about New America, he could not see Martha in the same way he once had. Kevin and Chloe had assured him that she meant every word of her own teachings. He wasn't sure if that was more upsetting than if she had been playing some elaborate joke on them all.

Gaylen's heart pounded in his ears, and his hands shook almost like a frightened bird. Still, he raised his weapon, made sure it was set to stun, and then fired at Martha. Her eyelashes fluttered closed, and she tilted forward, dropping her handscreen.

Quickly, Gaylen moved forward and picked her up, hardly able to believe what he was doing. He had his nation's greatest cultural and political icon right here in his arms. Her body felt warmer and heavier than he had expected. She had a slight scent of roses.

His whole body shaking from adrenaline and fatigue, he went through the painstaking process of moving back through the hallways of the White House, this time slowed by his weighty burden.

Then he headed through the city toward where the Lightbringers would be waiting to make their broadcast.

He couldn't believe he'd pulled it off. He wondered where it would go wrong—what he was missing. It couldn't be this easy, could it?

When Nick recognized the girl with the purple dreadlocks walking ahead of him in an underground tunnel, glee broke through his rage and pain, and he grinned. Fate had sent her to him. She was one of Drew's smug little hangers-on—the perfect target for his rage.

He followed her topside. They emerged in one of the deserted areas of the city, an abandoned warehouse district turned into an extension of the underground. Nick trailed her at a careful distance, playing out his intentions in his mind to whet his appetite. When he found a baseball bat lying abandoned in a field, he grinned again and picked it up. It was too perfect.

He waited until they were in an alley between two warehouses, and then he picked up his pace to catch up to her. The painkillers worked well, and the remaining pain took a back seat to the glorious anticipation.

When the girl heard the sound of his footsteps behind her, she turned. He thrilled at the fear that registered in her eyes.

He wound up and struck her on the upper arm with the baseball bat. She yelped and staggered and turned to run. He lunged after her. His next blow crashed solidly into her right hip, and she fell.

He began to beat her as savagely as his own broken ribs would allow, although the huge dose of painkillers allowed him to work almost as if he were uninjured.

At first, her look was one of terror. She screamed. She tried and failed to fend him off with arms that were shattered by the force of his blows. Tears of pain ran down her face as she tried to crawl away on broken hands. It was all of Nick's favorite things.

But when she rolled over onto her back and looked up at him, he saw something unexpected in her expression. It was a look of resolve. She wasn't afraid anymore. She wasn't afraid to face him, and she was letting him know it.

He snarled at her and redoubled his efforts to break every bone in her body. He put into the beating every ounce of hatred and rage he had for every person who had ever offended him. She cried out, and she wept, but always, her eyes came back to his. And her gaze said that this wasn't about her at all. It was about him.

Her clear, unflinching witness of his brutality sapped his rage and nudged him toward a long-unknown feeling—shame. And without his rage to mask them, the pain and fatigue and shame had free reign. He couldn't keep going, physically or emotionally, and the painkillers added to his sense of disorientation.

He staggered backward and leaned on the baseball bat, panting, and stared at his victim. She lay on the ground, her injuries impossible to survive, her breathing labored. But she still looked at him with her one good eye.

It took him a while to register that the look was compassion. This girl felt *sorry* for him.

The realization twisted his stomach so that he nearly retched. He was the one with the power. He was the one in control.

He dropped to his knees and put his hands around her throat. He squeezed, staring her in the eyes all the while. He would put out that light. He would watch until it burned out, until the compassion was gone, until he had killed it, and then—

And then—

Then he was sobbing as he squeezed, every part of his body and soul hurting exquisitely, unbearably.

Then he heard footsteps, and he tore himself away from the girl with the dreadlocks and hid himself, trying to stifle his sobs, wild with some kind of grief he could not understand.

John Oldman stood with thirty-three escaped convicts at the base of a flight of stairs in the underground. Everyone panted from the long run. John let them catch their breath while he checked on Sierra.

As soon as she saw him, the little girl asked, "When do I get to see Mommy and Daddy?"

Unfortunately, this was about as far as John's planning had gone.

He looked into the little girl's hopeful eyes and knew that he had made an idiotic mistake in saying that both of her parents had sent him to get her. It would break her heart all over again if he didn't reunite her with both of her parents now. Yet what right did he have to put Serena and Gaylen back into contact with one another?

He sighed. One thing at a time. He certainly had to put her back together with at least one of her parents, and since she had been living with her mother most recently, that seemed to be the logical first step.

First, he put the green-haired boy in charge of the NCPs and directed him to take them to the Lightbringers' safe house. It seemed the safest course of action for them. The Lightbringers would break the truth to them much more gently than any denizen would. Maybe they could find them all new lives.

Then he took Sierra's hand and set off toward Serena's house.

When she had taken Sierra and left Gaylen, Serena had moved to the extreme end of town, beyond several checkpoints. John was afraid to go through them with his escaped NCP, so they went by foot through the underground.

By the time they got there, John was beyond exhausted, and his knees hurt so much, he could hardly think of anything else. The adrenaline that had been fueling him had long ago worn off, and every step was a test of endurance.

He hesitated at the nearest intersection to Serena's house. Was it so simple as to walk up and ring the doorbell? He tried to think of what he might have been missing.

He realized in retrospect that it was lucky he'd rescued so many people. Had he taken only Sierra, it would have implicated Serena. The DAA might have been here already, interrogating her. But now they had no particular reason to be here.

He remembered the words from Serena's file: *Watch list. Checks every five days until November 31, 2079.* Were such checks made in person or by wallscreen?

Sierra tugged at his sleeve. "Are we lost?"

"No, honey. Just thinking for a minute."

Try as he might, he couldn't think of any reason for the DAA to observe watch-listed NCPs in person.

A few minutes later, he rang the doorbell of Serena's house. The door opened, a beautiful, tall black woman appeared at the threshold, and Sierra shrieked, "Mommy!" Then the two were hugging, both of them crying.

John took a few steps back, to give them privacy. He scanned the street. Still no sign of any reason to worry.

Finally, the woman looked up at him. "Who are you? Where's her grandmother?"

Grandmother. Cute. So that's what Sierra's postcard had said. Grandma had probably been dusted decades ago.

"I'm John Oldman, ma'am, and I'm . . . with the government. I'm here to return Sierra to you. But we need to talk over a few things. Can you come with me, please?"

"Of course. Just let me get my purse. Come with me, Sierra." The two disappeared into the house.

John waited impatiently. It seemed to take forever before they came back, but finally

they emerged, and Serena shut the door behind them. As they walked down the sidewalk, she scanned the street, and then, seeming confused, she asked, "Do you have a car with you, Mr. Oldman?"

"No, actually . . . let's just walk a little way and I'll explain things. There's really no hurry."

Now, how in the world was he going to explain this?

Still carrying President Martha's unconscious body, Gaylen entered the warehouse from which the Lightbringers would be broadcasting.

The place was full of denizens, former prisoners, and revolutionaries, all in that uncomfortable state of suspense between bored idleness and eager waiting. The camera was set up, and everyone was ready to go at a moment's notice.

When Gaylen appeared, all eyes turned to him and the room fell silent as they saw the body over his shoulder. Drew, who had been sitting up against a wall, leaped to her feet. Any words she had been preparing to say died in her throat as she saw President Martha.

Gaylen lifted Martha's body off his shoulder and lay her on a nearby table. Her beautiful dressing gown was in marked contrast to the squalor of the warehouse, her soft, lightly tanned skin in contrast to the rough attire of the denizens who had rejected perfection and beauty.

"Is that really—" someone asked.

"Yes," Gaylen said. "Just stunned. We need her. Did Chloe tell you?" He looked around for the girl with the purple dreadlocks.

"No, tell us what?" Drew answered.

The others were crowding around, looking at Martha's body with fascination.

"Chloe isn't here? I sent her here . . ." Gaylen looked around again.

"No," Drew said. "I sent Kevin after both of you when you didn't—"

The door opened again, behind Gaylen. Drew's face froze in horror, and she began to run toward the door. Gaylen turned and looked, too, and his heart stopped.

Kevin carried Chloe in his arms. She was covered in blood, and her limbs hung awkwardly. It was clear at a glance that she was devastatingly injured.

Gaylen and Drew both ran to them, but Kevin motioned them aside. He barely glanced at President Martha's unconscious body on the table. "Move her," he ordered.

A couple of Lightbringers moved Martha away, and Kevin lowered Chloe to the table. She moaned, her voice garbled by the blood in her throat.

Gaylen stepped forward, looking at her body, seeing and not wanting to see, wanting to hold her and terrified to touch her.

Drew took her left hand, and Gaylen took her right one.

"I've given her a shot of painkillers and a shot of sedative," Kevin said quietly.

Her one good eye focused on him. "Gaylen?" she murmured. Her voice rasped as if she had been screaming.

"Yes," he said. "I'm here. I'm here, Chloe." His eyes filled with tears.

She looked at him again and tried to smile.

Gaylen couldn't find the words to ask what had happened or who had hurt her. "The doctor," he said to Kevin. "The one who healed me and Drew. Where is he? How do we get her there?"

She shook her head slowly. "No," she whispered. "Too late."

Kevin shook his head, too. His jaw was clenched, his eyes tight.

Gaylen looked at Drew. "No . . . please . . ." He wouldn't let it be too late.

Drew shook her head, too, and tears ran down her face.

Chloe turned her head and a rush of blood came out of her mouth. She fought for breath and gave him a look that said that arguing was pointless. His heart sank..

She smiled slightly and said, "I did good. I stayed in the light. I even found . . . I found compassion . . ."

Tears ran down both their faces. Gaylen wiped hers away. "I'm proud of you, Chloe. You're such a . . . such a *good* person." Gently stroking her cheek, he tried to smile at her.

"We love you, Chloe," Drew said gently.

Kevin visibly fought back tears as he said, "Yes, we do." He put his hand on her shoulder.

Chloe shuddered and tried to breathe. She swallowed, shifted, got another breath, and then whispered, "I should have told you before . . . Gaylen . . ."

"Shhhh," he whispered. "It's OK . . ."

"I should have told you . . . I was falling . . . falling in love with you . . . Gaylen . . ."

The words hit him hard. For a moment, he closed his eyes. He thought back over the awkward moments they'd had and her distance with him recently. It all made sense now. She'd rejected him only because she'd known that he didn't feel the same way . . . at least, not yet.

And now, not ever.

He said, "I'm sorry, Chloe. I didn't realize. I didn't understand. I'm an idiot." He'd missed what was right in front of him.

She grinned a little. "S'OK," she said again.

She said no more, and her breath came harder and harder and she began to cry and writhe with the agony and effort of trying to breathe. Both Drew and Gaylen held her hands until she suddenly convulsed, and then she died.

Gaylen held her body and sobbed.

He wanted to protect and comfort her, even though she wasn't there anymore. More than that, he wanted to turn back the days and relive them and this time take advantage of every possible moment with the sweet, pretty girl with the purple dreadlocks. He wanted another chance. And most of all, he wanted to have saved her—to have spared her this ending.

He stayed present and experienced every hard emotion that ran through him, as Drew had taught him when she grieved for Mercy. He was in a sort of darkness he had never encountered before—a rich, profound, multi-layered darkness. The light surrounded both him and the darkness, waiting for him to re-emerge.

Standing just outside the warehouse door, Nick listened to Chloe's death against his will. Every word added up to break down his mind by degrees. As the Lightbringers' grief ran its course, tears ran down Nick's face, too, but for some other reason he could not fathom. All he knew was that he had been pushed over some edge he hadn't even known existed. He felt like a hysterical lost child and a rabid wild beast pressed into one soul that could not endure either one of them. He had to do something. He had to make the pain stop.

And so, as someone drew a jacket over Chloe's still body and the Lightbringers regrouped, murmuring words of sorrow and regret, Nick stepped into the warehouse with his gun drawn.

When Gaylen saw him, Nick already had an old-fashioned revolver aimed at Drew's head from only a few feet away.

Gaylen shouted, "Drew! Look out!"

Drew looked around and saw Nick. She looked confused for a moment. She wiped away tears.

Nick looked insane—exhausted, stiff, wild-eyed, his face twisted with hatred.

Around them, the room fell silent again as the they saw what was happening. Gaylen and most of the Lightbringers pulled their weapons and trained them on Nick.

Nick said to Drew, "You think you know something, but you don't know anything. You think you're special. You are *nothing*. You are *no one*. We don't need you in our world." His gun was still pointed at Drew's face.

Suddenly, Gaylen realized what had happened to Chloe.

Drew looked at Nick for a long moment, and it seemed that she had come to the same realization that Gaylen had. She bowed her head and closed her eyes for a moment, wiping her face again.

"Look at me, bitch!" Nick screamed.

A moment went by before Drew raised her head and looked at him. Her eyes were weary, her face resigned. She spoke slowly, patiently. "Nick, you can kill me—you can kill us all, one by one—but you cannot kill the light. It will always be inside you, always telling you that who you have become and what you have done is deeply, deeply wrong. And you know it. And you will never *stop* knowing it."

Emotions ran across Nick's face—anger, fear, pain, fear again. "You have no right," he said. "You are *no one*—"

"We are the light," Drew said. "You will never be free of us."

Nick's weapon wavered and his face twisted.

"But you can always embrace it," Drew said. She took one step toward him. "It is never too late to step out of the darkness, out of what you have—"

Nick screamed, "Shut it! Shut up, you worthless, useless—!" His hand, and the revolver he held, trembled.

Gaylen stepped up quietly behind Nick, just out of the other man's peripheral vision.

"Shoot him!" someone screamed from behind him.

"No!" Gaylen shouted to the men and women around him. He had seen that Nick's finger was on his trigger. If anyone shot him, he might pull the trigger either deliberately or reflexively.

Nick started laughing. The laughter had an unhinged, wild quality to it. It was so rough and raw that it made Gaylen's throat hurt just to hear it. Then the laughter twisted and contorted into raw, naked sobs, painful to watch and hear. Nick staggered back and forth, his gun still pointed at Drew, as he vacillated between crying and laughing. Twice he lunged at someone in the circle around him, making them flinch and jump back. And then he stopped, screamed wordlessly, and, not even looking at Drew, pulled the trigger and shot her.

Gaylen saw it as if in slow motion. Drew jerked as the old-fashioned bullet struck her on the left side of her chest, spilling blood. Her green eyes unfocused, shifting from weariness to confusion, and then closed, and she collapsed in a crumpled heap.

All around them, gunfire erupted. Nick jerked and spasmed as dozens of beams and bullets struck him, and then he fell unmoving to the concrete floor.

Gaylen rushed to Drew. Others gathered around them as well, faces drawn and somber. The room had fallen silent for a second time. Nick's body went ignored.

Kneeling beside Drew, Gaylen turned her over carefully and touched her face. He knew immediately that the light had already left her body. He fell back into a seated position and stared into space. *Too much death. Too much.*

A long moment passed in silence, with all heads bowed in mourning. Then Kevin stepped up. Gaylen hardly processed his words. "My friends. I hate to ask you to do anything right now other than mourn, because you deserve the chance to mourn. But for now, the best way to honor them is to complete the mission that they died trying to accomplish. That mission awaits us right now, and it is time-sensitive. We must step up."

Around the room, heads reluctantly nodded.

Two Lightbringers came forward and gently, respectfully carried the women's bodies to the side, where they would be safe, and covered them. Two more carried Nick's body to a separate area and covered it as well.

"Gaylen."

It was Kevin again. The stocky man knelt down and looked at Gaylen intently. "Are you with me?"

Gaylen nodded reluctantly. He wanted to be anywhere but here. Here was a place so full of grief he could hardly bear it. But he nodded.

"Gaylen, you brought President Martha here. What's the plan?"

At first, Gaylen could hardly marshal coherent thought, let alone explain the plan. But he found himself stumbling through what Tommy had told him about the riots and the war and the DAA massacring everyone who couldn't be trusted to "forget" if the denizens lost and were driven back underground.

Kevin listened carefully, and then said, "You're the one with the plan. And you brought in Martha. No small thing. You take over from here, when you're ready." He offered him a bottle of water, which Gaylen gratefully took and drank.

He glanced again at the two slender bodies on the floor. It was the most outrageously unfair thing he could imagine, that these two women should have died while he still lived. He had to finish this, for them.

He went to President Martha, carried her to a chair and propped her up in it, and pointed the camera at her and turned it on. He called Tommy on Kevin's handscreen—they had no reason for secrecy now that everything was about to unfold—and told him to click the two icons to begin the transmission. And then he shook Martha awake.

Chapter Seventeen

Drew Ashling, Lightbringer:

I share with the denizens a love of individuality. I, too, believe that each person is sacrosanct, that he must make his own choices, that every path is individual. But the Lightbringers also teach that one must discover one's own conscience, in order to judge what is good or bad for one to do, for the sake of one's own well-being and clarity and strength. The denizens have no regard for the conscience and see no point in value judgments. That is where we differ.

John, Serena, and Sierra walked through the city, a couple of blocks from Serena's street. So far, Sierra and Serena had done most of the talking. John had explained only that Sierra had not gone to her grandmother, but that the government had taken her in to help her with missing her father.

"You missed Daddy that much?" Serena had asked, shocked.

Sierra had only nodded, evidently afraid of getting into trouble again, and clung to her mother.

"Well, I missed you, baby," Serena had said, hugging her daughter closely, her voice breaking. "Way more than I had ever imagined I could. I'm so glad to see you. I don't ever want to let you go again."

Now it was nearly eleven o'clock in the evening. Maybe thirty other people were on the street with John, Serena, and Sierra, going to or from a club or bar or restaurant. All of them were beautiful, young, and healthy. It was the perfection of New America.

Everything was calm, the air chilly but fresh and clear, the city beautiful. The evening broadcast was in the midst of Patriot Hour, which recapped glorious moments in American history. At the moment, it was the story of the Old Revolution, in which the United States of America had peacefully cast off the shackles of British rule by thinking of freedom and nothing else.

Then something happened that had never happened before, not in the memory of any living American. The wallscreens turned off—all of them.

Everyone stopped and stared. The silence was deafening.

A long series of beeps came through the speakers, and then the screens all lit up again and displayed the message, "Emergency Broadcasting System Activated."

A serious male voice said, "Your attention please. The Emergency Broadcasting System has been activated. This is not a—"

The wallscreens changed again. John recognized the man on the screen immediately.

"My fellow New Americans, my name is Gaylen Andrews, and I am a Lightbringer. And I have something to share with you all."

"Daddy!" Sierra cried out.

Serena's hand was over her mouth in shock.

The camera panned over to someone who looked like President Martha, but disheveled, groggy, and in her dressing gown, and in some dark, empty space—it looked almost like a warehouse. And Gaylen was pointing a gun at her.

Only John reacted to the gun. No one else knew what it was. But they did stare in alarm at President Martha's appearance.

"Are you President Martha St. Tala of New America?" Gaylen asked, trying to keep his voice steady. He wanted her to admit her identity so that no one could claim later that this broadcast was fake.

"Of course I am." She smoothed down her hair and sat up straight, her gaze sharpening by the moment. Without the smile she normally wore, this woman was intimidating. What Tommy had called her—Deadly Shining Martha—made sense now. She didn't even look at his gun.

"President Martha, this broadcast is going out to all of New America live, right now." He pointed at the camera with its red blinking light. "And before we begin, there's something we need to get out of the way.

"I happen to know that the denizens of the underground are about to come out and start rioting all across the country. And I need you to tell the DAA not to engage them, or we will be faced with an all-out war with far too many dead."

"No," Martha said crisply.

Gaylen froze, uncomprehending. "What do you mean, no?"

"I don't know what you're talking about, and I don't think it's of any interest to me. I will certainly play no part in it." Her gaze pierced him.

Gaylen waved his gun at her. "I would just like to point out that I'm holding a weapon here. I'm threatening you with this weapon. This thing is dangerous."

"I acknowledge nothing of the sort." She still did not look at the gun.

"I am *threatening* you. I can *hurt* you with this."

"No, you can't." It was a statement of fact. "Bring around a car to take me home." She settled herself in her chair and waited for compliance, not even looking at Gaylen.

Gaylen lowered the weapon. After all this, she could simply tell him no.

"Threats aren't going to work on you, are they?" he asked.

"No," she said.

He knew in his bones that she was right. His plan was not going to work. He had underestimated her.

For a brief moment, he almost wished he was an ordinary denizen who was willing to hurt her to force her to cooperate. But he also remembered Chloe's death, and he remembered Nick's photographs on his wall in his office and how Nick had demanded that he do something "despicable" in their first meeting, and he knew that he couldn't hurt someone like that. He was a Lightbringer. He was Gaylen.

He took a deep breath and looked at Martha again. Did she know all this about him somehow? "Why aren't you afraid?" he asked her.

"Because no harm can come to me," she replied, her expression calm. "I don't believe that you are any threat, and so you *are* no threat. Have you never learned any of the lessons I have taught you in positive thinking?"

She spoke as if she had personally instructed him. Perhaps she thought of all New Americans in that way.

"You're wrong," he said. "There are threats whether you believe in them or not." He had learned this many times in the past week.

"No," she said crisply. "Anything you experience, you have allowed. If you think you are experiencing something you do not want, it is only because your mind slipped while you were not paying enough attention. It requires discipline, son, but that is all. Then the world bends to your will."

"I'm not sure I'm bending to your will right now," he said. "You really think you 'allowed' this experience?" He waved his weapon at her.

"Yes," she said. "And my mind is quite disciplined. So since I have let you into my reality, it is for a purpose that is to my benefit."

Gaylen looked at her, stymied. Her confidence, the power she so casually represented, was absolute.

This woman, with her perfectionistic dogma, had perpetuated the society that had forced him to become a criminal and an outcast, that had hunted him down and attacked him. Because of her, people he knew and had grown to love had been hurt and killed. He had every right to hate every word President Martha St. Tala said.

Even if her teachings were true, he did not want them to be true. He did not want to believe that every miserable thing he had witnessed in these past days had been his fault—his co-creation with Chloe and Drew and Mercy and Nick and the others.

But he also remembered what Drew had told him so recently: *"There are no bad guys."* He tried to remember that it was true even for President Martha. She believed that she was in the right.

"DAA!" someone shouted from near a window.

Gaylen's heartbeat doubled. They had expected an attack, but not nearly this quickly. Something had gone wrong.

Kevin gave orders, his voice as calm as ever. "Delta Team, get ready. Five of you, stay on Gaylen and Martha, keep the transmission going as long as you can. The rest, with me."

Meanwhile, Gaylen examined what was happening in his body and mind. *Anger. This is called anger.* And resentment. And hatred.

He recognized his desire to lash out. He recognized the sickness of it. And he waited for the feelings to pass, even as Martha watched him and waited without expression.

In time, the feelings passed, and calm returned. Staring at Martha all the while, he then stepped from the darkness of helplessness into the light of power, and let it encompass him.

Martha continued to meet his gaze, undaunted.

It suddenly occurred to him to wonder, was President Martha in the light? He looked at her, at her perfection and her confidence, dressed in her lovely chestnut-brown dressing gown, her hands folded neatly in her lap—even while sitting on a plastic chair in a dark, dirty warehouse with a terrorist holding a gun on her.

"The darkness will never go away," Drew had said to him earlier. *"The harder you try to banish it, the more power you give it. The more you fight it, the more you fear it—and the more strength your fear gives it."*

He said, "Underneath, you must be afraid all the time. Even if you can never admit it."

She said nothing.

Gunshots and shouts came from outside the building. The five Lightbringers still in the room stepped outside to see their enemies coming. Then an unfamiliar noise—a rapid *ch-ch-ch-ch* sound—approached from the sky. Gaylen was almost out of time.

"Is it true that you don't even know about the DAA?" he asked. "Or the underground?"

Martha still said nothing.

"So, let me tell you something that you don't want to hear." He looked at the camera. "None of you will want to hear this, but you need to. You need to know the truth." He looked back at Martha. "There are secret prisons in this country where thousands of people are held against their will because they got sick or old or were too unhappy. And there is a secret police that executes hundreds of New Americans every day just because of those 'crimes.' What do you think about that?"

"I acknowledge nothing of the sort. You are not thinking correctly, that much is obvious. And your mental poison is only going to infect others if you don't stop immediately."

The *ch-ch-ch-ch* sound hovered over the building. More screams, more gunfire. The doors to the warehouse closed, and Gaylen and President Martha were alone together.

"Listen to me, young man," Martha said. "Abandon everything you are doing, this minute. Let go of this foolishness. Embrace correct thinking as you should as a good citizen of this perfect country. You are only doing a disservice to others with your wild untruths, upsetting them."

She looked directly at the camera. "My fellow New Americans, my dear children. You have nothing to fear, and neither do I. None of us do. Our lives are exactly the utopia that they appear to be. What is reality but what you see around you every moment? Simply look around."

A foreboding silence had fallen outside.

A door opened, and a nondescript man in a gray suit stepped in cautiously. He took in the scene at a glance, including the camera, and he seemed to choose his words carefully. "Ma'am, we've . . . handled the situation. And we've brought around a car for you."

Martha smiled.

Gaylen's heart sank.

"Shall we . . . take care of this one?" The man gestured toward Gaylen.

"No," she answered. "I have this under control."

The man closed the door behind him as he left.

"Time to walk away, son," Martha said. "Go think properly again until you're feeling better. And stop causing such trouble to others with your nonsense. This is not what productive citizens do."

She turned toward the camera again. "You see, this is what happens when you don't think properly. You cause all sorts of problems for others. Nothing good can come of it. One must focus on what is good and right in the world, always."

"No," Gaylen said quietly.

"Son, we've heard enough from you."

"No. No, you haven't. You really haven't."

His breath came hard. He was reaching a conclusion he could not escape, even as he wished he could. He couldn't hurt her, but . . . He remembered Drew's question again: *"Could you imagine finding a place of light that would allow you to push a button that would kill a million people?"* And he asked himself, *could I find a place of light that would allow me to pull a trigger that kills just one?*

Sweat trickled down his back.

He was out of time. If he walked away now, then Drew and Chloe and many others would have died in vain. Their coup—using the broadcasting system in this way—could never be used again. They might never have this chance again. And with every day that passed, more people died to serve a fanatical vision of perfection. He saw scales in his mind, with hundreds of thousands of innocent people on one side and Martha alone on the other.

Could he do it?

"Listen to me," Gaylen said. "You—you know for certain that the law of attraction is true. Right?"

"Of course it is."

"And your thinking is perfect."

"Yes, it is."

"So nothing bad can ever happen to you."

"That is correct."

Gaylen stopped to draw a deep breath. He asked himself, *am I in the light? At this moment, am I in the light?* He felt no anger, no vengeance, no hate. He felt tears starting to come to his eyes, for this thought that he was harboring, for this intention that was becoming more real by the second. He forced the words out. "So if I were to . . . shoot you and kill you, it would prove the law of attraction wrong. Forever. For everyone. Because your thinking is perfect, and if the law of attraction is true, you cannot be killed by a criminal such as me."

He gripped the weapon tightly in his hand.

Her gaze traveled to it for the first time.

The room was still and silent.

The door opened again. The DAA agent who had been there before stood in the doorway again. His voice was hesitant. "Ma'am?"

After just an instant, Martha shook her head at him, and he left.

Martha spoke to Gaylen, her head held high. "I refuse to entertain any such thought. Young man, walk away from this room, right now. Go back to your life. Correct your thinking."

"I wish I could. But I can't. Every helpless victim who has died at the hands of the DAA tells me that I can't. And I'm sorry. I really am. But this will be quick." He looked directly at the camera. "Sierra, if you're watching . . . don't look, baby. Please don't look." And he changed the setting on his weapon to the deadly setting, and he pointed it at Martha, and he pulled the trigger.

John stared at the wallscreen as Martha toppled from the chair. He felt like reality had taken a sudden turn and left him behind. He could not reconcile himself to what was happening. It was impossible. President Martha had always been there—his entire life, she had always been there. She would always be there.

Everyone had stopped whatever they were doing, had pulled over their cars or parked their bicycles, had put down their purchases and bags, to watch as the drama unfolded on the wallscreens. Now, they wept or yelled and pressed the "Request Assistance" buttons on the wallscreens over and over, but there was no response. Serena, her face drawn and horrified, tried to explain to Sierra what had just happened, but she couldn't find the words.

And then John heard war whoops and the roaring of motorcycle engines from the nearest subway tunnel entrance. As he stared, denizens erupted from the tunnel on motorcycles, recklessly riding up the stairs and speeding out into the streets. Then he saw that some carried guns—and suddenly they opened fire into the pedestrians and shops.

John grabbed Serena and Sierra. "Get down!" He half-dragged both of them behind a parked car. He made sure the cloaking device covered all three of them.

People screamed. Dozens of bystanders were mowed down where they stood, helpless. Suddenly, a series of explosions concussed the air—Molotov cocktails or something similar. Windows shattered, spraying glass.

John urged Serena and Sierra on into a building—a café—where they pushed past screaming, panicking patrons and employees into the interior office, which had no windows. "Stay low!" he screamed over the sounds of shouts and explosions and machine-gun fire. He put the cloaking device on Serena's hand.

Then he ran outside. He grabbed person after person, screamed at them to follow him, and rushed them into the office one at a time. When he could fit no more, he grabbed one sturdy fellow and ordered him to shut the door and barricade it with the desk. He cast one last look at where he knew Sierra and Serena huddled, invisible, and at the wallscreen there in the office, which showed Gaylen even now laying a jacket across President Martha's dead body.

Then he rushed outside and pulled more panicking people off the streets as the denizens tore through. He took them into the cafe itself and pushed them under tables that he shoved to the back of the deep room to give them all the cover he could. Then he drew his weapons and took up a post behind an overturned table near the door.

Outside, the roar of motorcycles continued, and the screams and staccato raps of gunfire. It would be a bloodbath out there. He could only save these few, but save them he would.

Instinctively, Gaylen lunged forward to catch Martha's body as it crumpled toward the floor. He looked down at her in his arms, her eyes open and staring, and it struck him how similar it was to when Chloe had died, and Drew. Gently, he laid her on the floor, and then he closed her eyes and laid his jacket across her body the way the others had done for Drew and Chloe. Then he knelt silently beside her body. His heart raced, his eyes welled with tears. He felt sick.

The woman who had guided him through every single day of his life was gone, silenced by his own hand, and he felt shockingly alone—orphaned. With all his heart, he wished he hadn't done it. He wished he could take it back.

As far as anyone knew, she had meant every word. She had meant to keep them all safe in a perfect world, free of sickness and death, free of suffering, forever. And he had killed her. What had he done?

He put his hands over his face. The mantra that Drew had taught him only days before found its way to his mind, and he recited it to himself. *Though I am surrounded by darkness, within me there is only light. And as I walk into darkness, may I never forget that it has no power over me that I have not given it* . . . Gradually, he regained his equilibrium. He remembered that he had not been in the darkness when he had acted. He had done it to bring the light.

Then, suddenly, he remembered that everyone in the country was watching him, and he stood up and turned toward the camera. He allowed words to arise in his mind.

"I'm sorry," he said. "I'm sorry to upset you in this way. I know this is shocking and terrible. I'm sorry that I did it. I couldn't think of any other way. I needed you to know, with absolute certainty, that the positive thinking teachings of President Martha are lies. Our whole society is a lie.

"I used to be just like you. Just a few days ago, I was just a regular person. And then I encountered the Lightbringers, and they told me the truth. And I want you to know the truth, too. There's nothing more important.

"What Martha taught us about positive thinking doesn't work. Our society isn't perfect. People fail the Wellness Confirmations all the time, and then they're taken away and executed. Accidents and natural disasters happen all the time, and the government covers them up. Crime is everywhere. The prisons I mentioned before—I've been there myself, I've seen them with my own eyes. The secret police—I've encountered them. They've tried to kill me. They almost did kill me, just a couple of days ago.

"What the Lightbringers taught me, what Drew, their leader, taught me before she was killed a few minutes ago"—he almost couldn't go on for a moment—"was that I wasn't alone. I thought I was the only person who wasn't happy. The only person in the whole country who wasn't happy. But it wasn't just me, and it isn't just you—we're all struggling.

"They showed me that sometimes things are actually wrong, and it's not our fault, and it's not because we're thinking wrong, it's because something outside of us is causing it. And then we have to do something about it, not just think something different.

"Drew showed me that there's another way. A better way. A way to feel . . . complete. Calm. Strong." He bowed his head, found his way to that place, and then raised his head and let the light shine from his eyes as he faced his country. "It's up to us to find the truth. It's up to us to bring the light. Stay with me, and we can do that. Together."

A slender, dark-haired man opened a door and walked into the room. His presence was striking—commanding and confident. Before Gaylen could think of what to say or do, the man went to the camera from the side, out of its view, and pressed a button. The red blinking light went off.

"Let's talk," the dark-haired man said. He pulled a chair toward Gaylen for himself and gestured to the chair that Martha had been sitting in. Then he took his seat and looked at Gaylen expectantly.

Gaylen sat down. "Who are you?" he asked.

"I'm Gau Bidarte," the man said. "The national head of the Domestic Awareness Agency." He looked at Gaylen with the smallest measure of annoyance in his gaze.

CHAPTER EIGHTEEN

Drew Ashling, Lightbringer:

*There is a way to greater meaning, peace, and happiness.
Life is meant to be joyous, it is meant to be full, it is meant
to be rich. And the way to a truly meaningful and satisfying
life lies with one another. Together, sharing true feelings,
true hopes and dreams. Sharing the truth. Together, we
make life worth living.*

Gau Bidarte.

Gaylen thought that he should have been surprised or alarmed,
but he simply nodded. It seemed clear that he was going to die very
soon. Yet he was calm.

"Are all of the other Lightbringers dead?" Gaylen asked, although he didn't want to know the answer.

"Some fled and no doubt survived." Bidarte crossed his legs and
straightened his jacket. "You have made strong choices, my friend.
You have earned the respect of many with what you have done. I am
impressed. And I have need of you now. Because the riots you mentioned have already begun." He gave Gaylen a significant look. "And
here is the truth: I don't want any part in this war that you have pro-
voked."

"Why not?"

"Because my men are outnumbered."

Gaylen blinked at the direct admission.

"I have many fewer men than there are denizens. Of course, not all of the denizens are coming up to fight. But more will join the effort, if it comes to all-out war." Bidarte brushed an imaginary bit of lint from his slacks and adjusted his position in the chair. "The problem is, there are a limited number of men who have the unique traits that make them valuable to me. It's impractical to replace them."

"You mean that they're sociopaths? Why do you value that so highly?"

Bidarte shrugged slightly. "I have my reasons."

Seeing that he was at a dead end, Gaylen went a different direction. "So you're not going to have the DAA fight back?"

"I'm afraid I don't have that option. You see, now that Martha has been proved wrong and removed from the equation—and I do thank you for that, by the way—I will be the new leader of New America. But the people will not appreciate my leadership if I allow the denizens to run free, killing and raping. No, that is not the politic way to begin a reign of power."

"Then I don't understand what you're saying."

"The denizens need to stop their rioting—which is, of course, what you want as well, since you don't want thousands of helpless sleepers to die—and right now you have quite a bit of sway with them. If you tell them to stop, they might listen to you. They will not listen to me, as we both understand."

Gaylen stood and paced for a moment. He hated the sound of Gau Bidarte having a "reign of power," but his immediate concern was the rioting. And the other man wanted that to stop, just as he did.

Bidarte checked his watch. "I would like to point out that with every moment we waste, an untold number of sleepers meet an unpleasant end."

Gaylen took a long, slow breath to re-center himself. "I don't think I have as much sway as you think I do. Yes, I know I . . . killed President Martha, but the denizens have been spoiling for this fight for years. I can't do it alone. You have to offer them something else. Something they'll value enough to be willing to stop."

"I'm prepared to offer that their crimes will be forgiven and they'll go free. Additionally, I can tell them that imperfection will no longer be criminalized. In fact, the denizens can rejoin society as they please. They will not be hunted by the DAA."

Again, Gaylen was taken aback. He wasn't sure that was desirable for the rest of society.

"I think we need more," Gaylen said. A bold idea had struck him.

Bidarte shifted in his chair. "What do you propose?"

"Set the prisoners free," Gaylen said. "All of them. Empty the prisons. Give a fresh start to every single New American." He held Bidarte's gaze.

Bidarte nodding slowly, appraising. "You do realize that you will free dangerous people and set them loose on the sleepers."

Anger sparked in Gaylen, and he waited until it passed, then spoke calmly. "You and I both know that the vast majority of the prisoners are innocent people who simply got old or sick or unhappy."

Bidarte shrugged slightly, conceding the point.

"Excuse me while I make a few calls," he said, and he stepped away with his handscreen.

Moments later, he went to the camera and turned it back on, then went back to Gaylen's side to address the nation.

"My friends, my fellow New Americans, I am sorry to meet you in this time of difficulty. I am Gau Bidarte, a government official. Regrettably, a new Martha has not yet been chosen, and I am stepping in as interim governor of New America, so that we will not go without leadership. Do not worry. You are in good hands.

"First, I must urge you to get to safety, if you have not done so already. Please take cover and barricade your doors. I have sent guards who will help protect you where they can.

"The rest of my message must, of necessity, be to those who are attacking you.

"Denizens of the underground, hear me now. I am Gau Bidarte, and I have an offer to make you. One which this man, the killer of President Martha, will vouch for."

Because there was no spokesperson for the denizens who could treat with them, all Bidarte and Gaylen could do was make their offer and then watch what happened.

Bidarte showed Gaylen what was being broadcast on the wallscreens on his own handscreen. He had patched in various live feeds so that everyone could witness the proof that Bidarte was not sending the DAA to kill denizens, but only to protect homes.

Standing shoulder-to-shoulder with the man who controlled the secret police, the man who had the greatest power of any person in this country—even before President Martha's death—Gaylen felt that everything had become unreal.

He noted that Bidarte had a slight five-o'clock shadow and that he smelled faintly of cologne. It was a strangely gentle, yet exotic scent, perhaps sandalwood. He noted that Bidarte was almost exactly his own height. That a slight scuff marred the outside edge of his right shoe. That the background image of Bidarte's handscreen was of a sunset in the mountains. He wondered how a man such as this—surely a socio, if anyone was—felt about sunsets.

They made no idle chitchat. Despite their casual cooperation, neither maintained a pretense of friendship.

Once the denizens had begun to settle down—neither getting the war they'd wanted nor finding a nation of helpless victims—Bidarte spoke to the camera again.

"New Americans, I regret that I must confirm some of the things you heard from Gaylen Andrews here. There was, indeed, a secret police, and secret prisons. President Martha had been keeping these secrets from you. I promise that these secrets will be no more.

"In fact, I tell you now, if you have received a post card from a loved one in the past month saying that they moved away, the truth is that they are in prison now. I promise to have your friends and loved ones released from these prisons—not someday in the future, but this very moment. Now that I am empowered to do so by President Martha's passing, I have already made the calls to make it happen. And I will show you the proof momentarily. Go now to the Bureau of Provision in your city and wait outside of it. Your loved ones will be reunited with you in moments.

"Denizens, this applies to you as well. Your loved ones are being returned to you now. We make this peace offering to you and ask you to stand down from your violence in return. Indeed, you are free now to rejoin our society in whatever way you choose, from now on. All your crimes, past and present, are forgiven."

Bidarte and Gaylen watched the handscreen for some time in silence. The offer to release the prisoners seemed to have the desired effect: the violence dwindled, though it was not entirely extinguished. It was not the war Gaylen had feared.

Within half an hour, all of New America watched as the doors of the Bureaus of Provision across the nation opened and tens of thousands of people came spilling out to be reunited with their loved ones.

Gaylen could not help but look for Sierra and Serena, in the moments that the screen showed D.C.'s Bureau of Provision. He didn't see anyone he knew.

As the reunions concluded, Bidarte signaled that the feed should return to the warehouse. "Denizens of New America, you need no longer fear the DAA because of how you look or what you say. Previously illegal entertainments will be permitted. Consider this your welcome-home party. You need not return to hiding. As your new governor, I promise you this."

He opened his mouth to speak again, but Gaylen stepped forward and placed a hand firmly on Bidarte's shoulder. The other man tensed. Gaylen's nonverbal communication was clear: *It's my turn.*

With the camera rolling, Bidarte had to be gracious. He stepped aside.

Gaylen faced the camera and spoke steadily. "People of New America, know this: I am not this man's ally. I do not vouch for Gau

Bidarte. I know that he used to be the head of the secret police, and that he has appointed himself our new ruler, and I don't trust him. I don't know what his reign will hold for New America, but I will have no part in it. I am a Lightbringer. And if you want to know the truth—no other agenda, no other purpose—find the Lightbringers. We survived for decades under Martha's tyranny. We will continue to survive, and we will continue to bring the light."

He looked full-on at Gau Bidarte for a moment.

The other man walked to the camera and turned it off, then turned back to Gaylen.

"OK," Gaylen said. "I said what I needed to. You can kill me now." He faced Bidarte squarely, unflinching.

"No," Bidarte said. "I can't kill you, actually." He faced Gaylen just as squarely, and rocked slightly up on his tiptoes and back down.

Gaylen looked at him and waited.

"Especially after what you just said to me on national television"—and his voice could not have been more cold, more brittle—"you're a celebrity, a hero among the denizens. If you simply disappear, they'll know why. They'll riot again. They'll make my men pay for it. For now, I need you alive and kicking."

The accompanying threat was unstated, but clear to read in his eyes: *Someday, Gaylen Andrews, I will not need you. And then, I will kill you with my own hands.*

Gaylen said nothing, though a corner of his mouth turned up in a slight smile. He turned and walked out of the building.

Gaylen stepped outside the warehouse to find a perimeter of dozens, if not hundreds, of DAA agents, many of them turning to face him, and all of them holding dust guns. The sight stopped him in his tracks. But they did not shoot him, nor did anyone speak, nor did a single expression shift. The October wind came through the warehouses, whistling through some piece of aluminum on a roof somewhere—the only sound.

Gaylen walked toward the semicircle of agents. As he reached the perimeter, two men stepped aside to give him passage. They gave him looks that made him feel like the rabbit in a dog hunt. He moved through and kept walking, even as he expected to hear the whine of a dust gun at any moment. But it didn't come.

Not far outside the perimeter, Gaylen was met by four Lightbringers, including Kevin.

Kevin shook his head when he saw Gaylen approaching. "Well, that was impressive. And crazy."

Gaylen put a hand on the other man's shoulder. "I thought for sure that you were dead."

"Just stunned—right in the beginning. I missed almost everything," Kevin said. "But I heard that last bit with Gau Bidarte. I hope you know you just signed your own death warrant."

Gaylen nodded. "Yeah. I do." He looked at the four of them. "Everyone else is dead?"

Kevin took another drag off his cigarette and looked away, his jaw set.

They all stood in silence for a moment, listening to the wind.

"Where to now?" Gaylen asked.

"What do you advise?" Kevin asked.

Gaylen thought for a moment. "Back to the safe house, I guess. Maybe there will be other survivors from Team Beta." He sighed. "We'll need them to collect our dead from here."

The group of them returned to the last safe house, the abandoned condominium.

As they entered the building, Gaylen was shocked to see a crowd of at least fifty people waiting in the lobby—but that surprise was trumped when he saw Goldfinger waiting with them. He approached cautiously, uncertain. The last he'd known, Goldfinger had been expelled from the Lightbringers for being a DAA agent.

"I found some new recruits," Goldfinger said, gesturing at the people in the lobby. The man looked exhausted and exhilarated at the same time, his cheeks ruddy.

Gaylen realized that the agent wasn't wearing his mask.

He didn't know what to say.

"And someone else wants to see you," Goldfinger said meaningfully. "Serena."

Gaylen could only follow him silently, too surprised to speak, into what used to be the condo's management office, where Serena sat at a dusty conference room table. She looked up at him. Her hair was disheveled, her eyes red.

Goldfinger left them alone.

They looked at one another for a long moment. Gaylen had thought a hundred times of the things he would like to say to her if he ever saw her again, but now his mind was a blank. Anxiety made his stomach turn over. He ran one hand over his face.

"I saw what you did," Serena said, her voice husky and trembling. "You killed her. She's *dead*. She's not going to come back."

Gaylen nodded. He found himself gripping the back of a chair as if it would keep him steady.

"The things you said . . . that other man said . . ."

Slowly, her hands came over her mouth. Gaylen wasn't sure if she was going to throw up or cry. Then she began to sob.

Instinctively, Gaylen went to her side. He knelt next to her and took her in his arms, the feel of her body at once familiar and strange.

"Nothing is what I thought it was," she cried.

"I know." Gaylen closed his eyes, breathing deep, finding the light within him, finding compassion, finding strength.

"I don't know what to do," she wailed. She shook violently. Gaylen became alarmed for her. She'd never encountered so much fear and violence before. She had no idea how to handle it.

He remembered the moment in the underground after the DAA's attack, the room with the blinking light, Drew's kind eyes anchoring him. He pulled away. "Serena, look at me. Look at me." He shook her gently, and her eyes focused on his. He met her gaze with his full presence, letting the light pour out of him, letting it cradle her in its warmth. "Look at me and breathe. Take long, slow breaths."

He held her shoulders and gazed into her eyes as she breathed, and gradually she calmed. The shaking subsided to a tremble. The frightened animal he saw in her eyes became human again.

He took her in his arms again, to cradle her as if she were a child or a lover, the way Drew had held him after his confession. "You're safe here. Everything will be all right. Breathe deeply. Let all your muscles relax and let go."

Her body relaxed in his arms, and she let her head rest against his chest for a few moments. Then, gently, she pushed her way back into a sitting position on the floor next to him.

"I have no idea who you are," she said. "You are not the man I married."

"No," he said. "I'm not." He let out a slow breath, letting his own tension go.

"I thought everything was perfect," Serena said bitterly. "Everything was always perfect, until I left you, Gaylen—because Sierra kept crying for you. She wouldn't just be OK and I didn't know how to fix it. They told me she went to her grandmother's, Gaylen. John brought her to me, that man outside? He saved her from the DAA. He had just brought her to me, and then . . . then you were on the wallscreens, and you killed Martha. You proved she was wrong. And that man . . . he showed us those prisons, all those people coming out—and the rioting—I thought I was going to die. John saved us. And you . . . you're not the same. I don't know you." Her gaze traced the contours of his face.

She had said that Sierra was safe. That was the important thing.

He tried to decide how to explain all of this, but so much of it was still new to him, still unprocessed. "I found another way, Serena. If you just . . . let yourself feel . . . then you can let it go, and you can face whatever it is, even when it's hard." He looked at her. "Even when it's impossible. And you can do whatever it takes, whatever you need to do."

He knew that it was true. There was a rock-solid center in him now that grounded him. He could find it whenever he needed it.

Slowly, she nodded. She swallowed. "I want you to teach Sierra. I want her to know the truth, to grow up knowing everything. I want her to be strong like you are now."

Joy surged in Gaylen. He would get to see his daughter again. "Of course. Of course I will."

Serena stood up and opened a door to another room. "Sierra. Come on, honey."

Gaylen thought his heart would stop as he saw his beloved child take a hesitant step into the room. Her face lit up as she saw him. "Daddy!" she shrieked.

Gaylen dropped to one knee and put his arms out, and Sierra rushed into them. They hugged hard.

"I'm here, baby," he told her. "I'm here. I love you. I'm not going away again, OK? Never, never, never again."

Serena stood nearby, watching them both with her hand over her mouth again. Gaylen wiped away his tears and looked up at her. His chest hurt. "Promise me you won't ever take her away again. Please promise me."

Serena's eyes were wet as she said, "I won't. I'm sorry, to both of you. I'm so sorry."

Gaylen stood and the family embraced.

The three of them went back out into the lobby a few minutes later, their tears dry for now. Gaylen held his daughter as if he would never let her go again. John came to them, and Gaylen put out his hand, and the two men shook hands. His tone heartfelt, Gaylen said, "Thank you. With all my heart. I can never repay you for protecting my family."

John simply nodded. "I know you would have done the same for my children." Unexpectedly, there were tears in his eyes.

"Will you join the Lightbringers? For real this time?"

John nodded slowly. "I'm pretty sure I already have." The two men shared an understanding look.

Gaylen laughed in relief when he saw Tommy approaching them. He was ashamed to realize that he hadn't thought about the other man since the broadcast had begun.

"Hey, man," Tommy said, offering his hand. "Nice job, man. Seriously, nice job."

They shook hands.

"How'd you get out?" Gaylen asked.

"Oh, I just fought my way out. Heroically. Against all odds," Tommy said. "And by that, I mean I hid in a closet until everyone else had left." He shrugged and Gaylen laughed.

Kevin stepped up, holding out his handscreen. "Gaylen, Don wants to talk to you."

Gaylen took the handscreen and stepped into another room where it was quiet, still carrying his daughter. "Yes?" he said.

"Gaylen. This is Don. The head of the Lightbringers nationally." The other man's voice was resonant, his tone somber. "What you did tonight was . . . powerful, and the implications are going to be unfolding for years to come." He paused. "Tell me something, Gaylen. And this is important. When you killed Martha, what was your inner state?"

Gaylen closed his eyes to concentrate, to remember. "I was not in the darkness, I know that for sure. I had let go of my anger and resentment and hatred. I just felt that it had to be done, that it was our one best chance to make sure everyone learned the truth. I did it for the truth. Nothing else."

Don was silent for a moment. "What do you feel about it now?"

Gaylen contemplated the question. He felt his way through the layers of emotion until he reached a solid place—somewhere cold and hard and heavy. He remembered it from when he had told Drew about the worst thing he had ever done. "Guilt. I took a life, and I can never undo that. Even though I thought I had a good reason . . . I still killed someone. And I hope I never have to do it again." He meant it.

The other man sighed. "I know that Drew has fallen. I'll have more to say about that in a moment, but right now, I'd like to know whether you would consider taking on the leadership role for the D.C. cell. I have a feeling that a lot of people are going to be looking for you, wanting to learn the truth."

"Replace Drew? Me? I don't really feel qualified for it . . . sir."

"I understand. Kevin told me that this is your third day with the Lightbringers."

It hardly seemed possible, but it was true. He laughed, a short bark. "Yes, sir."

"Given the heavy casualties your cell has sustained, you're the most qualified person available right now. And you're the face that everyone will recognize. Those are two very good reasons to choose you." Don paused again. "It won't be an easy job, Gaylen. You've seen enough to know that. And we don't know yet how the rioting, the return of the denizens to society, and Gau Bidarte's new leadership are going to work themselves out. It's an uncertain world. All we know is that there will be major challenges that we will need to be present for, bringing the light however we can. From what I've seen, you can do that."

Gaylen sighed. He held his daughter close. At the moment, all he wanted was to cuddle up and read her a bedtime story and forget everything that had happened since he had last seen her. "All right. I'll do it." Even as he said the words, he felt the weight of responsibility settle over him.

"Good. I knew you would." There was a smile in the other man's voice for the first time. Then he fell silent for a moment, then went on with a serious tone again. "About Drew . . . and Chloe. We need to hold a memorial service to tell their stories. And I believe we should build a monument to them, and to all the fallen. Will you organize it?"

"I will," Gaylen said. "Also . . . Drew's tradition—the Lightbringers books of names. We need to publish those books. She meant for them to be published after she helped bring the light. And I think she did."

"Let's do it. Make sure everyone has a chance to write something on Drew's and Chloe's pages first." Don paused. "That's all

I have for you now. We'll be in touch regularly from here on out. Take care, Gaylen."

"You, too," Gaylen said.

He ended the call and set the phone down.

He still held his little girl in his arms, and for a while, she was all that existed to him. She laid her head against his chest and nibbled on her thumb, and he swayed with her like he used to when she was just a baby and he was trying to soothe her to sleep. Tears came to his eyes. He would trade absolutely anything for just a dozen more moments like this one.

"I love you, Sierra," he said. "And I will always, always take care of you."

"I love you, too, Daddy."

About the Author

H.C.H. Ritz has a degree in theatre from the University of Houston and directs community theatre in her spare time.

Originally from rural Mississippi, she has lived in Houston, Texas long enough to have turned into a city person.

She is married to a wonderful human being and has a young son and a tortoiseshell kitty named Roxy Underfoot.

Connect With HCH Ritz

Email
hchritz@gmail.com

Facebook
facebook.com/hchritz

Grey Gecko Press

Thank you for purchasing this book from Grey Gecko Press, an independent publishing company that focuses on new and emerging authors, bringing readers the best in fiction and non-fiction at reasonable prices in all formats.

With books in nearly every genre of fiction and non-fiction, there's something for everyone, and you can be sure that buying books from us leads directly to the support of independent authors like H. C. H. Ritz. Grey Gecko pays our authors some of the highest royalty rates in the business and strives to produce only high-quality books.

Visit our website to purchase our titles, pre-order upcoming books at a discount, sign up for our free monthly newsletter, and find out about two great ways to get free books, the Slushpile Reader Program and the Advance Reader Program.

And don't forget: all our print editions come with the ebook absolutely free!

Authors First!

www.greygeckopress.com

store.greygeckopress.com

www.ingramcontent.com/pod-product-compliance
Lightning Source LLC
Chambersburg PA
CBHW051258210726
48287CB00002B/559